Jack's Last Class

A narrative Bible study for Zoom and other small groups

William Hawkins

<u>*Jack's Last Class*</u>

ISBN 978-1-7337586-0-4

A property of Spora Publications LLC

First print:2019; Second print:2021

Txt: 0927zmamzoh2219-1

Dedicated to our grandchildren

—Griffin, Jake, and Eli—

to their children,

and to their grandchildren

Amazon Reviews and Ratings

Swaliga
5.0 out of 5 stars
Enjoyed Immensely!
This book is the best way to explore the teachings of the Bible, a relationship with Christ and yourself. Written in lesson style, it is a great read by one or in a small group.

Mysterym
5.0 out of 5 stars
A Must Read!
There has never been a time in my life that I haven't known God, but even for someone who is a life-long Christian, this is a must read! The writing is creative, heartfelt and insightful. The reference material is broad and eye opening. This book doesn't merely skim the surface, but goes deep and wide. No matter who you are or what your beliefs are, you will be challenged to THINK. I appreciate the perspective that the author provides. There is no judgment or condemnation. There is only love and truth. Order a copy today. It will not disappoint. I've already placed orders for friends and family I want to share this with.

Dave W.
5.0 out of 5 stars
Great Insight Into the Christian Faith
The setting of this book is the last class of Jack Kirk, a longtime teacher at his church, who is moving away and will no longer be able to teach there. The "last class" is a series of lectures in which the author, through his character Jack, shares his understanding of the answers to several central questions regarding Christianity. Examples: What is the Uppermost Sin?, Who is the Holy Spirit?, Who is God?, Who is Christ?, Who is Satan?, and What is Salvation?. The author shares his knowledge, but also quotes liberally from other great thinkers such as C.S. Lewis and Alexander Solzhenitsyn. This book is valuable for a seasoned Christian who wants to gain a deeper understanding of the Christian faith, but also for a non-Christian who wants to understand what Christianity is all about.

G. D.
5.0 out of 5 stars
Encouragement to Think about your Faith
This read will be a great encouragement to those who want to study the Bible, discuss and get insights to their Christian faith. An excellent source to use in a Bible study setting- the church, sin, Holy Spirit, God, Christ, Satan, salvation, your mission in life?

Brent B.
5.0 out of 5 stars
A powerful read to strengthen your faith!
An enlightening and good read. We leveraged this study in a small group setting, but I see where it can be very effective in leading an individual through the questions they have on establishing their faith. This study is written with real-life characters and situations that make it relevant to what many of us experience and question. Don't let the low price mislead you on the value of this publication.

Auriana

5.0 out of 5 stars

Absolutely Phenomenal!

This book has helped me grow closer to God in so many ways. Each week I would go through a certain chapter and I would discover a truth I desperately needed to know in order to combat lies I believed for a long time. I struggled with being more religious than having an actual living relationship with Christ, and this book has helped me see God on a more personal level and has helped me to live in the freedom Christ has called me to. I recommend this book to anyone! I like to call this book a Bible study with a twist, because the author writes it in a VERY creative way.

Daniel T.

5.0 out of 5 stars

Light a fire

Great study for "seasoned believers" and new Christians alike. Great 'third person' presentation by the author. Light a fire into your Bible study discussion, or help a "wondering wanderer" on their journey.

SC

5.0 out of 5 stars

Jacks Last Class!!!

I highly recommend Jacks Last Class for any group looking for a bible study. I have participated in many and this one has made a huge impact on me! Great for couples, groups or whoever is searching!

Jerry B

5.0 out of 5 stars

Intriguing Bible study full of insight and enjoyment!

This book is an excellent way to bolster your faith foundation in both an enlightening and encouraging manner. Whether a brand-new believer or someone who has walked the Grace Journey for years, I think this book will enhance your understanding of Biblical truths and help you to grow deeper in your Faith walk.

Bryan R.

5.0 out of 5 stars

Unique and instructive

The unique instructive style and perspective make this a good read or a great gift for anyone who likes to think.

germ

5.0 out of 5 stars

A Biblical Story

This would be a great Bible study that would last about 12 weeks. It is very teachable as a story.

MM

5.0 out of 5 stars

Very inspirational narrative of the meaning of being a true Christian.

A wonderful book written by a true disciple of Christ. You will be engrossed as you follow Jack's journey in teaching and learning. You will learn alongside of him and come to know our Lord better. Worth the read. Very insightful and inspirational.

Introduction

To the Author, History, Mission, and Hope of "Jack's Last Class"

I wish we were at Starbucks

Inasmuch as a Bible study is a very personal thing, so, it seems, should be the information you have about its author and how the study came to be. To that end, I wish you and I were in a quiet corner at Starbucks and, over coffee and bagels, I was personally telling you its history.

How the book came to be

The first thing I would say is that I began *Jack's Last Class* in 2002. I wrote for about an hour a day, five days a week, for almost two years until most of the 12 chapters I had planned were completed.

Thanks to Dr. Bruce Wilkinson

Next, I would tell you that in 2008 Dr. Bruce Wilkinson (author of *The Prayer of Jabez*, *Secrets of the Vine,* and founder of *Walk Thru the Bible Ministries*) earned my deepest and lasting gratitude when he became an unexpected encourager and mentor, leading me to complete the last two chapters.

Why copies are so inexpensive—or free

Since then, I have given away hundreds and hundreds of copies. I continue that practice to the best of my ability in this arrangement with Amazon by pricing paperbacks at the minimum they will allow—just enough to cover their paper, printing, and production costs—with no increase to compensate me.

Stated another way, I receive 0% royalties.

The reason for this pricing policy is that this has never been a for-profit endeavor. Nor is it now*.

My hope for others through you

As stated above, over more than a decade I have given away hundreds and hundreds of copies… to family members and friends, colleagues and strangers, Bible study groups and deployed military Chaplains. My highest hope is that someday you, too, will find yourself giving a copy to a friend, an acquaintance, or a stranger.

A unique Bible study

I formatted *Jack's Last Class* in the traditional Bible study style of 12 chapters which are to be read at the rate of one per week and discussed at weekly meetings. But tradition ends there as the book unfolds in the best style for teaching—as a *story*.

This is a story rich in love

This is a story rich in the love of Jack Kirk—the fictional teacher I created—for his wife, his class, and his God.

This is a story rich in wisdom

This is a story rich in the wisdom, the warnings, and the teachings of Christian leaders; Scripture from the NIV, KJV, NKJV, ISV, ESV, NCV, ASV, NASV, and Amplified versions; details from time-tested encyclopedias and commentaries; and definitions from English, Hebrew, and Greek dictionaries.

This is a story rich in purpose

And this is a story rich in the feelings Jack has for his class—a feeling and a purpose any experienced teacher will recognize—as he strives to lead, to inspire, and to challenge its members to study, to write, and above all to *think*.

How this birthed my Mini-Mission

Though I have been a Christian since childhood, until 2002 I never planned to write, never really planned to publish, and certainly never planned a broad distribution of what I had written. But I found that this book… this *story*… was a remarkable gift from God through which small groups—as well as individuals—could comfortably address and openly discuss matters of faith.

Maybe your Mini-Mission too?

I hope you find this most unorthodox Bible study one you want to share.

In fact, I hope you and I form something of a quiet partnership… that together—with my providing low-cost materials and through your interest in your family, friends, and extended circle of influence—we reach hundreds whose lives will be enriched, service will be enhanced, and futures will be assured.

As we do, my single request is that—unless doing so as a fundraiser in a nonprofit—you avoid any add-on costs. This because my motivation is to freely share with others this which has been so freely given to me. And if I cannot make them absolutely free with Amazon, I can make them profit-free.

Because of my age, health, and season of life, it is not likely you and I will ever meet, or even correspond. Yet in Him—and in this partnership—you and I may form a bond of common service. That because this, for me as you'll read in Chapter 12, is my Mini-Mission.

Perhaps it will become yours.

I hope so.

Bill Hawkins,
Author, *Jack's Last Class*

*The mission of *Spora Publishing LLC* is to—as a nonprofit—cast forth the story of faith as taught in the Matthew, Mark, and Luke parables. That mission is also reflected in the LLC's name, the Greek word for casting, spreading, and sowing: *sporá*.

Style and Format

The purpose of this page is to make you aware, early on, of some style and formatting decisions I made.

Reverential Capitalization

The first style decision was related to what is called "reverential capitalization", the practice of capitalizing the first letter of pronouns identifying God, Jesus, and the Holy Spirit, and the growing countertrend by leading Christian guides—including Zondervan's *Christian Writers Manual of Style*—of *not* capitalizing them. I have followed this guide and, except where quoting Scripture, used lower cases.

Quotation Marks

The second style decision was related to quotation marks. I quote a great deal of Scripture and material from other sources. To avoid the tedium and confusion of multiple quotation marks—particularly around quotes within quotes—I only placed marks around statements made by speakers and placed all other quoted material in italics. I also placed emphatic words and silent thoughts of Jack's in italics.

"Your Takeaways and Action Items from this Chapter"

You'll find these two pages at the end of each chapter. If you like to underline or highlight, you'll find this a handy place to summarize those thoughts and ideas you most want to remember ("Takeaways") and those you want to put into practice ("Action Items"). The pages will also serve as a source of discussion points in weekly small group meetings (see page 176).

Bill Hawkins
Author, *Jack's Last Class*

nar·ra·tive /ˈnerədiv

noun

1. A spoken or written account of connected events
2. A story

Source: Oxford Languages, online dictionary

Contents

Prologue

Jack Kirk is moving after years of teaching a class he loves in a church he helped build. There is much on his heart. There is much he wants to say. There is little time to say it.

The room is full but will welcome one more—you.

So, settle in for one of the most intense, thought provoking, and unconventional series of lessons you've ever experienced.

Settle in for a new perspective on this brief life we're living.

Settle in to be changed… by *Jack's Last Class*

Why the Vine?

Chapter 1 - Sunday, May 8

I did not expect this, Jack Kirk thought as he looked over the rapidly-filling room. This was the third consecutive Sunday his class had been moved to a larger space—this time to an area usually partitioned off as overflow for weddings and receptions.

Where classroom chairs were normally arranged in a small circle, these were being arranged in rows, theater style. And where he was accustomed to a small group of regulars, those walking in now were from other classes and the broader church membership.

He was unclear as to why they were coming. But he was pleased that there would be this kind of interest in his last few lessons, or this sort of display of affection at his and Kelli's departure.

This moment actually began several weeks earlier when it became known that he and his wife were—after almost 20 years in this church and 12 years of teaching—moving to another city.

It was then that Jack decided that his last days of teaching would be his farewell series, and that they would focus on things of his heart rather than denomination-prescribed materials.

Sitting a few rows from the front was a first-time visitor named Dianne Downing. Next to her was Sandra Blake, a fairly new member of Jack's class who was particularly conscious of what it was like to be a newcomer.

Sandra introduced herself to Dianne and, after a few moments of chatting, was asked what she knew about the teacher. Sandra said that he was an executive, married to his college sweetheart, and the father of two grown children. She said he seemed to study constantly and had written a book. She added that—at his request and for reasons she'd tell her later—he originally used a pseudonym as the author. His work, she continued, required him to travel a great deal and that he probably used the hours on flights and evenings in hotels to write.

Dianne asked what she liked best about his teaching. Without hesitation Sandra said that he was always prepared, encouraged discussion, and kept discussions on track. She said she also liked the breadth of his lessons and his use of outside resources. But, she added with a smile, the thing she liked most were his questions—because they made her *think.*

Dianne was pleasantly surprised at her answer and settled back in her chair as a woman named Beverly approached the front of the class, called the group to order, extended a good morning, and began the class with prayer requests.

A few minutes later Jack walked to the front, stood behind a small wooden music stand that was going to serve as a temporary lectern, smiled and said, "I add my good mornings to Beverly's, and to those from Bob's, Janet's, and Chuck's classes that have taken a special sabbatical to join us—as well as those who are usually in the 11:00 service at this hour—I extend a special welcome. You honor me more than you might imagine.

"Because of the time it took to set up the chairs, I'm going to get right to it. As I do, I'll tell you that, due to our numbers, I'll be standing and teaching in a lecture format though I prefer sitting and talking in a discussion circle. Our class time will be divided into thirds with my lecture/lesson during the first third, your completion of a question/answer sheet during the second, and our discussion of your thoughts on those sheets during the third.

"I'll also tell those who are joining us for the first time that this is not an orthodox series of lessons. Rather, this is a very personal series in which I am talking about several of my favorite Scriptures in the context of my three favorite questions—the only questions, by the way, on the Q and A sheet you'll complete. Those three questions are...," Jack said as he turned to the whiteboard that had been placed behind him, picked up a black marker, and wrote,

Three questions of all Scripture:

1. *WHAT is said?*
2. *WHY is it said?*
3. *HOW does it apply to my life?*

"What? Why? How?" Jack continued as he again faced the class. "These are the three essential questions which lead us to *read*, lead us to *understand*, and lead us to *apply* Scripture in an effective, operational, life-changing way.

"Today we are finishing a study started three weeks ago from what is, singularly, my favorite passage in the entire Bible." Distracted by movement, he looked at the third row where he saw several old class members smiling at him. He smiled back and continued, "I'm getting that I-know-where-you're-going-with-this look from those in our regular class because they know how I feel about this passage. They know how I've referred to it as one of the five writings I'd want on my island if I were ever stranded because it is so passionate, so powerful, and so complete that one could read this and this alone and have a clear understanding of how we are to be filled with God's *love*, how we are to be filled with his *peace,* and how we are to be filled with his *joy*. This is not the essential story of how we are to be saved, but the core story of how we are to live.

"The passage is John 15:1-11. So that everyone will be up to speed on the first question, I'd like for you to turn to it, mark it, and close your Bible until we read it together in a few minutes."

As the soft sound of flipping pages filled the air, Jack continued, "Before we read it, I want to remind you of the setting: It is Thursday night. Five days earlier, on Sunday, Jesus had ridden into Jerusalem on a donkey… ridden into the crowds gathered there to observe Passover… and ridden into the minds of three different groups in three different ways.

"First, he had ridden into the *hopes* of most that this was, at last, the promised Messiah and king who would liberate them from Roman rule and re-establish Israel as an independent state. John 12:13 captures the scene in the city and the mood of the people when it says: *So they took branches of palm trees and went out to meet Him, shouting, 'Hosanna! How blessed is the One who comes in the name of the Lord, the King of Israel!'*[1]

"Second, he had ridden into the carnival-like *curiosity* of many to see if this magician—this Nazarene who had for three years healed the sick, raised the dead, and challenged the Pharisees—would do it again.

"Third and finally, he had ridden into the *fears* of a few—a very *elite* few—who saw this man as a clear and present threat to their near-deity stature at the top of a religious system that enforced a *spiritual* oppression more severe than any *political* oppression imagined by Caesar.

"The five days that followed could only be described as tumultuous and made all the more so by Jesus' actions—specifically his open... persistent... denunciation and condemnation of this privileged group. If there was a word or a deed that could publicly confront or indict these religious leaders or their financial patrons, Jesus seemed to seek it out. In Matthew Chapter 21 we see him violently turning over tables and driving money changers from the temple... and in 23 we hear him charge the Pharisees with a blistering litany of failures."

Stepping to the side of the stand, Jack recited the charges from memory, quoting their failures with a firmness and freshness that made them as relevant to the class as they had been to the crowds:

> *"Woe to you, teachers of the law and Pharisees, you hypocrites! You shut the door of the kingdom of heaven in people's faces. You yourselves do not enter, nor will you let those enter who are trying to...*
>
> *Woe to you, teachers of the law and Pharisees, you hypocrites! You travel over land and sea to win a single convert, and when you have succeeded, you make them twice as much a child of hell as you are...*
>
> *Woe to you, blind guides! You say, 'If anyone swears by the temple, it means nothing; but anyone who swears by the gold of the temple is bound by that oath.' You blind fools! Which is greater: the gold, or the temple that makes the gold sacred?*
>
> *Woe to you, teachers of the law and Pharisees, you hypocrites! You give a tenth of your spices—mint, dill, and cumin. But you have neglected the more important matters of the law—justice, mercy, and faithfulness...*
>
> *You blind guides! You strain out a gnat but swallow a camel...*
>
> *Woe to you, teachers of the law and Pharisees, you hypocrites, you clean the outside of the cup and dish, but inside they are full of greed and self-indulgence... Blind Pharisee! First clean the inside of the cup and dish, and then the outside also will be clean...*
>
> *Woe to you, teachers of the law and Pharisees, you hypocrites! You are like white-washed tombs, which look beautiful on the outside but on the inside are full of the bones of the dead and everything unclean...*
>
> *You snakes! You brood of vipers! How will you escape being condemned to hell?"*[2]

Jack stopped, letting the significance of what Jesus had said permeate the room. Quietly, he then said, "That is the big picture... this is the small: It is dark. Jesus and his disciples have finished what we know as the Last Supper. He has established the sacrament of communion or Eucharist. He has told them that he would be betrayed. He has washed their feet. They have left the Upper Room. They are outside the city wall. They are walking toward the Garden of Gethsemane.

"Suddenly he stops and in the deafening silence made all the louder by the events of the last few days—and though he *knows* the Pharisees want to kill him, *knows* Roman law will allow it, and *knows* Judas is, at that moment, betraying him—the teacher gathers his chosen for one last lesson."

Jack paused, then said, "Now, if you were hearing this story for the very first time… if you were not already familiar with what Jesus says…what do you *think* he *could* be saying? Don't cheat, don't go to what you know… tell me what you *think* he *could* be saying."

The room was silent.

After a moment, Chuck Wilson—an old friend and one of the teachers taking a sabbatical—spoke slowly, searching his thoughts, looking for words to describe the picture forming in his mind. "He could have said, 'This night will be the longest of your life… and of mine… for I am about to be arrested and about to suffer *extreme physical torture*. Extreme even by Roman standards. Extreme because some soldiers will beat me for sport in a feeding frenzy with their comrades… because some will beat me to demonstrate their prowess to commanders from whom they seek promotion… because some will beat me for their allegiance to Rome and the threat they believe I represent to the Empire."

Chuck continued, verbalizing notes he was making on the back of a church bulletin even as he wrote them, "I am about to suffer *extreme mental anguish*. Extreme because it will seem that all of Israel …all of you… even my father… will have betrayed me.

"And I am about to suffer the *extreme death sentence*. Extreme because it will not be by sword …or spear… or fire… but by crucifixion. This will be so extreme that in time the word *excruciating*—meaning out of the cross—will be commonly used to describe the most unspeakable, unbearable, unendurable pain.

"I tell you this," Chuck concluded, "because I want you to know of my love for you, and what in that love I have done for you… because I want you to know of the cross I bear for you so that it will lighten the cross you must now bear for me… and because I want you to know the resolve with which I give all for you so that you will—with the same resolve—give all for me."

For a few seconds the room was silent, imagining that which Jesus knew was coming, absorbing that which he could have said.

After a moment, Jack said, "Thank you, Chuck. No one could have put it better. And I agree with you… Jesus *could* have, at that moment, subtly but effectively, established *this-is-what-I-have-done-for-you-and-now-you-are-obligated-to-do-for-me* as the Great Premise of Christian service. Not of *salvation*, but of *service*.

"This idea of a quid pro quo… of a debt we now owe that must be repaid with service… is so disturbing to me and so foreign to God that I am compelled to spend this additional moment to make this critical point. God does not want our *service*… I'm not sure he even wants our *love*… if our *motivation* is *obligation*. He does not want it any more than you want the love of your child if the motivation is to somehow repay you for the bicycle, the piano lessons, or the two jobs you worked to cover tuition.

"Those were *gifts* from you to them.

"Jesus was a *gift* from God to us.

"In both cases the motivation was love. Not only can gifts not be repaid but attempts to do so are offensive. So, if you are one of those whose service has been driven by guilt and debt and grimness, rather than by love and grace and joy, I have good news: That is *not* what he said. That is *not* what he wants.

"Listen to what he *did* say… and hear what he *does* want… as recorded in this most memorable of all lessons," Jack said as he opened his Bible to John 15 in the New International Version and read the first 15 verses:

> *I am the true vine, and my Father is the gardener. He cuts off every branch in me that bears no fruit, while every branch that does bear fruit he prunes so that it will be even more fruitful. You are already clean because of the word I have spoken to you. Remain in me, and I*

will remain in you. No branch can bear fruit by itself; it must remain in the vine. Neither can you bear fruit unless you remain in me.

I am the vine; you are the branches. If a man remains in me and I in him, he will bear much fruit; apart from me you can do nothing. If anyone does not remain in me, he is like a branch that is thrown away and withers; such branches are picked up, thrown into the fire and burned. If you remain in me and my words remain in you, ask whatever you wish, and it will be given you.

This is to my Father's glory, that you bear much fruit, showing yourselves to be my disciples. As the Father has loved me, so have I loved you. Now remain in my love. If you obey my commands, you will remain in my love, just as I have obeyed my Father's commands and remain in his love.

I have told you this so that my joy may be in you and that your joy may be complete."[3]

Closing his Bible, Jack looked at the class and asked, "Do you hear any *you-owe-me* theology?

"Do you hear any *cross-you-must-bear* covenant?

"Do you hear any call to a *thin-lipped, sacked-clothed, long-suffering* life?

"I don't.

"I see one point: Joy.

"*Joy*!

"Joy in being loved… joy in being groomed… joy in being in Christ."

Stepping back behind the lectern, Jack continued, "Stay with me now as we shift from *what* he said to *how* he said it."

Jack paused as he realized that the 'how' would make little sense to many who were just joining the class, then said, "By way of background, a few months ago we spent several Sundays viewing a remarkable series of videos called *Faith Lessons: Old Testament*[4] which placed Scripture in an extraordinary historical, cultural, religious, and geographical context. They were produced by Dr. James Dobson's *Focus on the Family*, filmed onsite in Israel, and taught by one of the most gifted teachers and historians I've ever heard, Ray Vander Laan. This is a must-see series, and I encourage you to do so.

"In one of the programs, Vander Laan described the difference in the way Western and Eastern minds work. As an example, to the question, 'what is God like?', a Westerner would use familiar *words*… we would say that he is *loving* or *powerful*.

"On the other hand, an Eastern mind would use familiar *imagery*… they would say that he is like a *father*, or his presence like a *shepherd* leading to *still waters*.

"That being the case, we should not be surprised at the 'how' of this passage… that Jesus used imagery… in this case the vine.

"But," Jack said as he closed his Bible, stepped to the side of the music stand to be nearer the class, and asked, "Why the *vine*?"

He paused, let the quiet and the question fill the room, then said: "*Why* when speaking to his physically and emotionally exhausted disciples… *why* when making his last statements to those he loved most and on whom all now depended… *why* when trying to communicate with them in a clear, simple, unmistakable parable… did Jesus choose a grapevine?

"We know from his ministry there were dozens of other images he could have chosen. He could have chosen a lamb or a fish… a donkey or a dove… wheat or tares… stones or sepulchers. He could have chosen baskets filled with bread, nets filled with fish, or fields ripe for harvest. He could have chosen the Jordan River, the Sea of Galilee, or the Dead Sea. He could have chosen the walls of Jerusalem, stones of the Temple, or a manger in Bethlehem.

"But he *didn't*… and here, my friends, is where Scripture ends and speculation begins. And here are my personal—*very* personal—speculations.

"First, he may have chosen a vine because it was convenient… simply because a vineyard happened to be adjacent to the path they followed from the Upper Room through the Kidron Valley to the Garden of Gethsemane.

"Or it may have been that on this last night… this *end* of his Earthly ministry… he chose a vine because he wanted symmetry with the *beginning* of his ministry… that he wanted those who saw it *start* with the miracle of changing water into wine at a wedding see it *end* in a vineyard, the source of wine.

"Or it may have been that he wanted them to see the role *wine* played in celebrating the covenant of marriage between a man and his bride as a parallel to the role his *blood* would play in celebrating the new covenant between himself and *his* bride, the church.

"As I thought about these, I generally rejected them in favor of this thought: I think he chose a vine because it was the best *physical* representation of an abstract relationship… the best *visual* model of an invisible association… the best *tangible* illustration of the intangible bond that exists between God and man.

"And I think he chose it because no other plant requires the care, and no other crop produces a fruit as delicate nor as vulnerable as the grape.

"That leads us to the third question," Jack said as he turned back to the whiteboard, circled the last question, and read, "How does this apply to my life?

"I believe," he said turning back to the class, "that there are seven answers to that question …answers I have come to think of as the seven lessons of the vine.

"The first lesson is this," he said as he wiped the board clean and wrote:

Seven lessons of the vine:

1. It is God—not man—who does the work.

Facing the class, he continued, "One cannot carefully examine this model Jesus gave us without seeing a remarkable truth: *The vinedresser does all the work.* It is he that holds the master vision of what the vine is to become and what it is to produce. And then it is he who carries the water, hoes the weeds, washes the leaves, deflects the insects, snips the buds, ties the tentacles, turns the soil, shovels the fertilizer, watches the temperature, chooses the season, and picks the crop. It is this working—constantly…

lovingly… tirelessly—that most surprises me. I know that God loves me, and I know that he has plans for me, but I somehow never had in mind that which is so clear in this image that Jesus chose: and that is that God works indefatigably at making me into what he wants me to be.

"The Second lesson is this," he said as he wrote on the whiteboard:

Seven lessons of the vine:

1. It is God—not man—who does the work.
2. Man wants leaves. God wants grapes.

Turning back to the class, Jack said, "Left to itself, a vine will produce more *leaves* than *grapes*. It is the nature of the plant." He reached down and picked up a beautiful coffee-table book from a chair, opened it, and said, "I want to read to you a part of chef and vintner Michael Chiarello's magnificent book, *Napa Stories*. In it he quotes Doug Fletcher, a winemaker who holds an MBA from UCLA Davis and who guides the winemaking at the Chimney Rock Winery in California. Fletcher says,

> *When a cane gets to be about four feet long, you have enough leaves to ripen the fruit. If you let the cane grow to six feet instead of four, you're wasting sugar [growing more leaves on longer cane] that could have gone into the fruit. Young leaves take sugar to grow; only a mature leaf puts sugar toward the grapes. So if you have a vine that is continually growing [out of control], you're sending sugar to the wrong place.*
>
> *...But if you know that you want your vines to produce, say, two hundred leaves each year, you can leave ten buds on each vine. When you prune, you expect that each bud will generate a cane that will produce twenty leaves and stop growing where you want it to... at about four feet.*
>
> *Vines managed this way are 'balanced.' Leave too many canes and they won't produce enough leaves per cane to ripen the grapes... leave too few and they will grow too long, wasting sugar and shading the fruit."* [5]

Closing the book, he said, "As I read this the first time, I was amazed at the precision required by this art of growing grapes, unlike raising wheat, herding sheep, or catching fish—other metaphors Jesus could have chosen. And if *vinekeepers* do this much work to produce Cabernet, Chardonnay, and other grapes, imagine *God's* care when he wants to groom us to produce Galatians 5 fruit—love, joy, peace, patience, kindness, goodness, faithfulness, gentleness, and self-control."

Turning to the board he said as he wrote, "The third lesson is an extension of the second and is this:"

> Seven lessons of the vine:
>
> 1. It is God—not man—who does the work.
> 2. Man wants leaves. God wants grapes.
> 3. Only God can produce grapes.

He reopened his Bible to the section they had been reading and said, "Listen to what Jesus says in John 14:10—just before he begins the parable of the vine in John 15: *Don't you believe that I am in the Father, and that the Father is in me? The words I say to you I do not speak on my own authority. Rather, it is the Father, living in me, who is doing his work."*[6]

Jack stood silently to let the thoughts and the words sink though minds to hearts, then quietly said, "This tells me that I can no more *naturally* produce more spiritual fruits than the unattended vine can *naturally* produce more grapes.

"And this tells me, 'Jack, don't be disheartened because *neither could Jesus.'* This tells me that Jesus—the person—did *nothing*. This tells me that it was God—in the form of the Holy Spirit—who did *everything*. This tells me that Jesus merely did what he understood, what he discerned, what he perceived his father wanted him to do, and then left the results—the grapes—of that action to God.

"This thought reminds me of a personal conviction that came out of my experiences as a young lieutenant serving with a tank battalion. During two combat tours in which there was no place safe from rockets, mortars, grenades, RPGs, sappers, snipers, and small-arms fire—and a place where you could *not* lead men and do your job if you chose to hang back or hide in a bunker incased in a flak jacket and helmet—I developed the philosophy that *my only responsibility was to act responsibly... and leave the results of those actions to God.*

"I rely on him today as I pass through the perils of life... with the same peace... with the same confidence... and with the same certainty as that with which I passed through the perils of war—knowing that my *only* responsibility is to *act* responsibly as I discern his word, my prayers, and the indwelling Spirit leads me."

Turning back the whiteboard, Jack said, "The fourth lesson is this:"

Seven lessons of the vine:

1. It is God—not man—who does the work.
2. Man wants leaves. God wants grapes.
3. Only God can produce grapes.
4. Only God should give direction.

"Looking again at the allegory, I think it is important that we see that the vinedresser gives the vine its direction for growth by carefully wrapping it around a wire or tying it to a trellis… and doing so repeatedly." Jack again opened the book and read from *Napa Stories*:

> *"Every winter, when the vine stands bare, vineyard workers undertake one of the year's most critical tasks: pruning. Vine by vine, they remove last year's growth and choose how many buds to leave for the coming year. Their actions determine what shape the vine will take and help control the quality of the crop….*
>
> *The three principal methods of pruning are cordon pruning, cane pruning and head pruning. A cordon is a permanent cane—a cane tied to a horizontal trellis when young and left on the vine year after year. Some vines have one cordon, others two, trellised in opposite directions to the vine to look like a 'T.' New canes emerge from spurs on the cordon and these canes are trained upward on catch-wires to keep both the leaves and grapes in the sun.*[7]

"This lesson four is important to me because it tells me that—even though I don't understand why something is happening… or don't know God's 'plan' for my life… or don't see how what I need for my family is going to be provided—God does know.

"I don't believe he *causes* much of the hardship in our lives any more than the vinedresser caused curling leaf mold or fatal root rot. But I believe he *knows.*

"I also believe that there is much in my life that he *does* cause or allow for reasons only he understands. Perhaps he wants me to live through a drought to experience his sufficiency… to endure a failure to become an example to others… to learn a new skill to permit my next professional step… to prepare me emotionally, move me geographically, position me vocationally to touch someone else's life… or to discipline me for sin."

Jack paused, "Before you dismiss this explanation of my accepting while not understanding as unsatisfactory, let me tell you about lesson number five." He then turned to the whiteboard and wrote:

> Seven lessons of the vine:
>
> 1. It is God—not man—who does the work.
> 2. Man wants leaves. God wants grapes.
> 3. Only God can produce grapes.
> 4. Only God should give direction.
> 5. Plant compared to vinedresser; man compared to God—the difference in understanding.

"I want you to picture Jesus talking to his disciples about the vinedresser and the vine, and how the dresser will prune the plant to make it more productive.

"Now here's my first question: How much do you think the *plant* understands about all this cutting and pruning and tying?

"If your answer is 'not much' because it is—relative to the vinedresser—a dull-witted plant, I would agree with you.

"Here's my second question: Was Jesus saying to his disciples that *man's* capacity to understand God's purpose is no greater than a *plant's* capacity to understand the vinedresser's?

"This was a revelation to me… when I began to see in this imagery that my intelligence compared to God's is like that of a plant's compared to a man's.

"A corollary thought is this: I find enormous personal peace in being loved and led by a God with such infinitely superior intellect."

Jack stepped to the board and wrote as he said, "This brings us to lesson six and one of the most interesting—if not initially most alarming—of the seven."

> Seven lessons of the vine:
>
> 1. It is God—not man—who does the work.
> 2. Man wants leaves. God wants grapes.
> 3. Only God can produce grapes.
> 4. Only God should give direction.
> 5. Plant compared to vinedresser; man compared to God—the difference in understanding.

> 6. God may want more than a nip and a tuck.

He turned back to the class, stepped to the side of the stand to be a little nearer, and said, "As I thought through lesson five, I found that this sense of peace… this calm… this comfort of being cared for by such an incomprehensible power with such an eternal perspective produced a tranquility beyond any I had ever experienced. As I thought of Jesus' admonition… that I should be prepared to be pruned in order to bear more fruit… I found myself accepting, even welcoming, the pain.

"And as I thought about the vinedressers of Napa Valley cutting the cane, trimming the vines, and counting the buds I found myself thinking that I could endure a nip and a tuck—frankly, I was prepared to endure them regularly—if it meant losing some leaves so that more light and more air would make me produce more fruit.

"And then I had this stunning thought: What if he wants to cut off more than a *few*… what if he wants to cut me back to the *trunk*… what if he wants me to give up *my* plans, *my* goals, *my* expectations… if doing so means more light and more air on *someone else's branch* so that *they* can produce more fruit?

"This thought haunted me for days. Then, I finally said, 'Yes… even trim me to the trunk if that's what you want.'"

Returning to the whiteboard, Jack wrote as he said, "Lesson number seven."

Seven lessons of the vine:

1. It is God—not man—who does the work.
2. Man wants leaves. God wants grapes.
3. Only God can produce grapes.
4. Only God should give direction.
5. Plant compared to vinedresser, man compared to God—the difference in understanding.
6. God may want more than a nip and a tuck.
7. God wants you to live in a state of joy.

Turning back to the class he said, "When I was a child, I pictured God as an immense being… somewhere… usually above me. As an adult I have accepted the fact that my mortal mind cannot comprehend God, that he exists in a dimension beyond my human senses.

"John 15 presents another mental model of what God, his family, and our roles in this life are like. The mental picture is that of a vineyard filled with *billions* of plants, and God patiently, persistently, and, somehow simultaneously, working on all of them, coordinating each for the good of the whole and for his ultimate purpose.

"Perhaps you can see yourself in that vineyard as I can see myself—dirty… frazzled… leafy—being carefully lifted and cleaned, gently re-trellised and re-tied, and confidently snipped and pruned by hands that love me, by a mind that empowers me, and by a vision that guides me.

"And perhaps you can hear Jesus say again those unimaginable words as he walked toward those unspeakable horrors: *I have told you this so that my joy may be in you... and that your joy may be complete."*

Jack stopped, stood silently, wanting to end the class, wanting this to be the last they heard, wanting these words to linger in the heart as refrains from a song linger in the mind. But he knew there was more to learning than hearing. There was thinking, there was doing, and, most effectively, there was writing. With that, he asked Beverly to pass out the sheets, made a few comments to familiarize them with the forms, and monitored for the next twenty minutes as the class completed the three questions from John—*What* is being said? *Why* is it being said? *How* does it apply to my life?—and shared new insights into this extraordinary passage. One point they discussed at length was what it meant for a person to abide. The consensus was that he intended us to reside, to rest, to dwell, to live, to await, to endure in his word, in his grace, and in his joy. And that we were to do all of that until... *until*... the fullness of his *season* for us.

As Jack concluded the discussion and prepared to end the class, he stepped to the side of the lectern again and said, "As we close, I do so with these last two thoughts regarding joy.

"First, it seems joy may be found in at least two forms. The first... the *highest*... is that of which Christ spoke regarding himself, and us, in John 15. This is a joy that exceeds all others in being personally fulfilling. It is one which comes from doing something for someone else. And—most importantly—doing that something, not because we *must*, but because we *want* to. It's a joy that follows any such act, from common to sacrificial... an act manifested in what Christ did for us... and an act which filled him with this supreme joy and a joy that is ours if we simply follow his example.

"Second, in addition to this highest joy of giving for others, it seems that God is obsessed with our living daily lives of inexplicable joy. I am not talking about silliness, foolishness, giddiness, or even happiness. I'm talking about joy—the quiet sense of well-being and contentment, of confidence and courage, that comes from knowing that we're loved *by* him and, because of that, he will be with us *through* all circumstances, *in* all places, *at* all times.

"We have just seen him teach this in the New Testament in John 15, and we can find it taught in the Old Testament, particularly in a verse from Psalm 33 that says, *...our hearts shall rejoice in him because we have trusted in His holy name.* This has been a favorite of mine for years, not only because of what it says, but because of what it does not say. It does *not* say that our hearts will rejoice in him because he has taken some action... saved us from some crisis... resolved for us some problem. *Gratitude* may follow, but not trust. Trust can only *precede* action. He is saying that our hearts shall rejoice *before* his action because we have trusted... *trusted*... him.

"I believe these, joy and trust, are two sides of the same coin, and I believe we cannot—*cannot*—have joy without trust. I am sorry to say that for me—even as impassioned as I am about this verse, as committed as I am to its principle, and as convinced as I am of its near-ten-commandment status—there are times when I can almost hear Jesus' persistent first-century question to Peter... *do you love me?...do you love me?...do you love me?...do you love me?,* restyled in his persistent 21st century question to me: *Jack... I know you love me, but do you trust me?...do you trust me?...do you trust me?"*

Jack stood quietly for a moment, looked over the full room, smiled, and said, "And that's the great question for you, too, because everything else—salvation... abiding... service... joy—follows your answer.

"It seems to me that Jesus must have known how difficult it was going to be for us to mature through those stages—from *salvation* to *abiding* to *service* to *joy*. I believe he must have known because, otherwise, I don't think he would have used this final opportunity—this *last* occasion before being arrested, these *last* minutes before being beaten, these *last* breaths before suffocating—to say these words if they did not reflect his highest hope for our living and our lives: *I have told you this so that my joy may be in you... and that your joy may be complete*."

Jack stood quietly for another moment then said, "And it seems to me that we may ask forgiveness for the sin of not living in *trust*, but rarely for the sin of not living in *joy."*

After yet another silent moment he said, "If you think that is an overstatement, come to your own conclusion. This week in your quiet time, reread John 15 then answer for yourself the question of whether Scripture places enough emphasis on joy that *not* living in joy is a sin. You'll be able to think of scores of reasons why abiding in joy is tough—you'll think of the pressure of work, the stress of family, the trauma of illness, the strain of finances, the loss of a loved one, and an infinite number of other legitimate causes. But whether it's *tough* is not the question… though it may have been the reason Jesus chose this as his *final* lesson."

Stepping back to the music stand, closing his binder of teaching notes, Jack said, "Next Sunday we will continue our examination of what it seems God intends *for* us… expects *from* us… and seeks to do *through* us."

With that, Jack smiled, turned to the woman at the left end of the front row and said, "Bev, please close us with prayer."

# # #

Your Takeaways and Action Items from this Chapter

Takeaway 1

(page__)

Takeaway 2

(page__)

Takeaway 3

(page__)

Your Takeaways and Action Items from this Chapter

Action Item 1

(page__)

Action Item 2

(page__)

Action Item 3

(page__)

Why "Church"?

Chapter 2 - Sunday, May 15

The pre-class clatter surrounded but did not distract Jack's wife, Kelli. From across the room, without blinking an eye, she watched her husband as he stood at the door, facing her, talking to visitors who had just been brought to the class. *All the better,* she thought as she visually stalked Jack, focusing on every nuance of his every move, waiting for that moment when she could pounce like a cat on a mouse. She didn't do this often, no more than once or twice a year, but oh how it annoyed him, and oh how she enjoyed it. And then it came. The prey stumbled. With a foolish glance at her, she caught his eye, froze him with a smile… and *winked.*

He smiled back with a slight turn of the head that said, "*Please... don't do that.*" She nodded an understanding—knowing how distracting this was at the beginning of a class when all his energies were focused on the lesson—and, like the thoughtful wife she was, she answered… *wink, wink.*

He laughed, gave her a leave-the-room look, explained to the visitors that his wife was harassing him, and sat down as Beverly opened the class.

With Kelli's ambush forgotten and announcements, prayer requests, and prayer time completed, Jack walked to the front of the class as he adjusted a new lapel mic. "Good morning. For those joining us for the first time," he said as he smiled and looked over the group that was a little larger than the previous week's, but starting to show signs of stabilizing, "I extend a special welcome. I also extend a warning that this is not your usual Sunday School fare, for me or for this church. As you may know, this is my last series of lessons, so instead of using standard teaching materials I am taking these remaining classes to do what I like to do best: to examine one of my favorite Scriptures from the perspectives of three of my favorite questions—*What* is being said? *Why* is it being said? And *How* does it apply to my life?

"Last Sunday I closed with what, for me, is God's most persistent… most pressing… most important question: *Jack, I know you love me… but do you trust me?* This is the quintessential, seminal, gut-level question for all of us. But it is not one we can fully grasp until we begin to fully comprehend how God *views* us… how he *loves* us... how he wants to *use* us. To have a better understanding, last week we examined—through the allegory of the vine—Jesus' final instructions to those who would soon lay the foundation for his church.

"This week I want to start with this question about the word I just used and one that we, for the most part, take for granted. Here's the question," he said as he turned to the whiteboard and said as he wrote:

When does the word <u>church</u> first appear in the Bible?

Some in the class responded with surprise, having never given it much thought, then set about scanning various Old and New Testament passages to see if there was a reference prior to the famous one to Peter. After a moment, Sue White said, "It appears in Mathew 16. Jesus has asked his disciples who people say he is. He then asked them who they say he is. Peter replies, quoting from my New King James Version *You are the Christ, the Son of the living God.* To which Jesus stated, *Blessed are you, Simon Bar-Jonah, for flesh and blood has not revealed this to you, but My Father who is in heaven. And I also say to you that you are Peter, and on this rock I will build My church…."*

"Thank you, Sue. Now," Jack said, "if you're like me, you've probably read or heard that passage hundreds of times, and each time have usually rushed by it. If we're not careful, we could do the same and thereby miss a watershed moment in Biblical history.

"Think about the political and theological context in which Jesus made that statement: The Roman Empire is ubiquitous; Jewish legalism is tyrannical.

"In this setting Jesus says: On this rock I will build my *church.*

"Not *temple…*

"Not *tabernacle…*

"Not *synagogue…*

"Not *kingdom…*

"Not *nation…*

"…but '*church.'*

"We need to ask ourselves why?" Jack continued, "But first we need to ask ourselves three other questions.

"First, is *church* a reliable translation of the Greek?

"Second, if so, did the word have any common usage or meaning to the disciples?

"And third, what did Jesus—based on any common usage—probably mean?

"First, is it an accurate translation? One of the interesting findings," Jack said as he opened his three-ring binder of teaching notes to a list he had made earlier, "is the uniformity in interpretation among various translations. As examples, *church* is used in the King James, the New King James, the International Standard, the New International Standard, the American Standard, Weymouth's New Testament, Montgomery's New Testament and other versions, while the word *assembly* is used in Young's Bible and Darby's Bible."

Returning the list, he said, "I think given the consistency of the interpretations we can assume that the answer to the first question is 'yes'—*church* seems to be an accurate translation.

"However, it may be that Young's and Darby's 'assembly' is closest to what Jesus intended because of the Greek *ekklesia*," Jack said as he turned to the whiteboard and added:

> When does the word <u>church</u>
> first appear in the Bible?
>
> Greek: ekklesia

Reaching down, he picked up a large, worn, hardcover book from a small stack on a chair and said, "I want to read a part of what the International Standard Bible Encyclopedia says about ekklesia:

> *"Although ekklesia soon became a distinctively Christian word, it has its own pre-Christian history; and to those—whether Jews or Greeks—who first heard it applied to the Christian society, it would come with suggestions of familiar things. Throughout the Greek world and right down to New Testament times, ekklesia was the designation of the regular assembly of the whole body of citizens in a free city-state, 'called out' (Greek ek,'out' and kalein, 'to call') by the herald for the discussion and decision of public business....*
>
> *The word thus came into Christian history with associations alike for the Greek and the Jew.... The pre-Christian history of the word had a direct bearing upon its Christian meaning, for the ekklesia of the New Testament is a theocratic democracy, a society of those who are free, but are always conscious that their freedom springs from obedience to their King."* [1]

Jack stopped reading, closed the book with his index finger as a marker, and said, "Here, then, it seems, we find that the answer to our second question is 'yes,' the word did have common usage and meaning. With that we can move on to the third and more important question which is: What do you think—based on common usage—Jesus meant?"

The class sat silently… sorting out impressions… searching for insights… imagining the disciples. Patricia Baker sat quietly, looking for the right words, started to speak, halted, then started again, speaking as her thoughts cohered, "The disciples must have been shocked. In their lives they had known nothing but political and religious domination. Roman governors, soldiers, and tax collectors overshadowed their physical and financial lives. Pharisees, Sadducees, and scribes overshadowed their spiritual and personal lives. And though both were oppressive, I don't think Jesus was talking about freedom from a dictatorial government, but freedom from a dictatorial religion—especially, freedom from the synagogue's minutia of rules and codes and regulations that their leadership had built over the centuries from Mosaic Law."

"I think that's true," Stan Wheeler said, "and I think that there might be something else here. I think he might be using an old style to teach a new truth. Jesus taught in parables… and it seems to me that this is another one. I think he's using something familiar to illustrate something unfamiliar… something they understand to explain something they don't understand. In this, Jesus is using the baseline of the known—how Greeks could assemble as free men to address public matters of common interest—from which he extends the idea that *his* followers could assemble as free *believers* to worship… to fellowship… to address spiritual matters of common interests."

"Good," said Jack as he opened the book again. "I want you to hear more of the Encyclopedia's discussion of 'church' that supports what you're saying and ask you to pay particular attention to its emphasis on the individual believer.

> *The fundamental note is faith. It was to Peter's confessing his faith in Christ that the promise came, 'Upon this rock I will build my church.'*
>
> *Until Jesus found a man full of faith He could not begin to build His church; and unless Peter had been the prototype of others whose faith was like his own, the walls of the church would never have risen into the air.*
>
> *Primarily the church is a society <u>not</u> of thinkers... or workers... or even of worshippers ...but of believers."*[2]

Looking up, Jack said, "In a future lesson we will look at the society… the body corporate… the assemblage of believers… the *Church*.

"But we can't go to that until we get this: Jesus did not look to the size, wealth, traditions, staffs, programs, prestige, code, creed, statements-of-belief, or articles-of-faith of any church to save its members. He looked to the individual to save himself. And to do so through *faith*, not works… to do so *permanently*, not temporarily… to do so according to *God's* plan, not man's… and to do so by accepting the profoundly simple promise from John 3:16: *For God so loved the world, that He gave His only begotten Son, that whosoever believeth in Him should not perish, but have everlasting life.*[3]

"Again, from the International Encyclopedia:

> *Hence, we find that 'believers' or 'they that believed' is constantly used as a synonym for the members of the Christian society....*
>
> *This church-founding and church-building faith, of which baptism was the seal, was much more than an act of intellectual assent. It was a personal laying hold of the personal Savior, the bond of a vital union between Christ and the believer which resulted in nothing less than a new creation."*[4]

Closing the book and picking up his copy of the International Standard Version of the Bible, Jack continued, "Not only was *salvation* to be personal, but so was *service*. Looking back at last Sunday's lesson… at the Seven Lessons of the Vine… we see Jesus speaking of himself as the vine… and each person as an individual branch… and then hear him saying *you* must abide… *you* must be pruned …*you* must produce fruits. What is clear in this is that the church corporately begins with us individually. Paul later emphasizes this in his letter to the Corinthians in which he says some are feet, some hands, but all are part of the body. Here, in part, is what he wrote as reported in 1 Corinthians 12:14-27:

> *For the body does not consist of only one part, but of many. If the foot says, 'Since I'm not a hand, I'm not part of the body,' that does not make it any less a part of the body, does it? And if the ear says, 'Since I'm not an eye, I'm not part of the body,' that does not make it any*

less a part of the body, does it? If the whole body were an eye, where would the sense of hearing be? If the whole body were an ear, where would the sense of smell be?

But at this very time God has arranged the parts, every one of them, in the body just as He wanted to. Now if they were all one part, where would the body be? So there are many parts, but one body. The eye cannot say to the hand, 'I don't need you,' or the head to the feet, 'I don't need you.'

On the contrary, those parts of the body that seem to be weaker are in fact indispensable, and the parts of the body that we think are less honorable are treated with special honor, and we make our less attractive parts more attractive. However, our attractive parts don't need this. But God has put the body together and has given special honor to the parts that lack it, so that there might be no disharmony in the body, but that its parts should have the same concern for each other. If one part suffers, every part suffers with it. If one part is praised, every part rejoices with it. Now you are Christ's body and individual parts of it." [5]

Jack closed his Bible, stepped to the side of the lectern and said, "Not only does this describe the difference in the parts of the body, but the unique role each part plays in the whole. Most noteworthy in Paul's writing is that each part must be dedicated… consecrated… to fulfilling its essential purpose. Perhaps nowhere is this dedication, this consecration, more clearly and frequently displayed than in his prolific use of the term 'saints' for 'those who believe.' He used it about 45 times in Romans, Ephesians, Philemon, Colossians, 1st Timothy, 1 st and 2nd Corinthians, and 1st and 2nd Thessalonians. In addition, other New Testament writers use the word for a total of about 65 references."

Stepping back behind the music stand, Jack again picked up the hardback book and said, "This use so many times suggests that we stop and give the same kind of examination to the New Testament word *saints* that we just gave to the word *church*. This is what the International Standard Encyclopedia says about the word:

A*nother dominant note of the New Testament church lay in the consecration of its members. 'Saints' is one of the most frequently recurring designations for them that we find. As thus employed, the word has in the first place an objective meaning; the sainthood of the Christian society consisted in its separation from the world by God's electing grace....*

The members of the church, as Peter said, are 'an elect race, a royal priesthood, a holy nation, a people for God's own possession' (1 Pet 2:9). But side by side with this sense of an outward and priestly consecration, the flame 'saints' carried within it the thought of an ethical holiness—a holiness consisting, not merely in a status determined by relation to Christ, but in an actual and practical saintliness, a consecration to God that finds expression in character and conduct. No doubt the members of the church are called saints even when the living evidences of sainthood are sadly lacking....

It is necessary for the ordinary reader constantly to guard against the idea that New Testament saintship was in any way a result of personal character, and consequently that it implied approval of moral attainment already made. Such a rendering as 'consecrated ones,' for example, would bring out more clearly the relation to God which is involved, but, besides the fact that it is not a happy translation, it might lead to other errors, for it is not easy to remember that consecration—the setting apart of the individual as one of the company whom God has in a peculiar way as His own—springs not from man, but from God Himself, and that consequently it is in no way something optional, and admits of no degrees of progress, but, on the contrary, is from the beginning absolute duty. It should also be noted that while, as has been said, to be a saint is not directly and primarily to be good but to be set apart by God as His own, yet the godly and holy character ought inevitably and immediately to result. When God consecrates and claims moral beings for Himself and His service, He demands that they should go on to be fit for and worthy of the relation in which He has placed them…." [6]

Jack paused, closed the book, and said, "For the next few moments I want you to think of yourself differently than you normally do: I want you to think of yourself—not simply as a member of this *church*—but as an essential member of a *royal priesthood*… as a member with *indispensable gifts*… as a member who along with others uniquely-gifted have collectively become in Paul's words, '*Christ's body*.'

"As you do, I want you to close your eyes and think of yourself in this first-century context. I want you to think of yourself as it appears God intended… and intends. I want you to think of yourself as being separate and apart, consecrated and called, to a special purpose for you and for those whose lives you touch. To help you visualize what I'm describing, for the next few moments I don't want you to think of yourself as Sue or Robert or Brad… but with neither merit nor pride, neither works nor worthiness, based solely on this separation and consecration to his purpose… I want you to think of yourself as *Saint* Sue… *Saint* Robert… *Saint* Brad. I want you to close your eyes and whisper to yourself… '*saint me.*'"

For a moment the classroom was silent. No shuffling of feet. No turning of pages. No sounds at all… except for the calm rhythm of gentle breathing as souls searched the depth and breadth of what this might mean, what it seemed God had intended, and how this might change their sense of service to him.

Eyes opened as Jack quietly said, "We can't think about this sainthood… about this consecration… about this being set apart, without coming to this disturbing thought: You and I are the only *Bible* some will ever read… the only *church* some will ever see… the only *saint* some will ever know."

Continuing quietly, Jack said, "And to that thought, most of us will say 'not me'… I'm not ready because I'm still figuring out if this whole Christian thing is a deal *I'm* going to take… or

"I'm not ready because I have no confidence in my ability to lead a representative life… or

"I'm not ready because others know me too well and have seen me fail too often.

"If you are part of the first group—still thinking that Christianity is the speedbump in life rather than life being the speedbump to eternity—you're in good company. C.S. Lewis and an infinite number of others have traveled the same road from questioner to believer. So, be patient. Keep looking. You'll get it."

Pulling an old newspaper from the back pocket of his three-ring binder, Jack said, "If you're in the second group, I want to tell you about the best definition of confidence I've ever read. It's the subject of a book reviewed in *USA Today*. The book is called *CONFIDENCE* and was written by Rosabeth Moss Kanter, a Harvard Business School professor.

"The book is the product of her research on how confidence affects performance. In it she talks about how *confidence* has impacted athletic programs like the University of Connecticut's girls' basketball team and corporate giants like Gillette. I admire her for both her perspective on this subject and her skill as a writer. With regard to the latter, look at how she defines confidence," he said as he turned to the whiteboard, erased it clean, picked up a marker, and read as he wrote:

> **CONFIDENCE:**
>
> **The 'sweet spot' between arrogance and despair.**
>
> **Where arrogance is the failure to see any flaws, and despair the failure to acknowledge any strengths.[7]**

"One of the things I like about this statement is its active rather than passive nature. Look at this," he said as he circled two words, '*sweet spot.*'

Turning back to the class he said, "Kanter could have chosen several other phrases to identify the midpoint between the extremes of 'arrogance' and 'despair'—which, by the way, could be the framework for another lesson with the sins of arrogance or pride at one extreme and despair or fear at the other—but that was not her point, nor is it mine. My point is this: instead of *sweet spot* she could have said the *line* between or *point* between or *border* between... all of which would have described something static, stagnant, lifeless. But she didn't. Instead, she chose the phrase full of energy, vibrancy, life... a phrase that anyone involved in any of several sports would instantly understand... *the sweet spot.*

"If you play golf or tennis or baseball you know about the sweet spot. You know of that ethereal, miniscule, invisible speck on your driver or racket or bat. You know that—if you connect there—the sport is easy, the world is good, and God, indeed, is in his heavens.

"Further, you know it is not a matter of 'trying harder' or 'swinging faster.' You know, rather, it is a matter of knowing the fundamentals... of playing within yourself... of being *patient* with yourself while actively *pursuing* a greater goal.

"You also know that it is, first, a matter of *playing*... of being *in* the game... of getting *out* of the cart and onto the tee, *off* the chair and onto the court, *away* from the dugout and onto the diamond with the intention—the *intention*—of doing well. And that, my friend, is all that God asks of you... and all that you can ask of yourself."

Stepping back to the lectern, Jack said, "If you're in the third group... the last group... the I'm-not-ready-for-that-because-they-know-me-too-well-and-have-seen-me-fail-too-often group, you're in with a pretty big crowd. You're there along with David, Abraham, and Jonah in the Old Testament... Paul, Peter, and Matthew in the New... and myself, those sitting on either side of you, and everyone in this room today."

He paused, looked at the class for a long moment, then said, "Hear me on this. As I said last week about the Seventh Lesson of the Vine—Jesus wants us to live in a permanent state of inexplicable joy. Not giddiness... not Pollyanishness... but quiet, abiding, sustaining joy.

"We can't do that if we live in a state of chronic low-grade guilt—much as a child may run a chronic low-grade fever—because we cling to real or imagined failures. These are those for which we will not forgive ourselves. These are those for which we relentlessly give ourselves mental lashings of

'I should have said this,' 'I could have done that,' 'If only I hadn't....' These are those that keep us in the muddy shallows of self-condemnation.

"If the failures are real, ask and God will forgive you. As you do, also ask for the power to forgive yourself. And, if others are involved, ask for the wisdom to determine what other remedial and reconciliatory steps you should take.

"But if they are not—and this is the point I want to make—stop beating yourself up!

"Go back with me to the parable of the vineyard: It is dark. Jesus is hours away from death. His time on Earth is over. Ending is his mission to recruit and train a team which will constitute the leadership and form the infrastructure of a new Earthly organization manifesting God's new covenant with man.

"As I read John 15 and as I try to imagine what he must have thought in those closing minutes, I have to ask myself: Did Jesus... even for a split second... think he had *failed?"*

Jack stood quietly for a moment, then elaborating said, "Did Jesus think he had failed with his disciples who were scared and confused... failed with Jerusalem, the city over which he had wept... failed with those he had fed and healed who still viewed his miracles as little more than magic... failed with those who expected his purpose to be a release from Rome, who never understood it to be a release from sin... failed with the Jews, the ones to whom he had been sent as the promised Messiah, who in a few hours would demand his death... and did he then pray, *Abba... Abba... I am so sorry."*

Jack stood quietly again. He gave the class a moment to think through the question. Gave them a moment to think through Scripture. Gave them a moment to think of their own answer.

He then said, "If we look at one of the most passionate prayers ever prayed as recorded in John 17, we can only conclude that Jesus *did not*. We can only conclude that he *knew* it would be difficult... *knew* there would be confusion... *knew* he could do no more than act responsibly... and *knew* the measure of judging the *success* or *failure* of that action rested in *God's* definitions of those two words.

"Not in *his*.

"And not in the *world's*.

"If you are one who constantly feels ineffective and unsuccessful in your walk, I encourage you to give God some credit... place in him some trust... and rely on him for grace to understand your efforts, your heart, your intentions.

"Then turn your eyes from yourself and see that Jesus, having earnestly lived his life as a servant *to*... in obedience *of*... and dependent *upon* his understanding of God's will, did *not* usurp his father's supremacy and presume that *he* had the right... that *he* had the perspective... that *he* had the privilege of judging *himself*. And, my friends—if you and I are to live a bold God-led, God-pruned, God-honoring life of fruitfulness and joy—neither do we have the right to judge ourselves if we live with God-focused, God-enabled, God-serving intent... *intent*!"

Looking to his left, he said, "Bev, will you pass out the sheets." Then looking back at the class said, "I want you to read Jesus' remarkable prayer in John 17:2-26, this from the New International Version, then write your answer to the question of what is being said, why is it being said, and how does it apply to my life."

For the next twenty minutes they completed the three questions after reading Jesus' remarkable prayer on the eve of being betrayed, beaten, and crucified:

> *Father, the hour has come.*
>
> *Glorify your Son, that your Son may glorify you. For you granted him authority over all people that he might give eternal life to all those you have given him. Now this is eternal life:*

that they know you, the only true God, and Jesus Christ, whom you have sent. I have brought you glory on earth by finishing the work you gave me to do. And now, Father, glorify me in your presence with the glory I had with you before the world began.

I have revealed you to those whom you gave me out of the world. They were yours; you gave them to me and they have obeyed your word. Now they know that everything you have given me comes from you. For I gave them the words you gave me and they accepted them. They knew with certainty that I came from you, and they believed that you sent me. I pray for them. I am not praying for the world, but for those you have given me, for they are yours. All I have is yours, and all you have is mine. And glory has come to me through them. I will remain in the world no longer, but they are still in the world, and I am coming to you. Holy Father, protect them by the power of your name, the name you gave me, so that they may be one as we are one. While I was with them, I protected them and kept them safe by that name you gave me. None has been lost except the one doomed to destruction so that Scripture would be fulfilled.

I am coming to you now, but I say these things while I am still in the world, so that they may have the full measure of my joy within them. I have given them your word and the world has hated them, for they are not of the world any more than I am of the world. My prayer is not that you take them out of the world but that you protect them from the evil one. They are not of the world, even as I am not of it.

Sanctify them by the truth; your word is truth. As you sent me into the world, I have sent them into the world. For them I sanctify myself, that they too may be truly sanctified.

My prayer is not for them alone. I pray also for those who will believe in me through their message, that all of them may be one, Father, just as you are in me and I am in you. May they also be in us so that the world may believe that you have sent me. I have given them the glory that you gave me, that they may be one as we are one—I in them and you in me—so that they may be brought to complete unity. Then the world will know that you sent me and have loved them even as you have loved me.

Father, I want those you have given me to be with me where I am, and to see my glory, the glory you have given me because you loved me before the creation of the world.

Righteous Father, though the world does not know you, I know you, and they know that you have sent me. I have made you known to them, and will continue to make you known in order that the love you have for me may be in them and that I myself may be in them.[8]

At the end of the discussion period, Jack said, "If you feel that God may be speaking to you about re-examining your purpose and your priorities in life… if you think there might be something to this being set apart and being consecrated… if you want to explore some means by which you might move from just *loving* God to *trusting* God… then you'll want to be here next Sunday as we talk about the all-important Requisite Start."

Then, turning to the woman at the end of the front row, he said, "Bev, please close us in prayer."

###

Your Takeaways and Action Items from this Chapter

Takeaway 1

(page__)

Takeaway 2

(page__)

Takeaway 3

(page__)

Your Takeaways and Action Items from this Chapter (cont.)

Action Item 1

(page__)

Action Item 2

(page__)

Action Item 3

(page__)

What Is the Requisite Start?

Chapter 3 - Sunday, May 22

As the large class went through what was now becoming their Sunday morning routine of greeting friends, shuffling chairs, and settling in, Jack talked with Dianne, a woman who had first visited weeks before. He was pleased that she was joining the class and that Sandra, the woman Dianne sat by earlier, appeared to be hosting her into the group.

He was also pleased to learn that one of the points he had made in the seven lessons of the vine—that given our relative intelligence, we can no more understand God's purpose in pruning us than a vine can understand a vinedresser's purpose in pruning it—had brought her a new level of peace and contentment. He said that he hoped she would find today's lesson equally informative but reminded her that his interpretations of the metaphor of the vine were his personal views—not Scripture—and fore-warned her that today's lesson also reflected his personal opinion. As she and Sandra took their seats and as Beverly greeted the class, asked for requests, then led them in prayer, Jack silently whispered, *My God... lead me to say what you want me say... the way you want it said....*

Jack walked to the old music stand, set several reference books on a vacant chair near the lectern, added his good mornings to Beverly's, then began the lesson by saying, "As I closed last week, I said that if you feel that God may be speaking to you about reexamining your purpose and your priorities in life... about being set apart and being consecrated... about moving from just *loving* God to *trusting* God... then you would want to be here today.

"I start our lesson with this simple expression universally used in reference to Jesus," he said as he turned to the whiteboard and in black marker wrote:

Lord and Savior

Tapping the phrase with his marker as he turned back to the class he continued, "Years ago, I wondered about the order of these words. It seemed to me that they should be reversed, rearranged into the chronological order like this so that we would speak of Jesus first as *Savior* of our souls before we spoke of him as *Lord* of our lives," then wrote on the board:

Lord and Savior

Savior and Lord

"While I may have wondered about the sequencing, I have never wondered about the dualism… that this phrase describes two distinct, interdependent, but isolated events: His role as my redeemer for eternity… and his role as my master in this life. Our focus over the next several weeks will be on the latter… his lordship of our lives.

"The main source of today's lesson is my wife, and the main point is the lesson she taught me years ago. As you know, Kelli and I have two children, a son and a daughter, both grown. They are exceptional adults today because they had an exceptional mother in their formative years. Kelli was not only good at parenting them, but good at tutoring me.

"One of the lessons she taught me by example was that they needed for me to spend *scheduled* time with them. I already knew that many of the moments to talk, to think, to share came when they were least expected… when it was just parent and child carpooling to school… or painting a bedroom …or making cookie dough. It was during these that the news about the betrayal of a friend… or hopes for the present… or dreams for the future came out.

"But she also taught me that in addition to these serendipitous moments of togetherness, they needed *structured* ones… they needed planned time when parent and child drew themselves away together… just to talk, just to share, just to be with one another.

"If you as a parent have had these, both planned and unplanned, and if you responded appropriately through the full range of the parent-child relationship—from thoughtful questions to disturbing moods to unexpected humor to surprising maturity—two indispensable things happened: First, your child received timely instruction and encouragement *from* you. Second, your child developed experientially-based trust and faith *in* you.

"This model for learning and trusting is obvious… at a human level for parent and child… at a spiritual level for God and man. And the indispensable ingredient for it is equally obvious: *time.*

"I believe that we as Christians will *never* become what God wants us to become… *never* move his son from Savior to Lord… and *never* become instruments wholly consecrated until we regularly set aside *structured* time for him to *teach* and to *lead*… and for us to *learn* and to *trust*.

"To that end," Jack said as he again turned to the whiteboard, wiped it clean, and said as he wrote, "I believe…"

> **God wants our first part of every day.**

Turning back to the class he continued, "I believe this for three reasons. First because of the example Christ set for us in Mark 1:35 where it says, *In the morning, while it was still very dark, Jesus got up and went to a deserted place and prayed there.*[1]

"Second, I believe this because of the writings of two authors for whom I have the highest respect: C. S. Lewis and Bruce Wilkinson."

Jack reached down to the small stack of reference materials, picked up a worn paperback and said, "C.S. Lewis was one of the intellectual giants of the twentieth century, an atheist turned Christian, and arguably the most influential Christian writer of his day. He was a Fellow in English Literature at Oxford University until 1954 when he was elected Chair of Medieval and Renaissance Literature at Cambridge, a position he held until his retirement.

"He wrote more than thirty books, including three icons in the Christian community: *Mere Christianity, The Chronicles of Narnia*, and *The Screwtape Letters.* The first—a compilation of radio talks made during the 1940s—has sold millions of copies worldwide and has served as a study in sensible reasoning for nonbelievers and a primer for daily living for new believers. I give you this long introduction in part because he is an author you should know, and in part because I so strongly recommend that you read these books." He turned to the page he had marked and said, "In *Mere Christianity,* he wrote this about the realistic aspect of living life as a Christian:

> *...That is why the real problem of the Christian life comes where people do not usually look for it. It comes the very moment you wake up each morning. All your wishes and hopes for the day rush at you like wild animals. And the first job each morning consists simply in shoving them all back; in listening to the other voice, taking that other point of view, letting that other, larger, stronger, quieter life come flowing in...."*[2]

Jack returned the book to the stack, picked up another, and said, "The second author, Dr. Bruce Wilkinson, has touched the lives of millions through the *Walk Thru the Bible* ministry he founded, through the scores and scores of teaching/training materials he has written, and, in particular, through the three inspirational books he has authored: *The Prayer of Jabez*, *The Dream Giver,* and *The Secrets of the Vine.*

"Though I've never met Dr. Wilkinson, no spiritual leader has influenced my daily life more. I'll talk about the other two at another time, but right now I want to focus on this, *The Secrets of the Vine*, and the lesson it taught me—several years ago—from the lesson he was taught. He relates in chapters seven and eight how growth in the ministry he had founded was starting to slow down, how he was starting to feel used up, how he was starting to think of resigning… all because there were no more hours in a day he could give to it, no more energy he could bring to it, no more resources he could invest in it. He was, in a few words, exhausted… depressed… tapped out.

"He took the step of flying to California to meet for three days with an advisor who had counseled hundreds of others in similar circumstances. Wilkinson held nothing back as he described his work and his hopes, his fears and his frustrations. After hearing it all, the advisor's recommendation was stunningly simple… and complex.

"It was this: Do less. Pray more.

"Translated, Wilkinson was told that his talent and enthusiasm had taken his ministry as far as it was going to go, and that—for it to go farther—he had to have the *discipline* and the *faith* to do the unthinkable: to *work* less and to *fellowship* more.

"This meant, if his day started at 6:00 a.m., it was not with a period of scheduling or managing, training or leading, writing or reading. This meant it was with a period of prayer… of fellowship… of talking… of listening. This meant that he would have to somehow trust the improbable equation that less time 'producing' meant more 'production.'

"I'm glad he listened. Someday I'll tell you what this time is like for me. Suffice it until then to say that this man, and this book, have shaped my mornings and thus my life.

"And third," Jack said as he returned the book to the stack and picked up his Bible, "I believe this because of my own experience, and because I believe my role in God's work… my calling to his service… is no less important in his design of things—though in a much, much smaller way—than his call to Martin Luther, Charles Spurgeon, or Billy Graham. Stated another way, I don't believe ministry is just left to ministers… the clergy… the cloth. I think God intends for you and me to touch lives, influence thinking, and bear witness in our circle of influence… whether we are in a board room, classroom, cubicle, or kitchen… whether at a sales convention, family reunion, restaurant, or graveside… whether developing strategies, leading troops, hiring trainees, or babysitting.

"As an example of this, I want you to hear one my favorite stories from the New Testament and one that represents the mental model I carry for how God uses the most obscure of us at the most unanticipated of times. This event takes place three days after Paul's Damascus Road experience where he was blinded, fell to his knees, and heard a voice saying, *Saul, Saul, why are you persecuting me?*[3] Would someone find and read Acts 9:10-17?"

The sound of fluttering tissue-thin pages again filled the room, then Don Crane said, "I have it," and read from the NIV:

> *In Damascus there was a disciple named Ananias. The Lord called to him in a vision, 'Ananias!'*
>
> *'Yes, Lord,' he answered*
>
> *The Lord told him, 'Go to the house of Judas on Straight Street and ask for a man from Tarsus named Saul, for he is praying. In a vision he has seen a man named Ananias come and place his hands on him to restore his sight.'*
>
> *'Lord,' Ananias answered, 'I have heard many reports about this man and all the harm he has done to your holy people in Jerusalem. And he has come here with authority from the chief priests to arrest all who call on your name.'*
>
> *But the Lord said to Ananias, 'Go! This man is my chosen instrument to proclaim my name to the Gentiles and their kings and to the people of Israel. I will show him how much he must suffer for my name.'*

Then Ananias went to the house and entered it. Placing his hands on Saul, he said, 'Brother Saul, the Lord—Jesus, who appeared to you on the road as you were coming here—has sent me so that you may see again and be filled with the Holy Spirit.'

Immediately, something like scales fell from Saul's eyes, and he could see again. He got up and was baptized, and after taking some food, he regained his strength."[4]

"Thanks, Don," Jack said, then continued, "Now… here's the thing I like about this story. I used the word obscure a moment ago, and I'll use it again now. In all of Biblical history this man Ananias is heard of once… just *once*. He steps out of obscurity, touches Paul's life, and returns to obscurity. I am conscious of this story all the time… particularly as I fly. I have never known strangers to speak more candidly nor more quickly than they will on long, late-night flights. They will talk about marriages getting better, children running loose, and businesses pressing bankruptcy with an abandonment that their spouses would love, their children would heed, and their bankers would loathe. And often the talk turns to deeper issues of life… of values… of spiritual matters. I see these situations for me as being similar to that of Ananias'… for me to be used for a moment if that is God's purpose, then, with contentment, slip back into anonymity… into obscurity.

"Finally, I believe there is another similarity—though again much, much smaller—between myself, Martin Luther, Charles Spurgeon, and Billy Graham… and that similarity is that they were active rather than passive believers, and that they *proactively* studied God's word, searched for God's purpose, spent time in God's presence. This proactive *posture* is critical… this *time* with God is critical … and this *fellowship* through the Holy Spirit is critical."

Jack began to speak, then hesitated. There was silence for a few seconds as he looked at the floor. He slowly looked up and said, "…As I think about it, I believe it would be appropriate for me to pause here and give you a sidebar on my view of the Holy Spirit. You will forgive me if this sounds blasphemous… but I believe that—though the Bible is the inspired word of God—without the interpretation, explanation, and application by the Holy Spirit it is nothing more than ancient, dusty, sometimes interesting history with no more relevance, importance, or meaning to my life than the earliest Chinese, Greek, or Celtic writings. Further, I believe that the Holy Spirit cannot—can *never*—*fully* interpret, *fully* explain, and *fully* apply God's word to me if I only give him a couple of *seconds* of prayer before a meal, a couple of *minutes* of prayer before bedtime, or a couple of *hours/days/weeks* of prayer before a child in crisis, a job that is going bad, or an incurable medical condition is resolved."

Jack paused again… more seconds of silence ticked by… then began speaking, "While I am on this extraordinarily personal note, I am going to tell you what this daily time is like for me. I don't suggest this for you, but it is what I do and perhaps it will help you… how did I put it a few minutes ago… *regularly set aside structured time for him to teach and to lead."*

Once more Jack stood wordlessly, looking down, his thoughts darting, thinking, *My God, what have I done… this was not planned… where does this end… where does telling them much become too much… is it not enough to look at the teaching from Scripture… I am no model and what I do is no paradigm.*

Looking up and into their faces, he continued, "I'm going to tell you what I do, what I *try* to do, every day. Many days I can't because mornings are filled with travel, family, business, and scores of other inflexible demands leaving little time. So on those days I do this: I spend the first five minutes—over my first cup of coffee before the day's wave of plans, problems, and opportunities engulf me—in a quiet place, in prayer.

"It's that simple: The first five minutes

"It may be in a hotel room in the dark, in our bathroom with the door closed, or in our den with the lights off... but I'm there, saying good morning, thanking him for the night's safety, preparing for the day by re-calibrating my spiritual compass toward God as my magnetic north. It's almost like taking that one big quick gulp of fresh air before jumping in the water."

Jack paused, then said, "That is Plan B. This is Plan A."

Jack paused again, then continued, "I sit quietly.

"I am preparing to meet my creator.

"I am preparing to meet my father.

"I am preparing to meet his son.

"I am preparing for fellowship with them through the Holy Spirit.

"It is *similar* to Plan B in that it is the first thing I do every morning. It is *dissimilar* in that I set aside 30 minutes or more for it... *dissimilar* in that it is more a time of prayer, of conversation, of companionship... and *dissimilar* in that I sometimes open it with a devotional reading from something like Sarah Young's *Jesus Calling*, Billy Grahams' *Hope for Each Day,* or Alistair Begg's modern version of Charles Spurgeon's *Morning and Evening.*

"Other times I open with Scripture. At the moment I am working my way through Zondervan's *Parallel New Testament in Greek and English.* I'm doing this at the rate of about fifteen verses a day. It is slow... wonderfully slow... because this book lays out, side by side, three versions —the original King James Version, the New International Version, and the Nestle Greek Text. On the Nestle pages under each Greek symbol is the word or phrase in English. It's interesting to see the subtle differences in how some words are translated into the two English versions. As another sidebar, if you're interested in translations, I recommend *Strong's Complete Dictionary of Bible Words.* It's big and comprehensive. It contains *every* major word in the KJV, in alphabetical order, with a list of *every* Hebrew, *every* Aramaic, and *every* Greek word that can be translated into English. Like I said: It's big."

Jack paused a third time, took a breath, then, reluctantly, pressed on, "Next, on many mornings, I write a prayer. I write because it's early and writing helps me stay awake. I write in a spiral notebook. I start with a fresh page every day. I date each page. And—because I understand that Jesus rather than using the formal word '*father*' prayed using the more affectionate, more personal, more relational '*papa*'—I often remind myself of the relationship God wants with *me* by beginning with this word: '*Dad.*' So, I open my written prayer with these three words, *Good morning, Dad,* then write of the things heaviest on my mind.

"On other mornings, usually in the dark, I simply talk to them—the Trinity—as if I were talking to my birth dad, leaving to the Holy Spirit the transmission of my prayers. I don't 'talk' verbally, of course, but mentally. I begin with adoration, recognition of his supremacy, submission to his sovereignty. Next, I ask for forgiveness of sins, thank him for blessings, and then expand my one-way conversation to cover the full spectrum of my concerns... for my family, my friends, my country... for his will, his clarity, his enabling... for my health, my stewardship, my witness. Again, all through this I pray comfortably, informally, unceremoniously, as if I were talking to my birth father, trying to bring, to give, to share with him that which I think he wants most: *fellowship... with me.*"

Jack paused yet again, hating himself for where he had led things, repulsed by the idea that anyone should know any of this, wanting to stop this speeding slide down this slippery slope. To disclose any details of this most personal, most private, most intimate relationship of his life... more personal, more private, more intimate than even that with Kelli... was to violate—simply, unconditionally, and seemingly unforgivably—a trust.

The pause became half a minute. His eyes were fixed on the floor. Finally, looking up, with a resolve to continue but with regret that he'd ever started, he quietly and reluctantly said, "Often, during this fellowship, I go through a process for which I don't know that there is a name. It begins with me mentally stripping away all those things that might inhibit my focus... that might distract me from the purity of this moment. I try to strip away all my identities as a human and try to become the essence of what I am as God's child. I try to set aside the fact that I am a husband and everything associated with that role, that I am a father and those responsibilities, and the responsibilities associated with my work, my friends, my church, my neighbors, my extended family, this class. Sometimes I see myself like an onion, gently peeling away all the important and unimportant earthly layers... to get to my core... knowing that in doing so I will resume the roles and the responsibilities in a few minutes.

"With that core bare, I sit, doing what I suppose would be praying... it is a time of communion ...fellowship... guidance. It is frequently for me a time in which I say 'God, I know there is more to our relationship and to my life than what I'm aware of... more than what I'm experiencing. Take me, I ask, to that next level of understanding, that next level of revelation.

"And it is often a time in which I don't try to pray as one normally does. Specifically, I don't try to construct sentence-prayers because they are so cumbersome, and I frequently don't try to address particular issues of others because I am not aware of them all. Instead, it's a time when I simply hover my mind over a name or a face for a few moments, as on my laptop I hover a cursor over an icon, to tell the Holy Spirit that it is this person that I want him to take before God for me.

"It is quiet. There are no words from me. If I were to try to imagine what it looks like, it would be that which you used to see on your old computer when you opened an e-mail and watched the small sheets of paper arch from the file on the left to the file on the right. The messages were indiscernible. They were transmitted in a code, within a medium, and at a speed that could only be read by the local server and its remote server. And in these moments, I am attempting to allow the Holy Spirit to do the same for me... to do what Paul describes in Romans 8:26, *...the Spirit helps us with our weakness. We do not know how to pray as we should. But the Spirit himself speaks to God for us—even begs God for us—with deep feelings that words cannot explain."*[5]

Jack seemed to catch himself mid-thought, then said, "Someday, not today, but someday, I may tell you more about these extraordinary moments. I *will* tell you that this quiet time has not been easy for me over the last several months... maybe even years... as Kelli and I have sought to buy the company that is taking us from here. As many of you know, it is small and one we hope to build into a much larger one.

"That in itself does not make these times of spiritual focus difficult. What does are the three Horsemen of my personal Apocalypse—not the four of Revelation—my three. Under the banner of this business they thunder into my prayers with unbridled abandon, throwing dirt and grit and distraction into meditation and reflection and fellowship.

"The first is named Pride, swollen with satisfaction in how far we've come from humble beginnings.

"The second is named Fear, smelling sour with cold sweat from predawn thoughts on what could go wrong? How much could be lost? Where are the years to recover?

"The third is named Idolatry, sultry and seductive, promising forgiveness for Pride and release from Fear if I but embrace this business as the source of sufficiency for the emotional needs of myself and the financial needs of my family.

"These are the three great sins I fight. Some days I do well. Those are the days in which I see this business for what it is—God's project over which he has made me steward, those days in which I know his highest hope for me is—as unbelievable as this is going to sound—to simply hold on and enjoy the ride. Other days, I don't do well. The worst are those when Pride sees this as the fulfillment of a note I made about myself in the margin of a book on leadership twenty years ago: *Some men are born to climb mountains. I was born to build one.*"

Jack stopped, looked at the floor, then looked up and said, "Today I have shared with you more than I intended—both the good and the bad. Maybe this last, the bad, will give you encouragement with your own horsemen.

"The good—if it can be called that—needs to be stamped with a warning, for I think there is a great danger in anyone—particularly a teacher—describing in detail that which I have this morning because there can be a tendency for a class member to consider my words, my habits, and my interpretations to be Scripture. They are *not* Scripture, and no one's words or habits or interpretations should be elevated above those found within the four corners of your Bible.

"Will you be influenced *by* others? Yes!

"Will you be an influence *to* others? Yes.

"But never should the example set *by* others for you, nor the example set by you *for* others be elevated above Scriptural examples.

"This is especially true if you look at me as a teacher or anyone else who appears to be a spiritual leader. This is true irrespective of how much they are esteemed, how much they are revered, or how profound their contribution... whether it is your pastor, the president of your denomination, or one of the world's most influential preachers like Billy Graham... whether they pounded a thesis criticizing indulgences on a church door on the eve of All-Saints in 1517, spent their life as a missionary in the darkest most barbaric culture, or started a soup kitchen in Dallas.

"It matters only that they were common men and common women called to uncommon purposes. And it matters only that *you* be available for *your* uncommon purpose—that for which God wants to set apart and consecrate you… that for which he wants you to trust and rely on him… that for which you have become *saint me*."

Jack hesitated… feeling he had said all that needed to be said… debating whether to continue or bring the class to an early close... then, deciding on the latter, said, "I have one last thought I want to share with you this morning, and that is this: I don't think God wants us to commit… consecrate… dedicate what, in his view, is the superficial… the external… the exterior.

"Specifically, I don't think he wants our skills if we are surgeons, our words if preachers, or our legislation if politicians… I don't think he wants our land if farmers, our rigs if truckers, or our books if authors… I don't think he wants our employees if employers, our students if teachers, or our children if parents.

"In fact, not only does he not want them, I don't know that he particularly *cares* if we are surgeons or preachers or senators or farmers or truckers or authors or employers or teachers or parents. I don't think he cares because that is not what he created us to be.

"He created us to be *his*.

"Now he wants us to consecrate to him our *souls*.

"He wants this because—irrespective of where our interests have taken us professionally, where we live geographically, how we have done financially—it is through the Holy Spirit's union and communion with our *souls* that God leads us to *his* work. And that work is to touch the lives of those he brings into our *spheres of influence*. I will speak more on another Sunday about this topic of sphere of influence, but for the moment will simply say that these are the people we influence: for good or bad… intentionally and unintentionally… consciously and unconsciously… directly and indirectly… by word and by deed… momentarily and eternally… through action and—so often and so surprisingly—through *in*action. These are those who are immediate family members and close friends… work associates and casual acquaintances… total strangers and avowed enemies.

"And, touching those lives does not *begin* over a dinner table or conference table… in rush hour traffic or a packed elevator… at a ball game or a mall. It *begins* while the world is still asleep, while the sky is still dark, and while the day is still new. It begins while you humbly, obediently, expectantly meet the one who will prepare you for… then lead you through… this patch of time called day."

Jack stopped. Stood silently. Then said, "I want to tell you one more thing, one more of a list of things that are personal opinions, one more of things I'm saying this morning I thought I'd never say to anyone privately, let alone a room full of people publicly.

"That is this: too often we pray with our *mind* rather than our *soul.*

"The problem with praying with our mind is that it is a terribly cluttered thing—full of wants and thanks, praise and pleas, names and needs. All of these are important, of course, but they are only a part, a *part*, of prayer.

"The other part, the part that precedes prayers from the mind are prayers from the soul.

"And prayers from the soul are a matter of simply becoming quiet, closing your eyes, shifting the focus of your mind *from* your mind *to* your soul, and—free of all thought… free of all clutter—allowing *your* soul to become one with *God's* soul."

Glancing at the clock he saw that there was time for one more point, stepped to the side of the music stand, and said, "I've talked about what prayer means to us, means to others, means to God in his calling us to service, giving us direction, enabling us to do more with less.

"But I would be remiss if in this morning's reasons for time with God I didn't repeat what I believe to be his *initial* and perhaps *highest* reason: *fellowship.*

"For our look at this, I want to go back to the beginning, back to Genesis, back to the first time there's a written record of God and Adam and Eve together. Would someone read Genesis 3:8-9?"

Darrell Stone said, "I have it in the NIV," then read:

> *Then the man and his wife heard the sound of the LORD God as he was walking in the garden in the cool of the day, and they hid from the LORD God among the trees of the garden. But the LORD God called to the man, 'Where are you?'*[6]

"Thanks, Darrell," Jack said.

Then Jack, feeling the peace of the moment that God seemed to feel, said to the class, "… *walking in the garden… in the cool of the day*. What a lovely picture. This suggests to me that this was something of a gentle routine for God… that it was not uncommon for God to be there… that it was not uncommon for Adam to be there… that it was not uncommon for *God* to go to *them*. And we have to stop and ask ourselves *why... why* is God doing this? *What* would motivate *God* to go to *them*? If he simply wanted to *see* them, if he simply wanted them to *see* him, why not send Gabriel out with a flaming sword to *drive* them to his *throne*?"

Jack stopped. Waited. They had to see it. They had to come to their own conclusions.

Then said, "You tell me: Why?"

After a moment a voice said, "*Fellowship.*"

A second voice said, "I agree: fellowship."

And a third said, "I also agree. Fellowship."

Then Jack quietly said, "I think you got it—as I finally did—that from this Scripture it seems that what God wants *from* us, wants *with* us, and wants *routinely* is fellowship. And maybe, just maybe, this—*fellowship*—is the principal reason God created us."

Jack paused, then stepping to the side of the lectern, said, "I'm going to share with you one last very personal thought. Recently, I found in my quiet time that I tried to write poetry to express my feelings. I found this an odd experience as I'm not really a fan of it and have never tried to compose a poem. But I wrote this… this realization:

How long have we been meeting in this darkness before dawn
For this quiet meditation, for this closeness that I yearn
For this talking, for this listening, for this joining of our souls
For this fellowship on Earth with the One who makes me whole
I am humbled beyond measure when I feel and when I see
You yearn with equal passion, to spend this time with me."

Jack stepped back to the lectern, more exhausted by this hour of teaching than any in memory, hesitated, then—seemingly deciding what he wanted to do—closed his three-ring binder and said, "Bev, would you pass out the sheets?"

As they were being distributed, Jack said, "No three questions this morning. Instead, we are going to use the last part of this period for silent prayer, and we're going to do it this way: I want you to turn the sheets over to the blank side, then write as much as you want… about anything you want… taking as much time as you want… after starting at the top of the page with this," and, turning to the whiteboard, Jack wrote:

Good morning, Dad

As time to end the class approached, Jack returned to the lectern, interrupted the silence, and brought the class to an early close by saying, "You and I have walked a very personal path this morning… one I never intended to walk, and one I intend to never revisit in front of a class. Next week, back on lesson plan. This week, each day, I encourage you to continue the practice you have begun this morning of writing a prayer. Fold these, tuck them away in your purse or pocket, then file them in a confidential place when you get home."

Jack asked Beverly to close them in prayer, briefly visited with a few class members, met Kelli at the door, took her by the hand, and rather quickly left the room.

As they walked across the parking lot to their car, Kelli said, "Good class."

Jack said nothing, remained uncharacteristically quiet, preoccupied, almost moody.

Kelli asked if something was wrong.

Jack replied, "I said too much."

Kelli looked at him, somewhat astonished, and said "Believe me… you didn't."

She then squeezed his hand, looked away, and silently prayed with a smile, *Okay, God, time for a little post-class action here. What do you want me to do… homeschool him on last week's lesson about not judging ourselves… about not beating ourselves up… about your definition of success? Just name it.*

As they approached Jack's classic white roadster parked on the far side of the lot, the answer came: *Let's start with a springtime, top-down, tree-lined drive through the curveys to the lodge.*

Reaching the car, still holding his hand, she forced him to the passenger side, opened the door, set him down, walked around to the driver's side, got in, popped the top, and said as she started the mellow-muffled engine of the ground-hugging two-seater, "Brunch at the lake… on me… for my favorite teacher… whose job it now is to sit back, breathe in the morning, and—quoting his most memorable words from one of his best-ever classes—hold on and enjoy the ride."

Jack, as she hoped, began to smile.

###

Your Takeaways and Action Items from this Chapter

Takeaway 1

(page__)

Takeaway 2

(page__)

Takeaway 3

(page__)

Your Takeaways and Action Items from this Chapter (cont.)

Action Item 1

(page__)

Action Item 2

(page__)

Action Item 3

(page__)

What Is the Uppermost Sin?

Chapter 4 - Sunday, May 29

Jack stood at the door welcoming class members and guests. His attitude had improved materially over the week, in part because the focus of today's class would be off himself and on Biblical characters, and in part because their profiles taught such great lessons about life. Further, this was a lesson he had been planning for some time, and he looked forward to getting into it.

He was delighted when Tom Taylor, another new member, stopped for a moment to say that he had bought two of the books Jack had recommended—*Mere Christianity* and *The Screwtape Letters* by Lewis—but less pleased when Tom asked him to sign a copy of his own book. Jack said, "Sure," signed the fly page and visited with him for a few more minutes, partially answering the frequently asked question about why he had chosen to first have it published under a pseudonym. As time to begin the class had arrived, Jack told Tom he would give him a full answer in a moment and excused himself.

After Beverly had greeted the group, completed announcements, called for prayer requests, and led them in prayer, Jack stepped to the music stand. He added his welcome to Beverly's and with a smile opened the class by saying, "I have been asked why I originally chose not to be identified in my book as its author. Since that question is so important, I'm going to answer it before I begin today's lesson.

"So, here's the reason: I was, quite simply, afraid.

"I was afraid to be known as the author because I thought I'd experience one of two emotions when people spoke to me about it. They would either say, 'I've read it and *don't* like it', in which case I would experience a degree of disappointment… or, 'I've read it and *like* it', in which case I would experience a degree of pride.

"Now with regard to the first—if you read it and *didn't* like it—I should not have been disappointed *if*, as it should have been, I was merely recording what the Holy Spirit was leading me to write.

"With regard to the second—if you read and *did* like it—I should not have felt pride because that… *pride*… is, in my view, among the worst of all sins. And I'm not the only one who feels this way."

He looked to the left side of the row of chairs and said, "Tom, did you bring your copy of *Mere Christianity*?" Tom said that he had and handed it to Jack. Jack opened the book, quickly scanned a few pages, found the section he wanted, and said, "I want to read to you a few paragraphs from Chapter 8, which is titled The Great Sin. Lewis says:

> *I now come to the part of Christian morals where they differ most sharply from all other morals. There is one vice of which no man in the world is free; which everyone in the world loathes when he sees it in someone else; and of which hardly any people, except Christians, ever imagine they are guilty themselves. I have heard people admit that they are bad-tempered, or that they cannot keep their heads about girls or drink, or even that they are cowards. I do not think I have ever heard anyone who was not a Christian accuse himself of this vice. And at the same time I have very seldom met anyone who was not a Christian, who showed the slightest mercy to it in others. There is no fault which makes a man more unpopular, and no fault which we are more unconscious of in ourselves. And the more we have it ourselves, the more we dislike it in others.*

The vice I am talking of is Pride or Self-Conceit; and the virtue opposite to it, in Christian morals, is called Humility. You may remember, when I was talking about sexual morality, I warned you that the centre of Christian morals did not lie there. Well, now, we have come to the centre. According to Christian teachers, the essential vice, the utmost evil, is Pride. Unchastity, anger, greed, drunkenness, and all that, are mere fleabites in comparison; it was through Pride that the devil became the devil; Pride leads to every other vice; it is the complete anti-God state of mind.

Does this seem exaggerated? If so, think it over. I pointed out a moment ago that the more pride one had, the more one disliked pride in others. In fact, if you want to find out how proud you are the easiest way is to ask yourself, 'How much do I dislike it when other people snub me, or refuse to take notice of me, or shove their oar in, or patronize me, or show off?'

The point is that each person's pride is in competition with everyone else's pride. It is because I wanted to be the big noise at the party that I am so annoyed at someone else being the big noise. Two of a trade never agree.

Now what you want to get clear is that Pride is essentially competitive—is competitive by its very nature—while the other vices are competitive only, so to speak, by accident. Pride gets no pleasure out of having something, only out of having more of it than the next man. We say that people are proud of being rich, or clever, or good-looking, but they are not. They are proud of being richer, or cleverer, or better-looking than others. If everyone else became equally rich, or clever, or good-looking there would be nothing to be proud about. It is the comparison that makes you proud: the pleasure of being above the rest.

Once the element of competition has gone, pride has gone. That is why Pride is essentially competitive in a way the other vices are not. The sexual impulse may drive two men into competition if they both want the same girl. But that is only by accident; they might just as likely have wanted two different girls. But a proud man will take your girl from you, not because he wants her, but just to prove to himself that he is a better man than you. Greed may drive men into competition if there is not enough to go around; but the proud man, even when he has got more than he can possibly want, will try to get still more just to assert his power. Nearly all those evils in the world which people put down to greed or selfishness are really far more the result of Pride...

...It is Pride which has been the chief cause of misery in every nation and every family since the world began. Other vices may sometimes bring people together: you may find good fellowship and jokes and friendliness among drunken people or unchaste people. But pride always means enmity—it <u>is</u> enmity. And not only enmity between man and man, but enmity to God.

In God you come up against something which is in every respect immeasurably superior to yourself. Unless you know God as that—and therefore know yourself as nothing in comparison—you do not know God.... It is a terrible thing that the worst of all the vices can smuggle itself into the very centre of our religious life. But you can see why. The other, and less bad, vices come through our animal nature. But this does not come through our animal nature at all. It comes direct from hell. It is purely spiritual: consequently, it is far more subtle and deadly... for at the heart of it... power... over others... is what Pride really enjoys." [1]

Jack stopped momentarily and said, "Lewis goes ahead to say that we must guard against some possible misunderstandings and makes these three points. He writes:

> *(1) Pleasure in being praised is not Pride. The child who is patted on the back for doing a lesson well, the woman whose beauty is praised by her lover, the saved soul to whom Christ says 'Well done' are pleased and ought to be.*
>
> *(2) We say in English that a man is 'proud' of his son, or his father, or his school, or his regiment, and it may be asked whether 'pride' in this sense is a sin... Such admiration is, of course, very far from being a sin.*
>
> *(3) We must not think Pride is something God forbids because He is offended at it, or that Humility is something He demands as due to His own dignity—as if God Himself was proud. He is not in the least worried about His dignity...."*[2]

Jack closed the book, handed it back to Tom, and expressed his thanks.

He then turned to the whiteboard and said as he wrote, "Let's stay with this topic, and let's begin with this:"

Find and read three Scriptures warning against pride.

A soft puff of pages turning, their muffled sound reminding Jack of small wings fluttering, briefly filled the room. Then Bob Smith in the fifth row said, "I have Proverbs 6:16-19 in the King James which says:

> *These six things doth the Lord hate: yea, seven are an abomination unto him: A proud look, a lying tongue, and hands that shed innocent blood, an heart that deviseth wicked imaginations, feet that be swift in running to mischief, a false witness that speaketh lies, and he that soweth discord among brethren."*[3]

"What does that suggest?" Jack asked.

"It reminds me of something I've found before to be astounding, and that is that God doesn't distinguish between attitude and action. What does surprise me is that he finds pride—something which to me is pretty innocent—to be as abhorrent as murder."

"Thank you, Bob," Jack said, then asked who had another passage.

Kay said that she did, that she was looking at a parallel King James/New International Version, and that the former used *pride* where the latter used *arrogance*. She then read 1John:16 from the NIV:

For everything that is in the world—the desire for fleshly gratification, the desire for possessions, and worldly arrogance [pride]—is not from the Father but is from the world." [4]

"Thank you, Kay," Jack said, then asked, "What does this suggest?"

She answered, "I think it is saying that sins of the mind—specifically lust, greed, and pride—are not only wrong, but *equally* wrong."

"Good. Thanks. Okay," Jack said, "One more?"

Cliff said, "I have one from Malachi 4:1," and he read from the Amplified Version:

"For behold, the day comes that shall burn like an oven, and all the proud and arrogant, yes, and all that do wickedly and are lawless, shall be stubble; the day that comes shall burn them up, says the Lord of hosts, so that it will leave them neither root nor branch...." [5]

"Comments?" Jack asked.

Cliff said, "It is not so much the stubble burning and being left rootless that strikes me in this... it's that pride merits such harsh judgment. It's treated here as a felony-level fault when I've thought of it as a simple misdemeanor."

"Thanks, Cliff. Now that we have looked at three passages of Scripture regarding pride—and there are many more in both the Old and New Testament—I want us to look at one Biblical character who teaches us by *example* the *consequence* of pride.

"That person is, surprisingly," Jack said as he turned, wiped the board clean, then wrote:

Moses

Jack turned back to the class and said, "I would argue that there are few more prominent, more influential, more renowned characters in the whole of Jewish history than Moses.

"Take him out of the Bible and you have no Exodus from Egypt and no delivery of the Children of Israel to the Promised Land.

"Further, you have no plagues, no Passover, no parting of the Red Sea...

"No manna, no sweet water, no guiding pillar of cloud by day nor pillar of fire by night...

"No annual feasts, no harvest celebrations, no establishment of the Levitical priestly tribe...

"And no Tabernacle, no Ten Commandments, and no Mosaic law which influences Jewish worship, culture, commerce, and customs to this day.

"Arguably, most of these events would have happened anyway—with or without Moses—and we would simply be speaking of them using someone else's name.

"But they didn't.

"It was *Moses* God recruited through the burning bush to lead the Exodus,

"*Moses* he empowered to confront Pharaoh,

"*Moses* he chose to transform oppressed slaves into a theocratic nation, and

"*Moses* he trusted to lead this nation into the land he had promised Abraham.

"Further, it was *Moses* who persuaded God not to '*smite them with the pestilence*' because of their fearful reaction to the majority report of the spies who reconnoitered that land… who then shared the consequence of their fear by leading them in the desert for 40 years… and through whom—for those 40 years—God continued to reveal himself to his people.

"And it was to *Moses*—at the end of those 40 years—that God in essence said: Because of your *pride* and your *arrogance*… because of your *conceit* and your *self-importance*... because of your honoring *yourself* rather than *Me*... you will *not* enter the Promised Land."

Jack stopped.

Silence filled the room.

Stepping to the side of the music stand Jack said quietly, "Did you hear me? I'll say it again. God tells *Moses*—after almost a half-century of service—*You are not going in*."

Jack stood there.

"Nowhere in the Bible do we more clearly see God's absolute condemnation of pride… God's complete disregard for how *important*, how *essential*, how *indispensable* any person *thinks* he is… and God's unconditional commitment to the commandment that we will have no other god before us—be that god an inanimate thing like a private *statue*, or an intoxicating thing like our own public *stature*."

"This condemnation happened at the *Second* Meribah.

"*First* Meribah… *Second* Meribah.

"These two events are for Moses like bookends on the 40-plus years between leaving Egypt and entering the Promised Land.

"We can't understand the Second until we understand the First, so we begin there… about three brief months out of Egypt. The Children of Israel are free. They are on the move. *In* Egypt they witnessed God's *power* as he brought the 10 plagues. *Out* of Egypt they have witnessed God's *sufficiency* as he delivered them from being trapped between the Red Sea and the pursuing Egyptian army… from being without food… from having only bitter water.

"Surprisingly, *shockingly*, they have with *each* new threat—the sea, the food, the water—raised to Moses and to God the same cries: *Were there no graves in Egypt? Why did you bring us out here to die?"*

Jack paused to let the absurdity of what they said reverberate through the silence.

He continued, "Then, at what became known as the First Meribah, they did it again. Would someone read Exodus 17:1-17?"

Ron Cole said, "I have it," and began reading from an Amplified Version:

> *"All the congregation of the Israelites moved on from the Wilderness of Sin by stages, according to the commandment of the Lord, and encamped at Rephidim; but there was no water for the people to drink. Therefore, the people contended with Moses, and said, Give us water that we may drink. And Moses said to them, Why do you find fault with me? Why do you tempt the Lord and try His patience?*

But the people thirsted there for water, and the people murmured against Moses, and said, Why did you bring us up out of Egypt to kill us and our children and livestock with thirst? So Moses cried to the Lord, What shall I do with this people? They are almost ready to stone me. And the Lord said to Moses, pass on before the people, and take with you some of the elders of Israel; and take in your hand the rod with which you smote the river [Nile], and go. Behold, I will stand before you there on the rock at [Mount] Horeb; and you shall strike the rock, and water shall come out of it, that the people may drink. And Moses did so in the sight of the elders of Israel.

He called the place Massah [proof, testing, strife] and Meribah [contention] because of the faultfinding of the Israelites and because they tempted and tried the patience of the Lord, saying, Is the Lord among us or not?" [6]

"Thanks, Ron.

"Notice God's patience. Though he heard their cries, there is no punishment, no recrimination, no rebuke for their lack of faith at this the First Meribah.

"We now fast forward a few more weeks. They have arrived at Mt. Sinai. They will spend most of a year here. I need to summarize that year because there is not sufficient time this morning to look in detail at the magnitude of this change for the Children of Israel… for this people who 400 years earlier had freely entered Egypt as a *family* of about 70 and now exit as an enslaved *mass.* A mass—based on the census God later ordered in Numbers—of over 600,000 fighting men… plus women, children, men too old to fight, and the tribe of Levi… bringing their total numbers—according to some scholars—to 2,500,000. If this total is near accurate, the mass would have roughly equaled the combined populations of today's Delaware, Rhode Island, and Vermont.

"I say mass because they are just that. They are—like the chemical-element mercury—without any *form* of their own. They have no *societal* form, no *governmental* form, no *cultural* form, Like mercury, the *only* form they have is that defined by the space into which they are *allowed* to flow, that *indulged* by their owners, that which they have known as *slaves.*

"They need *form* and it is here, at Mt. Sinai, they are to receive it. Think of it as a 50-week crash course in which they are to be radically *transformed:* transformed from being governed to governing… from being owned-property to being property owners… from being indistinguishable members of a marketable *commodity* to being individual *persons* of unique value. The magnitude and minutia of this forming may best be seen in the sheer volume its description takes in the Bible—more than three of the first five books.

"It is here that they are to be transformed… transformed by the Ten Commandments, by instructions on building the Tabernacle, by division into 12 tribes, and by declaration of the laws, holidays, and cultural institutions essential to any cohesive people.

"But, most importantly, transformed by the very *presence* of God himself.

"And it is Moses… God's spokesman, adjudicator, and confidante… that endures the whining, complaining, and rebellion of this *mass* which has not yet—which may never, he must wonder—become the *nation* God intended.

"Near the end of the year, with formation complete, they leave Mt. Sinai for the Promised Land. The whole story may be found in Numbers 10. But again, due to time this morning, I must be brief. In fact, most of this story you probably already know: You know their travel time from Mt. Sinai to Kadesh on the border of Canaan is a brief couple of weeks… you know upon arriving they send 12 men in to reconnoiter the land… you know the spies are in the country 40 days… you know when they come out, two report that it is a land of milk and honey ready to be taken, and 10 report that there is much to be feared, that it is a land dominated by men so large that *We seemed like grasshoppers in our own eyes, and we looked the same to them.*[7]

"You probably also know—or might now guess—the response of the people. Would someone find and read Numbers 14:1-4?"

Ted Street said, "I've got it," and read:

> *"That night all the members of the community raised their voices and wept aloud. All the Israelites grumbled against Moses and Aaron, and the whole assembly said to them, "If only we had died in Egypt! Or in this wilderness! Why is the LORD bringing us to this land only to let us fall by the sword? Our wives and children will be taken as plunder. Wouldn't it be better for us to go back to Egypt?"* [8]

Jack said, "Thank you, Ted. Please go ahead and read God's reply beginning with verse 28."

Ted continued.

> *"As I live, declares the LORD, what you have said in my hearing I will do to you... your dead bodies shall fall in this wilderness.... But your little ones, who you said would become a prey, I will bring in, and they shall know the land that you have rejected.... But as for you, your dead bodies shall fall in this wilderness. According to the number of the days in which you spied out the land, forty days, a year for each day, you shall bear your iniquity forty years, and you shall know my displeasure."*[9]

Jack said, "And so—with Moses leading—the Children of Israel leave the borders of the Promised Land and began their forty years of wondering in the wilderness."

Jack stepped to the side of the stand and said, "We now fast forward through those forty years... fast forward to their return to Kadesh Barnea... fast forward to the *Second* Meribah. Would someone read Numbers 20:1-13, then 23 and 24."

Toni, also holding an Amplified Version, began to read,

> *"And the Israelites, the whole congregation, came into the Wilderness of Zin in the first month. And the people dwelt in Kadesh. Miriam died and was buried there. Now there was no water for the congregation, and they assembled together against Moses and Aaron. And the people contended with Moses, and said, Would that we had died when our brethren died [in the plague] before the Lord!*
>
> *And why have you brought up the congregation of the Lord into this wilderness, that we should die here, we and our livestock? And why have you made us come up out of Egypt to bring us into this evil place? It is no place of grain or of figs or of vines or of pomegranates. And there is no water to drink.*
>
> *Then Moses and Aaron went from the presence of the assembly to the door of the Tent of Meeting and fell on their faces. Then the glory of the Lord appeared to them. And the Lord said to Moses, take the rod, and assemble the congregation, you and Aaron your brother, and tell the rock before their eyes to give forth its water, and you shall bring forth to them water out of the rock; so you shall give the congregation and their livestock drink.*
>
> *So Moses took the rod from before the Lord, as He commanded him. And Moses and Aaron assembled the congregation before the rock and Moses said to them, Hear now, you rebels; must we bring you water out of this rock? And Moses lifted up his hand and with his rod*

he smote the rock twice. And the water came out abundantly, and the congregation drank, and their livestock.

And the Lord said to Moses and Aaron, Because you did not believe in Me to sanctify Me in the eyes of the Israelites, you therefore shall not bring this congregation into the land which I have given them.

These are the waters of Meribah [contention, strife], where the Israelites contended with the Lord and He showed Himself holy among them."[10]

"Thanks, Toni. Okay," Jack said, as he looked at the class, "... tell me what you see here."

There was silence as they reviewed the verses, then Bill Brown said, "At the first Meribah, God told Moses to *strike* the rock... at the second he told him to *speak* to the rock. He was obedient in the first, and disobedient in the second. But, I don't think obedience or disobedience was the problem. I think the problem was Moses' attitude... of arrogance or pride or self-importance. And we might wonder about who Moses meant when he used the plural 'we', perhaps trying to spin that he was speaking of himself and God. But it's clear that God did not wonder because, as my ASV puts it, *ye believed not in Me, to sanctify Me in the eyes of the Children of Israel."*[11]

"I agree," a voice from the back said. "My NIV says *'to honor Me'* in their eyes."

"My New King James says *'hallow'* me," another voice said.

Jack stood quietly. He turned to the whiteboard, wiped it clean, picked up a black marker, turned back to the class and said, "The message to me is clear... simple... fundamental. It is this:"

> God wants to be
> <u>acknowledged</u>, <u>honored</u>, <u>hallowed</u>
> for that which He does
> through us.

But Jack's conclusions could not be forced on others from the outside. They had to grow from the inside, and that meant thinking... and thinking meant writing... and writing meant worksheets. Jack turned to the left end of the first row asked, "Bev, would you pass out the sheets?" As she did, he said, "Today's three questions are—based on the assumption that this is a new insight:

"1. *What* is now your view of pride?

"2. *Why* is that now your view?

"3. *How* will that affect your life?"

After the sheets were completed and answers discussed, Jack glanced at the clock, saw that there was time, and said "I want to shift our attention to another lesson buried in the Exodus story. It is found

Numbers 14:28. We heard it read a few minutes ago. I'll quote it again: *...As I live, declares the Lord, what you have said in my hearing I will do to you....*[12]

"Those 18 words must be the most encouraging or most discouraging in all of Scripture... *encouraging* if God hears you expressing *faith... discouraging* if he hears you expressing *fear.*

"If you've read my book, you've read how I feel about fear. In chapter three I write:

I believe that if there were an 11th commandment, it would be 'Thou shall not fear.'
I believe this unequivocally, unambiguously, and explicitly.
I believe this because of Scriptural teaching.
I believe this because of Biblical examples.
I believe this because of rational examination."

"I'm not talking about the kind of fear that comes from speaking to a large audience, learning of a child's fall, or hearing a train whistle as you're crossing the tracks. Nor am I talking about the kind of personal fear I had of being known as the author of my book."

Opening his ISV, he said, "I'm talking about the kind of fear that comes from the feeling that resources are not going to be sufficient to meet the needs of life... the kinds of needs Jesus spoke specifically and directly about in Matthew 6:24-34.

> *No one can serve two masters. For either he will hate one and love the other, or be loyal to one and despise the other. You cannot serve God and riches! That's why I'm telling you to stop worrying about your life—what you will eat or what you will drink—or about your body, what you will wear. Life is more than food... more than clothing.... Surely your heavenly Father knows that you need all of them! But first be concerned about God's kingdom and his righteousness, and all of these things will be provided for you as well. So never worry about tomorrow, for tomorrow will worry about itself. Each day has enough trouble of its own."* [14]

Closing the book, he continued, "2nd Timothy 1:7 tells us, *For God has not given us a spirit of fear; but of power, and of love, and of a sound mind.*[15]

"Philippians 4:6 tell us, *Do not be anxious about anything, but in every situation, by prayer and petition, with thanksgiving, present your requests to God.*[16]

"1st Peter 5:6 says, *Humble yourselves, therefore, under God's mighty hand, that he may lift you up in due time.*[17]

"We could look at several other Old and New Testament passages that repeat this same message, but redundancy in this case would not breed clarity. Could it be clearer? I don't think so. I think we could style it in different ways, but it would still come back to the same question that I shared with you several weeks ago when I said that I can almost hear Jesus' persistent first-century question to Peter... *do you love me? do you love me? do you love me?* restyled in his persistent 21st century question to me: *Jack, I know you love me, but do you trust me? do you trust me? do you trust me?*

"I think overcoming the sin of *pride* is easier than overcoming the sin of *fear.* I think this because pride is so often rooted in emotions and attitude over which I have some control... and fear is so often rooted in economics and circumstances over which I have little or no control."

Stepping to the side of the lectern, Jack quietly said, "If you are there right now—fighting this demon, fear—you have a brother in me who has traveled through the same valley, fought for sleep in the same predawn darkness, sought resolution in every credible corner.

"It was years ago for me, first in college, then later when my career was just beginning. But I still remember it and I still fight the demon today. The difference between then and now is confidence.

Not in me. In God. Confidence from seeing his circumstantial leadership, as he closed this door, opened that. As he matured me. As he led me. As he used me.

"But I still remember… like black ink leached into a glass of clear water, fear seeped into my spirit, slowly curling, spreading downward. As this darkened my inside, opinions of me from those I respected clouded my outside. It was this that I feared as much as anything. And it was their opinions that I didn't want to hear, not at that moment.

"I didn't want to hear any preaching about living with the consequence of decisions I had made—not when I made them cautiously, prudently, prayerfully, based on the best information I had at the time. Not when I applied all my talents, intellectual, and physical resources to the task. Not when I believed that I was a small but important part of God's body, that he had an essential role for me to play, and for that purpose he had equipped me… trusted me… and, in a fashion I don't understand, *sanctified* me.

"The *only* preaching I wanted to hear was from God himself, saying, *'Hang in there, Jackie boy. I know what I'm doing.'* And that's what I *did* hear, not audibly through my ears from his voice, but visually through my eyes from his book. I had to have this, for nothing else would *remove* the ink. It could not be blotted out. It could not be willed out. It could not be cried out. It could only be flooded out… with fresh water of his words, reminders of his promises, and my frontal lobe knowledge that he who created me only demanded one thing of me at that moment: *trust*.

"God knows the ink in your life—whether it's health or job or family or finances or guilt. He knows what you're feeling. And he wants *you* to know one thing: *feelings have nothing to do with it.* He wants you to buck up, take a breath, read his word, pray for wisdom, and know that from *you* he only demands one thing at this moment: *trust."*

Jack paused.

Stopped.

He stopped talking.

He stopped teaching.

He stood silently as if ending the lesson, ending class, preparing to close.

He stopped because something from the first part of today's session gnawed at him… something was missing. He had not planned and thus had not spent hours preparing to teach this lesson about sin, about Moses, about the Meribahs. Had he planned it, this something-missing would have been foreseen, thought through, covered.

Then it struck him. Breaking his silence he said, "It's time to end this class but we *can't*… not here… not with this *tension* between Moses and God… not with this *rupture* in their relationship… and not without asking ourselves: What happened next… did they reconcile? … Did Moses continue to serve God?... Did God continue to use Moses?

"First, *Did Moses continue to serve God*? We can think it's possible that he didn't… we can think Moses might have thought that denying him entry into the Promised Land for this single transgression after decades of obedience was unjust, undeserved, and unwarranted punishment. And while we could *think* it possible, we don't *see* it in Scripture. In fact, we see the opposite. If we continue reading the next verses, Numbers 20:14-17, we see Moses—without so much as a whimper—forging ahead in a business-as-usual mode, negotiating safe passage for the Israelites through the Kingdom of Edom to the Promised Land.

"Next question: *Did God continue to use Moses?* We can think it's possible that he didn't… that he turned immediately to Joshua… that Moses' service was finished as well as God's recognition of any of it. And while we could *think* it possible, we don't *see* it in Scripture. In fact, we see the opposite… we see Moses elevated by God, to at least three prestigious positions, on three significant occasions.

"First, in the *Old Testament*, we see that it is *Moses*—before they are led by Joshua across the Jordan—delivering to the Israelites a speech covering every dimension of the life to be lived in the Promised Land… a speech of history and laws, promises and warnings, economics and leadership, customs and celebrations… a speech so important and so encompassing and so large that it constitutes the *entire* fifth book of the Bible… Deuteronomy.

"Second, in the *New Testament*, Matthew 17, we see that it is *Moses*—not Abraham, not David, not Jacob, not any other Old Testament character—who appears with Elijah at the *Transfiguration*.

"And third in *Revelation 15:3-4,* we see that it is the *Song of the Lamb… and of Moses…* that they sing."

Jack stood silently, then said, "That's it. The lesson is now complete… except for this last question: *What does this passage teach me?*

"I submit that it is this very *personal* promise from my very *personal* God: *Jack, expect from me no less… no less patience… no less love… no less grace."*

Jack continued, "And I hope you see that this *teaches*—and he *promises*—no less for you."

"Bev, please close us."

Your Takeaways and Action Items from this Chapter

Takeaway 1

(page__)

Takeaway 2

(page__)

Takeaway 3

(page__)

Your Takeaways and Action Items from this Chapter (cont.)

Action Item 1

(page__)

Action Item 2

(page__)

Action Item 3

(page__)

Who Is the Holy Spirit? (Part 1)

Chapter 5 - Sunday, June 5

Jack stood against the back wall, ready to teach the lesson postponed from last week, watching as Beverly went through the class-commencement process in what was now routine for this new group. People were generally sitting in the same areas and becoming acquainted with—in some cases friends with—those they were beginning to see regularly. Though over the years he had seen these dynamics dozens of time, he was always amazed that bonds between strangers could form so quickly. And particularly amazed at the candor with which people—in the midst of these strangers, new acquaintances, and old friends—would so openly express some very personal prayer requests.

This time each Sunday—this listening to them—was always tough for Jack. There were so many with critical needs… so many whose parents were failing, jobs were threatened, or health was at risk. But the toughest for him were those that went well beyond the financial or physical, that went to the spiritual. Most often these were from couples or single parents who had become Christians later in life, who were now praying that their children would follow. And—though usually unspoken—praying for a means of coping with their own feelings of guilt for not creating a different home environment during the formative years.

Their sense of *guilt*, their sense of *helplessness*, their sense of *hopelessness* weighed ever more heavily on him *this* morning as he—leaning against the wall, head down, arms crossed, eyes closed—listened… and as he felt his focus start to slip from his lesson plan to their spoken words.

With Beverly's 'amen', he walked to the front, stepped behind the music stand, said good morning, then paused. In less than a heartbeat, those who had been in his class for years knew that this hesitation… this moment of apparent rethinking… meant that Jack was going to abandon a lesson plan. *He* didn't know it yet. But they did.

He whispered a silent one-sentence prayer, then said, somewhat repeating himself, "I, again, join Bev in welcoming you."

He paused again.

Decided. Then resolutely looking over the class, said, "I welcome you to what I hope will be one of the most *illuminating*… one of the most *encouraging*… one of the most *applicable* of our last few classes together."

Leaving his notebook closed, he continued, "I'm going to postpone today's lesson until later this hour or even next week. Instead I want to speak to some of you about this morning's prayer requests.

"Specifically, I want to talk to those who asked for prayer for spiritual direction for your children. This, it seems to me, has become the most *frequent*, the most *urgent*, the most *important* of all matters lying on our collective hearts."

He stood silently for a moment as he mentally pulled together pieces and patches from 12 years of teaching, then asked Beverly to pass out the Q&A sheets. As she did, he checked to see if his stack of books included one by Billy Graham he had brought to loan to a class member. He found, opened, and marked a page in it, in his Bible, and in another book with 3x5 visitor's cards; wrote three points on the blank side of his lesson plan; and quietly spoke to Chuck Wilson on the second row.

He then stepped to the side of the music stand and said firmly, "Here's the two-word lesson for those of you who are trying to change your children: *Give up."*

Silence filled the room, the class not understanding what it had just heard.

"Hear me clearly on this: *Give up.*

"Give up three ways.

"First, give up trying to do it *yourself* because this is a change that can only be brought about by the Holy Spirit.

"Second, give up trying to do it *alone* because this is a change that needs the prayers of your friends as well as yourself.

"Third, give up *feeling guilty* because the past is history from *your* perspective—not God's."

He stopped.

He watched.

"I'm going to say this again: First, give up trying to do it *yourself* because this is a change that can only be brought about by the Holy Spirit.

"If you don't get that, it's because you don't get who the Holy Spirit is. So, we're going to start there by looking at a couple authorities on the subject: Billy Graham on *who* the Holy Spirit is and Jesus on *why* he sent him."

He opened the dogeared book to the page he had marked and said, "This is his classic, *The Holy Spirit.* The first chapter is entitled, 'Who Is the Holy Spirit?' and states clearly, explicitly, emphatically,:

> *Throughout the Bible it is clear the Holy Spirit is God Himself.*
> *This is seen in the attributes which are given to the Holy Spirit in Scripture....*
> *Without exception these are attributes of God Himself.*
> *He is eternal...*
> *He is all-powerful...*
> *He is everywhere present...*
> *He is all-knowing...*
> *The Holy Spirit is called God....*[1]

"Then Graham emphasizes this important point:

> *The Bible teaches that the Holy Spirit is a person. Jesus never referred to 'it' when He was talking about the Holy Spirit. In John 14, 15 and 16, for example, He spoke of the Holy Spirit as 'He' because He is not a force... or thing... but a person...."*[2]

Looking up from the book, he said, "Our own reading tells us in John 14:17 that the Holy Spirit *dwells* in us... in 14:26 that he *teaches*... in 15:26 that he *bears witness*... and in 16:13,15 that he *guides, speaks,* and *declares.* In Ephesians 4:30 we are told that he can be *grieved*... in Hebrews 10:29 that he can be *outraged*... and in Romans 8:27 that *...the one who searches our hearts knows the mind of the Spirit, for the Spirit intercedes for the saints according to God's will.*"[3]

Jack closed the book, moved forward from the lectern, and said, "That's a brief description of *who* he is and *what* he does.

"Now I want to look at *why* he is." He could not help but smile as he glanced at the group from his old class. "To the third-row gang who are about to give me that here-we-go-again look, I say 'you're right'… we're back in John 14 and 15."

Then, looking back at the class, he said, "I want you to hear part of what Jesus said on his last night with his disciples, moments before his allegory of the vine, and hours before his arrest. The setting is this: Jesus has washed the disciples' feet. He has predicted his betrayal, predicted his death, and predicted Peter's denials. The disciples are confused and two in particular, Thomas and Phillip, have spoken up—Thomas asking how they can go with him when they don't know where he's going, and Phillip saying that they will believe if he will simply show them the father.

"Jesus responds by saying that he is the way and that if they have seen him they have seen the father, then, in John 14:16, makes this astounding promise: *I will pray to the Father, and He shall give you another Comforter, that He may abide with you forever."* [4]

Jack stopped and stood silently for a moment to let the words fill the still room, then said, "This is one of those passages—those *promises*—that we get so used to that we, in time, fail to recognize its importance… its essentialness... its indispensableness… to God's connection, bond, and relationship with us… and us with him.

"I just quoted from the King James version where a *Comforter* is promised.

"The International Standard version uses the noun *Helper.*

"The New International Standard the word *Counselor.*

"As I've mentioned before," Jack said as he held up his Parallel New Testament version in his right hand, "I like this because it includes the original Greek."

Then, as he held up a copy of the International Standard Bible Encyclopedia in his left hand, he said, "And I like this because it allows me to look at a Greek word in the broader context of first-century semantics."

Laying the Bible in the chair and turning to the whiteboard, he wrote as he said, "The key word in this verse—translated into the three nouns *Helper, Counselor, Comforter*—appears like this in Greek:"

παράκλήτου

Facing the class, opening the encyclopedia, he said, "I want to read to you part of what this says about one of the translations: *comforter.* I want to do this for two reasons: First because of this morning's examination of who the Holy Spirit is and what he does.

"Second, because I want to demonstrate the importance of *studying*… specifically of *your* studying... of *your* researching… of *your* asking why, what, and how. Hear me clearly… God's great joy is in a *heart* that loves, a *soul* that praises, and an *intellect* that insatiably wants but one thing: *to know more.* To become that, you *must* develop the self-discipline of study… you *must* develop the mind of an independent thinker… and you *must* assemble a small, credible library of study resources.

"By 'discipline of study', I mean setting aside time every day… *every* day… for immersion in God's word.

"By 'independent thinker', I mean independent of the denomination line… and I say this irrespective of whether yours is a mainline or minor denomination. I say this because you have been created in God's image, not the denomination's. I say this because God has a special purpose *for* you that he wants to communicate personally *to* you, one that can never be wholly communicated in a general-purpose, denomination-wide, this-is-the-focus-of-study-for-the-quarter pamphlet. And your church leadership will be the first to encourage you as you eagerly seek the development of your personal relationship with your personal savior, and as you search for that unique calling for which God has set apart and sanctified you.

"By 'credible library', I mean at a minimum a small collection of three to five references on your shelves at home to which you turn for supplementary information as well as for highlighting, cross referencing, and penning margin notes. In addition to these, you may want to find free online or buy any number of Bible versions, commentaries, dictionaries, encyclopedias, and other references.

"The minute you begin to pursue this interest of independent Bible study, the question that will come to mind is: *'How do I do it? Where do I start? How do I bring about organization and direction?'* Until you develop your own system, I recommend that you simply buy a three-ring notebook, a packet of lined paper, and a set of clear plastic divider tabs. On the first page, write—without any attempt at prioritizing—a list of topics for study that appeal to you. They may be *word* studies such as grace, love, or redemption… or *character* studies such as Paul, Noah, or Moses… or *geographic* studies such as the Jordan River, Jerusalem, or the Sea of Galilee… or *event* studies such as Joseph's sale into captivity, the 12 spies in the Promised Land, or Pentecost… or *book* studies such as Job, Proverbs, or James… or *teaching* studies such the Sermon on the Mount, days in the wilderness, or 'I am the vine.'

"From there say a prayer, pick a topic, make a tab, begin researching, and start writing. The significance of this last step cannot be overstated. Sometime ago I heard a quote that said 'reading keeps us informed… conversation makes us interesting… but writing makes us *think.*' So write! *Write* as you explore your thoughts… *write* as you record your findings… *write* as you define your conclusions. My suggestion—again until you find your own style—is that you write answers to these three questions… *what* is being said... *why* is it being said... *how* does it apply to my life?

"Right now, we are doing what might best be described as a character study, *the Holy Spirit,* which at the moment has led us into a word study—*comforter.*" Jack opened the worn hardback encyclopedia to the last visitor's card, and said, "I want you to hear what this has to say about the word:

> *Comforter*
>
> *This is translation of the word patakletos, in the Johannine writings. In the Gospel it occurs in John 14:16,26; 15:26; 16:7, and refers to the Holy Spirit. The word means literally, 'called to one's side' for help. ...The translation 'Comforter' covers only a small part of the meaning as shown in the context. The word 'Helper' would be a more adequate translation.*

The Spirit does a great deal for disciples besides comforting them, although to comfort was a part of His work for them.... The word 'Comforter' being inadequate, and the word 'Helper' too indefinite... it would probably be best to transfer the Greek word into English... (see PARACLETE).”[5]

Turning to the whiteboard, Jack added:

Παράκλήτου = *paraclete*

Facing the class again he said, “I want you to hear parts of the discourse on the word *paraclete*:

This word occurs 5 times in the New Testament, all in the writings of John. Four instances are in the Gospel and one in the First Epistle.... 'Paraclete' is simply the Greek word transferred into English....

In general the word signifies: (1) a legal advocate, or counsel for defense, (2) an intercessor, (3) a helper, generally....

If we raise the question of what is the best translation of the term 'Paraclete' in the New Testament, we have a choice of several words.... 'Comforter' contains an element of the meaning of the word as employed in the Gospels, and harmonizes with the usage in connection with its cognates, but it is too narrow in meaning to be an adequate translation

'Intercessor' comes nearer the root idea of the term and contains an essential part of the meaning.

'Advocate' is a closely related word, and is also suggestive of the work of the Spirit.

Perhaps there is no English word broad enough to cover all the significance of the word 'Paraclete' except the word 'Helper.' The Spirit helps the disciples in all the above-indicated ways. The following are given as the specific forms of activity of the Holy Spirit:

(1) to show them the things of Christ,
(2) to teach them things to come,
(3) to teach them all things,
(4) to quicken their memories for past teaching,
(5) to bear witness to Christ,
(6) to dwell in believers,
(7) other things shown in the context such as 'greater works' than those of Christ,
(8) to convict of sin, of righteousness and judgment....”[6]

Jack stopped reading, closed the Encyclopedia and said, "Back to what Jesus was saying in John 14:16: *...I will pray the Father, and he shall give you another Comforter, that he may abide with you forever.*[7]

"With this Scripture we begin to see what I think of as the 'Second Great Transition.' In my mind, the 'First Great Transition' came about thirty-three years earlier when God became flesh... when he was born *through* a human... lived *among* humans... died *as* a human."

Jack paused as he finished the sentence, smiled, and said, "You will forgive me if I again share with you a rather unorthodox thought." Spontaneous laughter rippled through the room as if the class with a single voice was saying, "So... what's new?"

Jack smiled again, this time at the response, and still holding the Bible said, "What I'm about to tell you is symbolic only. By that I mean it is not Scriptural... not Biblical... not consistent with an omniscient God. But.. it is interesting. It reflects the fact the God has wanted a personal, enduring, abiding relationship with man. It reflects the fact that he wants that relationship so deeply that he will continue to pursue it through any failure on man's part. And it reflects the fact that he is so committed to that relationship that he will sacrifice anything... even his own son... to guarantee it.

"Now here's the symbolic view: It seems to me it might be argued that he first tried to establish that relationship with a *couple*... Adam and Eve. When that failed, it seems he might have thought he'd expand his efforts and try it with a *family*... Abraham's. When that failed, he expanded his efforts again and tried it with a *nation*... Israel. And when that failed, he said, I'll go *myself*... and did so in the form of his Son.

"With his Son's coming, The *First* Great Transition from God *above* us to God *among* us was completed. They even spoke of *Immanuel... God with us*. And then, with The *Second* Great Transition, he moved from being *among* us to being *within* us in the form of the Holy Spirit.

"You may have seen me speak to someone here at the front earlier. I was asking one of our guest teachers to help me team-teach part of this morning's focus on the Holy Spirit. Chuck Wilson is now going to talk about the beginning of the Second Transition as it appears in the Gospels and Acts."

Chuck and Jack were close friends. Years ago, they happened to meet as they shared a lunch table at an airline courtesy club during a snow-delayed flight at Chicago's O'Hare. Chuck was the pilot. Jack was a passenger. Then, a year later, they met again in a golf tournament and learned that they not only lived in the same city but that Chuck had recently visited Jack's church. Today they meet regularly through golf and Bible study.

Chuck walked forward from the second row, laid his Bible and an old Q&A sheet with his handwritten notes on its back on the music stand, and said, "I appreciate this opportunity to share a few minutes, co-teaching a part of Jack's last class because I am about to lose the fellowship of a dear friend and the companionship of a fellow traveler. The fellowship has grown during three years of golf in a monthly foursome... the companionship as a fellow traveler during two years together in Chicago's off-campus seminary program. The former, golf, has taught me much about his faith. The latter, seminary, has taught me much about the man. Now, you might expect that to be reversed... that golf would teach me about the *man* and seminary about his *faith*. And I would say that, in most cases, that would be true. But not in this case. And not with this man.

"This is mainly because of this 'Second Transition' as Jack has called it... as he believes it... as he lives it. Most people can accept the intangible idea that, *long ago and far away*, Christ died for their sins. But they cannot accept the tangible reality that, *at this moment*, living within them is the Holy Spirit.

" And if—as Rick Warren said in *The Purpose Driven Life*—God has emotions, I wonder if there has ever been a moment in his eternal history when he has been more full of joy than at the instant of this Second Transition. Think about it:

"He moved from *residing* in a tabernacle, to being *embedded* in the soul.

"He moved from *whispering* notions, to *being* thoughts.

"He moved from a *peripheral presence* occasionally interceding, to being the *central core* permanently guiding.

Chuck paused, then said quietly, "And at the same time, I wonder if anything has ever been—or still is—more disappointing... more disheartening... more annoying... more exasperating... more irritating... more frustrating... more bothersome... more trying... more aggravating... more vexing... more testing... more distressing... more upsetting... more dismaying... more grieving... more offending... more disconcerting... more displeasing... more troubling... more saddening to God than our persistent *marginalization* of this reality. I say marginalization because it is not as if we don't *know* it... it is not as if we don't *believe* it. Rather, it is as if it is *easier* to acknowledge something from the past than to trust something in the present... it is *safer* to intellectualize something from history than to faith something in the moment.

"In golf, there's the old saying that 'every shot makes someone happy.' That is no less true in this matter. Marginalization *does* make someone happy, and that someone is the deceiver, Satan. His first hope is that you don't become a Christian. His second, failing the first, is that you never realize life beyond salvation. At salvation, he lost *you.* But if he can keep you from growing, he will minimize losing *others*. The most effective means he has of stunting your growth is to keep you focused on the *past*—Christ's death and resurrection, rather than the *present*—your decisions and your service. And this is rather easy for him to do because the past is clear, defined, pasteurized and unambiguous, while the present is unclear, undefined, impure and very, very ambiguous.

"Another means of marginalizing is keeping us confused about what we should *expect* from the Holy Spirit. It's as if we have this persistent yearning to travel, to fly, but find ourselves content once we're through airport security—using, by the way, our new ID and a ticket prepaid by someone else. Once inside, we never board the plane, never lift off, never reach a destination. Instead, we are consumed with the hum and buzz, the hustle and bustle, the rattle and rush of *virtual* travel... thinking that this is the way it is supposed to be... thinking that Jesus' job was to get us through security... thinking that from here on it's our job to figure out where we are to go, what we are to do, how we are to serve. Never realizing that once inside, he wants us to linkup with a Tour Guide... an indwelling Tour Guide... who will show us where to go, what to do, how to serve.

"Jack's focus this morning is on you and your children, and his first point is that *you* cannot change them—only the Holy Spirit can. For those who may still question this premise, I want you to think about this," Chuck said as he turned to the board, wiped it clean, and wrote:

If JESUS could not change his disciples,

YOU cannot change your children.

Turning back to the class, Chuck said, "Jack has asked me to focus on the Holy Spirit in the Gospels and Acts, and I want to do so now by looking at three brief but remarkable passages that confirm what I just wrote. The first event takes place on Sunday, the day of his resurrection. Two men are walking on a road toward a village called Emmaus, about seven miles from Jerusalem. Jesus joins them, does not reveal his identity, and engages them in conversation. Would you turn to Luke 24: 17-21 and tell me what it says."

After a few seconds of silence, broken only by the soft sounds of books being opened and pages being turned, a voice from the right center said, "I have it" and Shirley White read from an International Standard Version:

> *"He asked them, 'What are you discussing with each other as you're walking along?' They stood still and looked gloomy. The one whose name was Cleopas answered him, 'Are you the only visitor to Jerusalem who doesn't know what happened there these days?' He asked them, 'What things?' They answered Him, 'The things about Jesus of Nazareth, who was a prophet, mighty in the things that He did and said before God and all the people, and how our high priests and leaders handed Him over to be condemned to death and had Him crucified. But we kept hoping that He would be the one to redeem Israel.'"*[8]

"Thanks, Shirley," Chuck said, "Read the last sentence one more time."

Shirley glanced down at her Bible and read: *But we kept hoping that He would be the one to redeem Israel.*[9]

"Now move ahead 40 days," Chuck said. "Would someone find and read Acts 1:3-6?" From the back row, somebody read from an ISV:

> *"After he had suffered, He had shown Himself alive to them by many convincing proofs, appearing to them through a period of forty days and telling them about the kingdom of God. While He was meeting with them, He ordered them, Do not leave Jerusalem, but wait for the Father's promise, about which you heard Me speak. For John baptized with water, but you will be baptized with the Holy Spirit not many days from now.*
>
> *Now those who had come together began to ask Him, 'Lord, is this the time when You will restore the kingdom to Israel?'"*[10]

Chuck said, "Read the last sentence again," and the words came: *Now those who had come together began to ask Him, Lord, is this the time when You will restore the kingdom to Israel?* [11]

"Thanks, Ryan," Chuck said and, looking at the whole class, continued, "Okay… tell me what this means."

The room was again silent as they reread the Scriptures, searching for an answer other than the obvious… and the unimaginable… which Sue Sharp finally verbalized: "They didn't get it! None of them. Not those who knew him casually. Not those who knew him personally. None saw him as anything but a politico… a liberator… King Jesus the First."

Brent Wheeler said of Acts 1:3-6, "I agree with Sue. I never realized this before, but here… the *first* question in the *first* chapter of the *first* book after Jesus' death and resurrection is not about faith… it's about politics… it's about the re-establishment of Israel as a kingdom through the promised Messiah of the Old Testament. You would have thought that they—after three years of Jesus' hands-on teaching and healing and discipling—would have asked about *their* power to preach and heal and disciple."

Barbara Lynch said, "I can somewhat understand the two men in on the road to Emmaus wondering because it was the day of the resurrection and they were probably still in shock. But the group described in Acts is less understandable because they had had time to think about the events and their meaning. They had time to think about the four predictions he made about his death and resurrection before it actually happened. They had 40 days with Jesus *after* his resurrection in which he was telling them about the kingdom of God."

Chuck paused, looked at the class, and said, "These snapshots tell me that Jesus—as a person—did not change them. There is no denying that he *influenced* their outward behavior to be more loving, more charitable, more forgiving. But I see no evidence that his presence, his teaching, or his examples changed their hearts… their cores… their souls.

"The third and last passage I want to look at—Acts 2:14-41—is only a couple of pages later in my ISV and probably the same in yours. It is rather long, so I'll read it.

> *Then Peter stood up with the eleven, raised his voice, and addressed them, "Men of Judea and everyone living in Jerusalem! You must understand something, so pay close attention to my words. These men are not drunk as you suppose, for it's only nine o'clock in the morning. Rather, this is what was spoken through the prophet Joel: 'In the last days, God says, I will pour out my Spirit on everyone. Your sons and your daughters will prophesy, your young men will see visions, and your old men will dream dreams. In those days I will even pour out my Spirit on my slaves, men and women alike, and they will prophesy. I will work wonders in the sky above and signs on the earth below: blood, fire, and clouds of smoke. The sun will turn to darkness, and the moon to blood, before the coming of the great and glorious Day of the Lord. Then whoever calls on the name of the Lord will be saved.'*
>
> *Fellow Israelites, listen to these words! Jesus from Nazareth was a man accredited to you by God through miracles, wonders, and signs that God performed through Him among you, as you yourselves know. This very man, after He was arrested according to the predetermined plan and foreknowledge of God, you crucified and killed by the hands of lawless men. But God raised him up and destroyed the pains of death, since it was impossible for him to be held in its power. For David says about him, 'I always see the Lord in front of me, for he is at my right hand so that I cannot be shaken. That is why my heart is glad and my tongue rejoices, yes, even my body still rests securely in hope. For you will not abandon my soul to Hades or allow your Holy One to experience decay. You have made the ways of life known to me, and you will fill me with gladness in your presence.'*

Brothers, I can tell you confidently that the patriarch David died and was buried, and that his tomb is among us to this day. Therefore, since he was a prophet and knew that God had promised him with an oath to put one of his descendants on his throne, he looked ahead and spoke about the resurrection of the Christ: 'He was not abandoned to Hades, and his flesh did not experience decay.' It was this very Jesus whom God raised, and of that we are all witnesses. He has been exalted to the right hand of God, has received from the Father the promised Holy Spirit, and has poured out what you are seeing and hearing. For David did not go up to heaven, but he said, 'The Lord said to my Lord, Sit at my right hand, until I make your enemies your footstool. Therefore, let the entire house of Israel understand beyond a doubt that God made this Jesus, whom you crucified, both Lord and Christ!'

When they heard this, they were pierced to the heart. They asked Peter and the other apostles, 'Brothers, what should we do?' Peter answered them, 'Repent and be baptized, every one of you, in the name of Jesus Christ for the forgiveness of your sins. Then you will receive the Holy Spirit as a gift. For this promise belongs to you and your children, as well as to all those who are far away, whom the Lord our God may call to himself.' With many more words he continued to testify and to plead with them, saying, 'Be saved from this corrupt generation!' So those who welcomed his message were baptized, and that day about 3,000 persons were added to them." [12]

Closing his Bible, Chuck looked at the class and asked, "Now… tell me… were they changed?"

Quiet voices saying 'yes' and heads nodding in the affirmative reflected the class's answer.

"What changed them?" Chuck asked, then stood silently as he awaited responses. The answers came quickly, quietly, randomly from across the room: "Pentecost… The Holy Spirit… Acts 2:1-4.

"You are right," Chuck said after a moment. "It was Pentecost. It was the Holy Spirit. Listen to this a few verses earlier, at the beginning of Acts 2:

When the day of Pentecost came, all of them were together in one place. Suddenly, a sound like the roaring of a mighty windstorm came from heaven and filled the whole house where they were sitting. They saw tongues like flames of fire that separated, and one rested on each of them. All of them were filled with the Holy Spirit…." [13]

Turning to the whiteboard, Chuck said, "I want to add this to what Jack wrote earlier:"

It was the HOLY SPIRIT that changed the disciples.

It will be the HOLY SPIRIT that changes your children.

Chuck closed his Bible, stepped from the lectern, and returned to his seat as Jack resumed his place at the head of the class.

As he did, Jack said, "In your Bible, turn to John 14:16. Your version may be a little different, but in essence you will read what I quoted earlier from the King James: *I will pray to the Father, and He shall give you another Comforter, that He may abide with you forever.* On your sheets write your answer to the three questions: *What* is being said? *Why* is it being said? *How* does it apply to my life? Don't rush… this may be the most important part of today's lesson."

The room was silent. Jack waited quietly while personal thoughts were recorded. Finally, into the silence, Jack tapped the board with a felt pen and said, "*It was the Holy Spirit that changed the disciples. It will be the Holy Spirit that changes your children.*" Knowing that anything he added to that which Chuck had said would cloud its clarity and diffuse its simplicity, Jack adjourned the class with prayer.

###

Your Takeaways and Action Items from this Chapter

Takeaway 1

(page__)

Takeaway 2

(page__)

Takeaway 3

(page__)

Your Takeaways and Action Items from this Chapter (cont .)

Action Item 1

(page__)

Action Item 2

(page__)

Action Item 3

(page__)

Who Is the Holy Spirit? (Part 2)

Chapter 6 - Sunday, June 12

After Beverly received requests, led the class in prayer, and sat down, Jack took his place in the front, extended his good morning, and said, "Today's lesson is the second and final part of last week's. By way of review, we are addressing the concern of so many in our group and so many in our church who are praying for their children, particularly… *especially*… those who are relatively new Christians who wish they had created different spiritual environments when their children were young and at home. Last week I said that if you are one of those trying to change your children today, give up!" Turning to the whiteboard, tapping each summary as he read it, he said, "Give up these three ways."

> Give up.
> 1. Give up trying to do it yourself because this is a change that can only be brought about by the Holy Spirit.
> 2. Give up trying to do it alone because this is a change that needs the prayers of your friends as well as yourself.
> 3. Give up feeling guilty for you are now doing what needs to be done. Plus: adults can change...you did!

Turning back to face the class, he said, "Our focus last week was on the first of these three, the Holy Spirit… on how in John 14:16 Jesus promised he would send an advocate, a helper, a comforter to *abide with you forever*… on how this represented the Second Transition, from God dwelling *among* us to God dwelling *within* us… and on how, as Chuck taught," he read as he turned, erased parts and added to the bottom of the whiteboard:

Give up.

1. Give up trying to do it yourself
2. Give up trying to do it alone
3. Give up feeling guilty, because:
   - If Jesus could not change His disciples, you cannot change your children.
   - It was the Holy Spirit that changed the disciples, it will be the Holy Spirit that changes your children.

"*This*," Jack said as he tapped Chuck's words for emphasis with the recapped marker, "is great teaching… *this* is great truth… and *this* leads us to examine the role of intercessory prayer in general and its transformation of the disciples in particular."

As he laid the marker in the tray and faced the class, Jack picked up his Bible and opened it to the book of John, to the chapter whose pages had been touched so often that they felt butter-soft, to the verses whose margins were filled with handwritten notes so tiny and tight that they looked like whaler's scrimshaw. With the book open, he said, "I want you to go back with me to that moment with which you are so familiar… back to the path to Gethsemane… back to the allegory of the vine… back to the night of his betrayal… and I want you to listen again to Jesus' intercessory prayer for his disciples." Looking down, Jack read from Chapter 17:1-26:

> *"Father, the hour has come... I have made your name known to the men you gave me from the world... I am asking on their behalf. I am not asking on behalf of the world, but on behalf of those you gave me… I am no longer in the world, but they are in the world, and I am coming to you. Holy Father, protect them by your name… I say these things in the world so that they may have my joy completed in themselves… I am not asking you to take them out of the world but to protect them from the evil one… I ask not only on behalf of these, but also on behalf of those who will believe in me through their message, that they may all be one. Just as you, Father, are in me and I am in you, may they also be one in us."*[1]

Closing the Bible, he said, "This is an example of an intercessory prayer by Jesus. We could look at another in Luke 23:34 when he prayed for those who were crucifying him as he said, *Father, forgive them, for they know not what they do.*[2] We could look at *Old* Testament examples, including Moses' habitual intercessory prayers for the wayward Children of Israel. And we could look at other *New* Testament examples, including Paul's frequent prayers for friends, coworkers, and members of the new churches.

"But, I want to look beyond Old and New Testament examples of *individual* intercessory prayers to the Bible's encouragement for *collective* intercessory prayers. And I want to do so because of this," he said turning to the whiteboard and reading aloud as he drew a "✓" by the phrase:

✓ 2. *Give up trying to do it alone*

Turning back to the class and speaking more firmly than he intended, Jack said, "Hear me clearly… the prayer of others for a concern of your heart is not a casual experiment in group feel-good. Not according to *your* Bible. Not according to *mine*. In Romans 12, Paul tells the entire church, *Be devoted to each other with mutual affection. Excel in showing respect for each other.... Be joyful in hope, patient in trouble, and persistent in prayer.* [3] In Ephesians 6 he tells the entire church, *Pray in the Spirit at all times with every kind of prayer and request there is. For the same reason be alert with every kind of effort and request for all the saints.* [4] And in 1st Thessalonians he tells the entire church, *'So then, encourage one another and build each other up, as you are doing… Always be joyful.... Continually be prayerful....* [5]

"It is *imperative*," he continued, still too firmly, "that you share your concern for your children with those who know your heart, know your love, and know your hope.

"It is *imperative* that they pray *with* you for the right kind of friends, right kind of experiences, and right kind of influences in the lives of your children.

"And it is *imperative* that they pray *for* you for the right kind of leadership, right kind of example, and right kind of words *from* you *to* your children."

Jack paused.

Few moments *in* his teaching… few subjects *of* his teaching… bore the sense of importance and the sense of urgency as did this moment and this subject. This came, he thought, from the experience he and Kelli had had over the years with the small prayer group they had formed. Two couples in that group had become Christians after their children had grown up and left home, and their children and grandchildren had become the focus of weekly prayers.

After a few seconds, Jack turned to another section of the New Testament and said, "I want to share with you this last thought… this last Scripture… as encouragement to join with prayer partners in praying for your children. In Matthew 18:18-20, Jesus says, *Truly I tell you, whatever you prohibit on earth will have been prohibited in heaven, and whatever you permit on earth will have been permitted in heaven. Furthermore, truly I tell you that if two of you agree on earth about anything you request, it will be done for you by my Father in heaven. For where two or three have come together in my name, I am there among them."* [6]

Closing his Bible, he said, "Take the hand of the person sitting next to you, close your eyes, and for the next few minutes pray for them. It is not necessary that you know them… know their needs …or know their hearts. It is necessary only that *they* know someone is praying for *them*… that *you* know someone is praying for *you*…."

For a few moments the room was silent until Jack quietly said, "Start a group. Today. Before you leave. Ask three people to meet you one morning a week, one lunch hour a week, one weekend night a week. Then pray. Pray for each other, pray for each other's families, and pray… as the four of you… *become* family."

Jack laid his Bible down, organized his next thoughts, then said, "As you begin this process of praying for others… particularly the children we've been talking about… you're going to have the deceiver attack you subtly, persistently, persuasively. He will attack from two different directions, from both ends of the humanistic spectrum: he will attack your *emotions* and he will attack your *logic*.

"He will attack your *emotions* and you will find yourself thinking things such as 'it doesn't *feel* as if my prayers are being heard.'

"He will attack your *logic* and you will find yourself thinking things such as 'it doesn't seem *probable* that my child will be saved.'

"Nowhere have I seen this onslaught of deception, this battle for your expectation, this fight for your foundation better combated than in a book I bought years ago," he said as from a chair he picked up a small Ziploc bag. From it he removed a thin paperback book. He removed it as if he were lifting a diamond from a jewel box. He lifted it carefully for it was old… it was worn… and, for Jack, it *was* treasure. The book was *The Green Letters: Principles of Spiritual Growth* by Miles J. Stanford. Various parts of the book were originally written as short letters from Stanford to interested friends. Over time, the letters were compiled into this book.

"A few weeks ago I encouraged you to begin a library. I want to share with you this favorite book from mine. As I do, you will notice that this is not a 1,000-page tome. In fact, it is barely 100 pages. I point this out because the library you build, the collection of resources you assemble, doesn't have to be ponderous… only pertinent. And few books have been more so to my life… particularly my early Christian life… than this one. And it's because we are talking in these lessons about new Christians that I share with you this that had such an impact on my early Christian development. I'm going to read to you a few paragraphs from a few chapters that will give you encouragement as you begin praying for your children."

The book's original forest-green cover was now dappled with large white patches where the color had been worn away, not only from Jack's use but, significantly, from use by those to whom he had loaned it. Slipped in the front was a handwritten note of appreciation from a colleague dated 18 years earlier. Other users had been a boyfriend of his daughter, a new Christian in their prayer group, and a member of his foursome. Its pages, once bound into a book, were now as free as cards in a deck.

Gently cupping the open book in his left hand, as carefully as a child would hold a chick, and with his right hand unconsciously pushing pages back between the covers, his finger and thumb lightly squaring their corners, he began to read, the words coming easily, smoothly, like lyrics from an old familiar song.

"In Chapter 1, Stanford writes of the role of *faith* in our development, saying:

> *Since true faith is anchored upon scriptural facts, we are certainly not to be influenced by impressions. George Mueller said, 'Impressions have neither one thing nor the other to do with faith. Faith has to do with the Word of God. It is not impressions, strong or weak, which will make the difference. We have to do with the Written Word and not ourselves or our impressions.*
>
> *Then, too, probabilities are the big temptation when it comes to exercising faith. Too often the attitude is, 'It doesn't seem probable that he will be saved.'….But Mueller wrote: Many people are willing to believe regarding those things that seem probable to them. Faith has nothing to do with probabilities. The province of faith begins where probabilities cease and sight and sense fail. Alexander R. Hay adds to this by saying, '...faith is not a force that we exercise or a striving to believe that something shall be, thinking that if we believe hard enough it will come to pass.' That may be positive thinking, but certainly not Biblical faith."*[7]

Jack continued, "In Chapter 2, Stanford writes of the role *time* plays in our development:

> *It seems that most believers have difficulty in realizing and facing up to the inexorable fact that God does not hurry in His development of our Christian life…. So many feel they are*

not making progress unless they are swiftly and constantly forging ahead. Now it is true that the new convert often begins and continues for some time at a fast rate. But this will not continue if there is to be healthy growth and ultimate maturity. God himself will modify the pace....

John Darby makes it plain that 'it is God's way to set people aside after their first start, that self-confidence may die down. Thus Moses was forty years (before being called at the burning bush)... Paul was three... after his first testimony.'

Dr. A. H Strong... wisely points out to us that 'growth is not a uniform thing in the tree or in the Christian. In some single months there is more growth than all the year besides. During the rest of the year, however, there is solidification, without which the green timber would be useless. The period of rapid growth, when wood fiber is actually deposited between the bark and the trunk, occupies but four to six weeks in May, June and July.'

In that the Husbandman's method for true spiritual growth involves pain as well as joy, suffering as well as happiness, failure as well as success, inactivity as well as service, death as well as life, the temptation to shortcut is especially strong unless we see the value of and submit to the necessity of the time element....

'So often in the battle,' says Austin-Sparks, 'we go to the Lord, and pray, and plead, and appeal for victory, for ascendancy, for mastery over the forces of evil and death, and our thought is that in some way the Lord is going to come in with a mighty exercise of power and put us into a place of victory and spiritual ascendancy as in an act. We must have this mentality corrected. What the Lord does is to enlarge us to possess. He puts us through some exercise, through some experience, takes us some way which means our spiritual expansion... so that we occupy the large place....' I will not drive them [Canaanites] out from before thee in one year; lest the land become desolate, and the beast of the field [wild animals] multiply against thee. By little and little I will drive them out before thee, until thou be increased' (Ex. 23:29, 30). [8]

"In Chapter 3, Stanford continues, touching on one of the most important... most elusive... most fundamental of all principles of spiritual growth: the basis on which God *accepts* us.

There are two questions that every believer must settle as soon as possible. The one is, does God fully accept me? And, if so, upon what basis does He do so?....

God's basis must be our basis for acceptance. There is none other. We are 'accepted in the Beloved.' Our Father is fully satisfied with His Beloved Son on our behalf.... J. N. Darby was very clear on this: 'When the Holy Spirit reasons with man, He does not reason from what man is for God, but from what God is to man. Souls reason from what they are in themselves as to whether God can accept them. He cannot accept you thus; you are looking for righteousness in yourself as a ground of acceptance with Him....

To believe, and to consent to be loved while unworthy, is the great secret
To refuse to make 'resolution' and 'vows', for that is to trust in the flesh
To expect to be blessed, though realizing more and more the lack of worth
To rely on God's chastening hand as a mark of His kindness
To 'hope to be better' is to fail to see yourself in Christ only
To be disappointed with yourself is to have believed in yourself
To be discouraged is unbelief, as to God's purpose and plan of blessing for you
To be proud, is to be blind, for we have no standing before God in ourselves
To preach devotion first and blessing second is to reverse God's order and preach law, not grace.'" [9]

Jack closed the book, marking the page with his index finger, and said, "I want to shift our focus to try to help with the last of my three points: *Give up feeling guilty because you did not create a Christian environment during your children's formative years*.

"I want to do that by reading more of this book in a moment, but first I want to share with you some other thoughts that would help me if I were you. I'll begin with the Old Testament which—though it may initially seem to be archaic law rather than grace-based faith and irrelevant in our New Testament era—I think illuminates for us an important part of God's nature.

"If we go back to Mt. Sinai, go back to the place and time that God issued the Ten Commandment, go back to his collateral instructions that accompanied those Commandments, we see in Numbers 15:27-28 that he speaks of 'sins of ignorance.' Particularly, he says that *the priest shall make an atonement for the soul that sinneth ignorantly, when he sinneth by ignorance before the Lord, to make an atonement for him; and it shall be forgiven him.*[10]

"I personally agree with Don Dunn, a pastor in Clinton, TN when he writes, '*...If children sin before they reach the age of accountability, they sin in "ignorance," the atonement made by our Lord Jesus Christ, our High Priest, provides such with forgiveness.'* This, I hope for you as a parent, is the first step toward dealing with a sense of guilt."

Jack paused, seeming to think through the second point, decided to postpone it for a moment, and said, "For some reason, this 'sin of *ignorance'* reminds me of a 'sin of *violation.'* Maybe it's on my mind because I have an adult friend who is trying to cope with something like that today. It wasn't so much a 'sin of ignorance' as a child as it was a 'sin of violation' as a young adult. I want to speak to this because I think God has a special heart for those who were victims of a sins of violation in their formative years. There are many forms, but three of the most damaging are these: Early immersion into a perverted church or doctrine or religion, some so extreme that they may be called cults... early sexual abuse, whether subtle or forthright, causing victims to hold in contempt anyone representing any form of faith... and early rejection, exclusion, even ostracization by friends, family, or mentors when, as a youth, victims began taking tentative steps into exploring this thing called faith."

Jack stopped, quietly looked over the class, knowing firsthand from this friend how traumatizing such an experience could be... knowing that probably violations like this—usually in milder forms—were why so many mature adults never revisited the idea of faith... and knowing that there was more which needed to be said, but hoping that recognition was a start toward healing. Jack concluded by saying, "I'll say it again: If you have been a victim, I think God has a special—a very special—heart and place and hope for you."

Pausing again, Jack said, "Back to my points on why you as a parent should not feel guilty. The second step is acknowledging that your parenting is not solely and totally, wholly and completely, entirely and exclusively responsible for every decision your children make once they reach maturity and begin making independent choices.

"The third and last step is recognizing the price you pay today in living a life saturated with guilt for yesterday—particularly in the coin of depression and remorse, stress and fear—and how that inhibits doing the very thing you want to do tomorrow: *draw your children to this faith you have discovered."*

Opening the book again, Jack continued, "In Chapter 4, Stanford speaks about God's preparation of us, and how that preparation *of* us leads others to him *through* us:

> *Once we know His eternal plan and purpose for us, plus His method of preparation and process to that end, there is rest and confidence. Now it so happens that God's basic ingredient*

for growth is need. Without personal needs, we would get nowhere in our Christian life. The reason our Father creates and allows needs in our lives is to turn us from all that is outside of Christ, centering us in him alone....

For both our growth and service it is all-essential that we see and understand this principle, which J. B. Stoney sets forth in a sentence: 'The soul never imbibes the truth in living power, but as it requires it.' As for our growth, needs cause us to reach out and appropriate by faith, from our Lord Jesus, that which we require. And in the matter of service, in witnessing and helping others, we must watch and wait for the hungry, the needy heart, if there is to be abiding fruit'....

Watchman Nee puts first things first in saying, 'The Lord does not set us here first of all to preach, or to do any work for him. The first thing for which He sets us here is to create hunger in others. No true work will ever begin without a sense of need being created. We cannot drive people to be hungry. That hunger is to be created, and that hunger can be created only through those who carry the impressions of God.'[11]

"In Chapter 9, Stanford continues his thoughts on leading others to him through us:

It might be good to stress several points just here. (1) Never was a believer brought into healthy spiritual maturity by means of pressure meetings, and constant exhortation, nor before he was prepared by the Spirit. (2) Healthy progress is based upon the apprehension, understanding and appropriation of the truths in Christ that make for real growth. (3) The experiential aspect of all truth and especially these so-called deeper truths, is closed to all but the needy heart. Until one is aware of his need to progress spiritually, he will never be brought beyond the birth truths—a mere babe in Christ. [12]

"In Chapter 16, staying with his theme from Chapter 9, Stanford writes defining what it means to *mature* from a babe in Christ:

Immaturity considers the Lord Jesus a Helper. Maturity knows Him to be Life itself... Christian living is not our living with Christ's help, it is Christ living His life in us.[13]

"And in Chapter17, Stanford summarizes the *whole* of his book, the *whole* of God's process:

Each of us must be thoroughly cultivated before He can effectively cultivate others through us. It is not that there will be no service for us until we are spiritually mature, but that most of our service on the way to maturity is for our own development, and not so much that of others....

Since the work of God is essentially spiritual, it demands spiritual people for its doing; and the measure of their spirituality will determine the measure of their value to the Lord. Because this is so, in God's mind the servant is more than the work.

If we are going to come truly into the hands of God for His purpose, then we shall be dealt with by Him in such a way as to continually increase our spiritual measure. Not our interest in Christian work; our energies, enthusiasm, ambitions, or abilities; not our academic qualification, or anything that we are in ourselves, but simply our spiritual life is the basis of the beginning and growth of our service to God.

We are not saved to serve; we are matured to serve." [14]

Jack stopped, closed the book, laid it on the stand, stepped to the whiteboard, tapped the statements, and said as he began reading each one, "I hope with all my heart these have helped."

Give up.

1. Give up trying to do it yourself
2. Give up trying to do it alone
3. Give up feeling guilty, because:
   - If Jesus could not change His disciples, you cannot change your children.
   - It was the Holy Spirit that changed the disciples, it will be the Holy Spirit that changes your children.

Jack looked over the class, took a step closer, and continued, "I hope—for all of us—these lessons have brought a fresh realization of *who* the Holy Spirit is… *how* he lives in us… and *why* he is essential in our relationship with God and his with us. And, particularly, I hope they have given encouragement and guidance to those coping with guilt and frustration.

"As the final step in this lesson," Jack said as he asked Bev to pass out the Q&As, "on the back of the sheet, write a paragraph beginning with these three words: *The Holy Spirit…."*

Later, Jack asked those wanting to share their comments to do so.

He then concluded the class with this simple prayer: "Our Heavenly Father, in hunger and humility we seek through the Holy Spirit to be matured into those who, finally, give up trying to live *for* you and instead allow you to live *through* us… to draw and to serve others. In Jesus' Holy Name we pray. Amen."

###

Your Takeaways and Action Items from this Chapter

Takeaway 1

(page__)

Takeaway 2

(page__)

Takeaway 3

(page__)

Your Takeaways and Action Items from this Chapter (cont.)

Action Item 1

(page__)

Action Item 2

(page__)

Action Item 3

(page__)

Who Is God?

Chapter 7 - Sunday, June 19

It was Jack's nature to plan. Almost an obsessive-compulsive about it, the habit had served him well in college, the military, and in business.

Characteristically, the habit had found form in the lesson plans he had laid out—Sunday by Sunday—at the beginning of this farewell series. At the start, he could have told anyone the topic, the chapter, and the verse that would be taught on any Sunday for sixteen consecutive weeks. Now, as he thought back over the first six weeks and the first six lessons, he could not help but smile, and not help but be pleased with the way the plan had disintegrated… and at the way a new plan had spontaneously emerged, Sunday by Sunday, as he had sensed the needs of the class.

The old nature, however, had raised its head earlier *this* week as he had seen the possibility of a six-lesson series, and he had called two friends from the university about teaching portions of it. They had accepted and were going to lead most of the morning's class.

As Beverly completed the recognition of visitors, called for requests, and ended the opening prayer, Jack approached the lectern and said, "I join Bev in extending a good morning and welcoming you to what is becoming a six-lesson series. The idea of doing this came to me Monday as I was thinking about our last two lessons that had focused on the Holy Spirit. It seemed a natural extension to add four more and address these questions," he said as he turned and read as he wrote on the whiteboard:

Sundays 1-2 (Last two weeks): Who is the Holy Spirit?
Sunday 3 (Today): Who is God?
Sunday 4: Who is Christ?
Sunday 5: Who is Satan?
Sunday 6: What is Salvation?

Turning back to the class and smiling again, he said, "Now we are nothing if not ambitious… or arguably naïve… to think that we can cover these last four topics—each of which has been the subject of centuries of study by monks in monasteries, scholars in universities, and pastors in pulpits—in four Sundays. But, as they say… with a little help from my friends… we can try.

"The first of these friends is Debora Devonshire. Known as 'Dee Dee' to her friends, 'Deborah Mireille' to her parents, and soon, as '*Dr.* Devonshire' to her students. She speaks fluent English, French, German, Russian, and Italian... can read and write Greek and Latin… holds an undergraduate degree in

European history, a graduate degree in comparative religions, and in a few weeks will hold her doctorate in cultural anthropology.

"This is one remarkable lady, and before she comes to this lectern you need to hear part of her story: Her father, a native of Illinois with a PhD in theology from the University of Bern, remained in Switzerland to become president of the Bernkirche Theological Seminary. During the Cold War, the primary mission of BTS had been to provide intensive training to Iron Country ministers who were permitted to leave Russia on short-term visas. In Geneva he met a young French woman named Mireille, a ballet student with l'Opera National de Paris. They met, married, and had a daughter, our guest speaker.

"Dee Dee's formative years were spent, by any measure, in one of the most interesting sites on Earth… whether that measure be spiritually, culturally, linguistically, politically, geographically, topographically, historically, or anthropologically.

"A few months ago she asked me to read a draft of her doctoral dissertation, *Man's Architecture of Faith: The Irrefutable Evidence of God.* I was so taken by her perspective and analysis that I have asked her to share her thoughts with you this morning as we address the subject: Who is God?"

Turning to her, he said, "Dee Dee, thanks for joining us."

With the grace of a lynx, she walked from her second-row seat to the small music stand, a young lady with her mother's ballerina-slim frame and her father's Irish-green eyes. She smiled, then said with the soft French accent that Americans found endearing, "Good morning. I am afraid Jack has overstated my résumé, though," she added with another smile, this one to him in appreciation, "I did enjoy hearing it."

Looking back at the class, smiling again, she said, "As you heard, I have been born to special circumstances… *wonderful* circumstances. I will add that these circumstances have also endowed me with a special potential… a potential I hope someday to fulfill.

"I welcome the opportunity to present to you my doctoral work. Because of its nature, I am going to redefine Jack's question slightly to ask '*Is* there a God?' rather than '*Who* is God?'

"And because the personal circumstances to which I referred are germane to my perspective on today's lesson and on the content of my dissertation, I will elaborate on Jack's history of me.

"I will begin at my age twelve. I had been for eight years a student of my mother's Geneva LeFinfintel Ballet Academic, obsessed with dance and, I thought, destined to be a principal dancer at the Ballet du Grand Théâtre de Genéve. However, during that summer, I joined my father on one of his 'trips' and my focus, my life, was changed forever. These trips were private annual study-tours hosted by the Seminary, financed by affluent benefactors, and attended by only three persons, all from BTS: The General Director of University Curriculum, the Chairman of the Department of Cultural Anthropology, and my father.

"These brief study-leaves were used by my father for advancing his own understanding of man and God… for refreshing his own pitcher from which he would serve students and staff… and for taking advantage of the extraordinary opportunity presented by momentarily being on that part of the globe, in that part of the world, to spend days—*days*—on significant archeological, anthropological, and religious sites, both Christian and non-Christian.

"Through the kind indulgence of his two colleagues, I was invited to join them on their trip to Egypt. There, near Cairo, in Giza, on the west bank of the Nile, I climbed one of the great pyramids. As I stopped midway to the top, breathing hard from the climb, my fingers tracing the enormous seam between two house-size stones, I discovered that that which was *most* noteworthy to others—that there were ten pyramids in this region… that the largest was built for Pharaoh Khufu… that it took 100,000 laborers 20 years to stack 2 million limestone blocks—was of *least* importance to me. The most amazing thing to me was that which our guide had just said, and that which I can still quote: *...according to many scholars, the pyramids were shaped as they were to help the soul of the king climb to the sky and join the gods.* It did not matter to me that they worshipped eight primordial gods of the Hermopolitan Ogdoad and as well as many lesser gods… or that these were gods to wisdom or writing or war or sickness or other issues… or that they were worshipped in the shapes of snakes or falcons or other forms. It only was important to me that here—more than 2,000 years before Christ—Egyptians believed that there were supernatural powers… that these powers were manifested in these gods… that these gods were to be honored, revered, worshipped.

"At age thirteen I was again invited, this time to Athens, to the Parthenon. As I stood among the columns in the central court of this huge… *huge*… temple, I was overwhelmed at the thought that here, on this spot, four centuries before the birth of Christ, men worshipped. That they worshipped Athena Parthenos, I did not care. That she was the favorite child of Zeus, was of no concern. That Greeks sensed a *something* which was greater, higher, more powerful than themselves… only *this* mattered.

"At age fourteen, we were at Stonehenge where I again had the thought that here… at this site… 3,000 years before Christ… men worshipped. Worshipped what, I did not know. Who they were, I did not care. That they sought the favor of a power, higher than themselves, only this mattered.

"The next year, during a trip to Ephesus, I began a journal. I began with notes I made as I stood at the excavation of the Temple of Artemis—or 'Diana' if you're Roman. The Temple was enormous… twice the size of the Parthenon… so massive it was one of the Seven Wonders of the world. It was built in the 6th century before Christ to honor the Greek goddess. It made Ephesus a major city, and it made its silversmiths—who crafted and sold statues of Artemis—wealthy. The latter explains why, as told in in Acts 19:21-41, Paul was the focus of the riots by these craftsmen when he preached that these idols should not be bought because gods made by human hands were not gods at all. But those were not the most important points to me… as I stood on the stones of the excavated foundation, I had the thought—again—that here, *centuries before Christ*, men acknowledged, sought the favor of, worshipped a superior power."

Smiling, pausing to gather her thoughts, conscious of the time, Dee Dee began her summary, "In my journal I recorded my *impressions* begun in Egypt and my *convictions* that grew from subsequent trips with my father to the Blue Mosque in Istanbul, the Wailing Wall in Jerusalem, the Temple of Heaven in Beijing, the ruins of the Buddhist Vihara in Bangladesh, and the Neolithic Rock Drawings of Valcamonica—particularly those representing 'oranti' or 'praying figures'—in the Lombardy region of Italy… that grew from my readings about the Alaskan totems, Navajo sand paintings, and the Mayan temples… and that grew from my study of archeological digs in Africa, India, and Indonesia."

Holding a thin bound booklet, she said, "That journal became the genesis for my thesis, that conviction became the title of my paper, and both are summarized in my opening Abstract, part of which I will read to you now." Dee Dee read:

> *This paper addresses the question: Does God exist?*
>
> *It examines this question as an atheist or agnostic might, searching for evidence from sources other than the Bible, Torah, Qur'an, Vedas, Tipitaka, or other religious writings, all of which are commonly used by believers to confirm but universally dismissed by doubters as self-serving.*
>
> *This paper proposes that the skeptic who rejects the written records of faith turn to the physical records, do so by searching the archives of archeology, and begin that search with the following definition of archeology as found on the website cyberpursuits.com: 'Archeology is the study of human past. Its initial objective is the study of cultural chronology. Its intermediate*

objective is the reconstruction of past lifeways. Its ultimate objective is the discovery of the processes which underlie and condition human behavior.'

This paper asserts that any person:
(a) framing their inquiry within the objective context of this definition, and
(b) accepting the physical evidence produced by the discipline of archeology, will
(c) conclude that man in virtually every society, in every millennium, in every part of the world has sensed an incompleteness, a hollowness, a void; has
(d) intrinsically believed that there exists a power higher than himself that alone could fill that void; has
(e) universally craved the forgiveness and acceptance, guidance and fellowship, wisdom and favor of that power; has
(f) sought this through every means imaginable by his mind—by wearing beads and shaking tambourines, by burning candles and singing songs, by whispering chants and sacrificing animals, by launching crusades and erecting structures; and
(g) that it is this last—these physical, enduring, architectural structures—that stand as the irrefutable evidence that as surely as there exists a power that draws the body downward there exists a power that draws the spirit upward, and man, acknowledging these inescapable powers, has named the former gravity and the latter God."

Closing the small booklet, she turned to the next teacher and said, "Dr. Mark, if you will permit me one more moment," then looked at the class and continued, saying, "I want to close my portion of this morning by adding this personal postscript to this academic paper—this may be what I believe here in America is called a personal testimony.

"I imagine it to be *improbable* that there is seated in this room a true atheist or agnostic. However, I imagine it to be *probable* that there is seated here the occasional doubter… one who wonders, even momentarily, if there is a God when employment is lost, or a child is ill, or a relationship is irreconcilably damaged.

"I imagine this to be probable because I, too—infused though I was from infancy with the tenets of faith and experienced though I am with the realities of God—have had moments. When I do, I look at the world, I look at its history, I look at its architectural remnants, and I see the physical evidence that there has always been a *hole*… a *hollow spot*… an *incompleteness* in man.

"Why would that be?

Pausing, she then said, "If you're searching for the reality of God, begin by answering that question."

She stood quietly for another moment. Then, turning to Jack, smiled and said, "*Jacque... merci.*"

Jack squeezed her hand as they passed, she to her seat, he to the music stand, where he said to the class, "You now know the secret to great teaching… find great teachers. The next of those friends that will help me is a gentleman, a fellow teacher, and one of the few truly brilliant people I know. I have divided today's lesson—Who is God?—into three parts… historical, scientific, and Biblical… and have asked him to teach the second part. Would you join me in welcoming a man you already know, Dr. Mark Taylor."

There was almost applause as Jack stepped from the lectern and Mark Taylor, taking the cue, walked from his seat to the music stand. Dr. Mark Taylor—'Dr. Mark' to his students—was chairman of the Physics Department at Madison-Mason University. And if ever there was a professor truly loved, widely revered, and universally enjoyed, it was Dr. Mark.

"Good morning," Mark said as he smiled, stepped behind the lectern and laid one book on the music stand. "I join the others in this room, Dee Dee, in saying thank you for a memorable lesson. And I join Chuck in his comment a few weeks ago in feeling honored to be a part of Jack's last class.

"As you just heard, Jack has asked me to speak on the question, 'Who is God?', from the scientific perspective. I, too, am going to take the liberty of redefining the question to the fundamental, 'Does God exist?' and give you two answers—one long, one short.

"For the long answer," Mark said as he picked up the 300-page hardback book, "I encourage you to read this: *The Case for A Creator* by Lee Strobel. I recommend this though I could refer you to scores of technical papers written by physicists specializing in the disciplines of Geophysics, Volcanology and Hydrology, as well as scores of others focusing on the broader sciences of Soil, Ocean, and Space—each of which speaks to the delicate, unlikely balance of an infinite number of factors that work in harmony to make Earth habitable.

"Mr. Strobel was educated at Yale Law School, was an award-winning journalist for the *Chicago Tribune*, and—note this—an atheist. Through the influence of his wife he became a Christian, and through his skills as a writer has produced a credible, readable, enlightening book about the scientific evidence that God exists… and certainly one more enjoyable than any written by my colleagues.

"Strobel examines the arguments *against* and the evidence *for* a creator through interviews with dozens of international leaders in the fields of mathematics, astronomy, biochemistry, and physics. The interviews cover familiar theories such as those advanced by Einstein, Hawking, Sagan, and Darwin as well as those that are less familiar to laymen but actively debated in the academic community. This is a must-read book, an essential addition to your personal library, and an indispensable resource for thoughtful reflection on this tipping-point question—is there a God?

"While this is a question impossible to cover in one class period, I will give you examples of three answers from his book. These are from chapters five, six, and seven… respectively titled *The Evidence of Cosmology, The Evidence of Physics,* and *The Evidence of Astronomy*."

Opening the book to chapter five, Mark said, "Strobel writes in the first person, walking you through questions and answers, making you part of the interview process, this one with Bill Craig. Craig was once a skeptic and now a prolific author of books and articles supporting the theory of a creator. I'm not sharing this with you to persuade you, for that's not my responsibility. I'm sharing it because we hear so little from this side of the discussion, and, frankly, much of what we do hear is so emotional or dogmatic or narrow that most people, myself included, simply dismiss it.

"This excerpt from a lengthy interview begins on page 105. Craig is speaking about Einstein's fundamental hypothesis that the universe was fixed… static… meaning that it was *neither* expanding nor contracting. This was a key underpinning in his theory… one that has proved to be *false* with enormous implications. Here's what Craig said.

> *When Albert Einstein developed his general theory of relativity in 1915 and started applying it to the universe as a whole, he was shocked to discover it didn't allow for a static universe. According to his equations, the universe should either be exploding or imploding. In order to make the universe static, he had to fudge his equations by putting in a factor that would hold the universe steady.*
>
> *In the 1920s, the Russian mathematician Alexander Friedman and the Belgium astronomer George Lemaître were able to develop models based on Einstein's theory. They predicted*

the universe was expanding. Of course, this meant that if you went backward in time, the universe would go back to a single origin before which it didn't exist. Astronomer Fred Hoyle derisively called this the Big Bang—and the name stuck.

Starting in the 1920s, scientists began to find empirical evidence that supported these purely mathematical models. For instance, in 1929, the American astronomer Edwin Hubble discovered that the light coming to us from distant galaxies appears to be redder than it should be, and that this is a universal feature of galaxies in all parts of the sky. Hubble explained this red shift as being due to the fact that the galaxies are moving away from us. He concluded that the universe is literally flying apart at enormous velocities. Hubble's astronomical observations were the first empirical confirmation of the predictions by Friedman and Lemaître.

Then in the 1940s, George Gamow predicted that if the Big Bang really happened, then the background temperature of the universe should be just a few degrees above absolute zero. He said this would be a relic from a very early stage of the universe. Sure enough, in 1965, two scientists accidentally discovered the universe's background radiation—and it was only about 3.7 degrees above absolute zero. There's no explanation for this apart from the fact that it is a vestige of a very early and a very dense state of the universe, which was predicted by the Big Bang model.

The third main piece of evidence for the Big Bang is the origin of light elements. Heavy elements, like carbon and iron, are synthesized in the interior of stars and then exploded through supernovae into space. But the very, very light elements, like deuterium and helium, cannot have been synthesized in the interior of stars, because you would need an even more powerful furnace to create them. These elements must have been forged in the furnace of the Big Bang itself at temperatures that were billions of degrees. There's no other explanation.

So predictions about the Big Bang have been consistently verified by scientific data. Moreover, they have been corroborated by the failure of every attempt to falsify them by alternative models. Unquestionably, the Big Bang model has impressive scientific credentials."[1]

Mark closed the book and said, "In chapter 6, Strobel examines creation from the perspective of physics with a focus on the improbable set of circumstances that had to occur for there to be—from the Big Bang, its discharge of gasses, and the velocity of travel of its released debris—our habitable pebble among the trillions and trillions and trillions of galaxies and stars and planets it produced. This improbable set of circumstances, this balance, for the universe as a whole and Earth individually, is called by many physicists, 'fine-tuning.' Strobel writes of his interview with Robin Collins, PhD, Northwestern University, speaker and author of numerous books on the subject:

'When scientists talk about the fine tuning of the universe', Collins said, 'They're generally referring to the extraordinary balancing of the fundamental laws and parameters of physics and the initial conditions of the universe. Our minds can't comprehend the precision of some of them. The result is a universe that has just the right conditions to sustain life. The coincidences are simply too amazing to have the result of happenstance—as Paul Davies said, 'the impression of design is overwhelming.'

I like to use the analogy of astronauts landing on Mars and find an enclosed biosphere, sort of like the domed structure that was built in Arizona a few years ago. At the control panel they find that all the dials for its environment are set just right for life. The oxygen ratio is perfect; the temperature is seventy degrees; the humidity is fifty percent; there's a system for replenishing the air; there are systems for producing food, generating energy, and disposing of wastes. Each dial has a huge range of possible setting, and you can see if you were to adjust one or more of them just a little bit, the environment would go out of whack and life would be impossible. What conclusion would you draw from that?'

The answer was obvious, 'That someone took great care in designing and building it,' I said.

'That's right,' he replied. 'You'd conclude that this biosphere was not there by accident. Volcanoes didn't erupt and spew out the right compounds that just happened to assemble themselves into the biosphere. Some intelligent being had intentionally and carefully designed and prepared it to support living creatures. And that's an analogy for our universe.'"[2]

Mark looked up from his book, glanced at the clock, smiled at the class and, obviously enjoying the reading, said, "I love this guy. He has digested the most complex of subjects into a book a fifth-grader could understand. I wish he were on our staff.

"We've looked at two chapters in which he describes the case for a creator from the perspective of cosmology and of physics. The last we'll have time for is three or four quick glances from the perspective of astronomy. Strobel writes in Chapter 7:

Earth's location, its size, its composition, its structure, its atmosphere, its temperature, its internal dynamics, and its many intricate cycles essential to life—the carbon cycle, the oxygen cycle, the nitrogen cycle, the phosphorous cycle, the sulfur cycle, the calcium cycle, the sodium cycle, and so on—testify to the degree to which our planet is exquisitely and precariously balanced.. [3]

"A few pages later, again speaking of our location, Strobel writes, quoting Guillermo Gonzalez, PhD:"

'There's a concept invented by astrobiologists called the Circumstellar Habitable Zone. That's the region around a star where you can have liquid water on the surface of a terrestrial planet. This is determined by the amount of light you get from the host star.

You can't be too close, otherwise too much water evaporates into the atmosphere and it causes a runaway greenhouse effect, and you boil off the oceans. We think that might be what happened to Venus. But if you too far out, it gets too cold. Water and carbon dioxide freeze and you eventually develop runaway glaciation.'[4]

"The third and last excerpts from his book speak of the moon, mass, and mountains:

...The moon actually stabilizes the tilt of the Earth's axis.... The tilt is responsible for our seasons. During the summer, in the northern hemisphere the North Pole is pointed more toward the sun. Six months later, when the Earth is on the other side of the sun, then the South Pole is more pointed toward the sun. With the Earth's tilt at 23.5 degrees, this gives us very mild seasons.... If the tilt were more like 90 degrees, the north pole would be exposed to the sun for six months while the south pole would be in darkness, then vice-versa....[5]

"There's much, much more that Strobel covers—too much for us to explore in these few minutes. Enough, however, to lead the strongest skeptic to ponder the question of *how* this all began ...and *why*... and *what*—or *who*—caused it."

Mark closed the book, laid it on the music stand, and said, "Now I'll give you my short answer to the question, does God exist, and I'll do it with these two sub-questions.

"Question one: If God exists, would he reveal himself?"

Mark paused.

"Question two: If he revealed himself, how would he do it?"

Mark paused again.

"My answer to the first is 'yes.' He would reveal himself because that would be the *only* way—along with what Christ revealed—he would have for *us* to know his *worship-worthiness.*

"My answer to the second is that he would reveal himself in ways that would be understandable to us, as humans, both collectively and *individually.* By the former, I mean he would reveal himself by meeting our *common* needs for food and shelter, love and joy, purpose and hope.

"By the latter, I mean he would reveal himself by meeting our *unique* needs, based on our *individual* interests and intellect, education and emotions.

"It is on this last—this *unique* revelation—that I want to speak as I address the subject of considering God's existence through science. And I want to do that by asking two more questions:

"First, if you were God, how might you reveal yourself to a curious four-year-old preschooler?

"Second, if you were God, how might you reveal yourself to a brilliant forty-four-year-old physicist?

"To the preschooler, you might do it with the color, the delicacy, the intricacy of a *butterfly.*

"To the physicist, you might do it with the color, the delicacy, the intricacy of *space.*

"God loves the forty-four-year-old as much as the four-year old.

"He wants to reveal himself to the physicist as badly as he wants to reveal himself to the preschooler.

"And to do that, he is just as *willing* and just as *able* to create a *galaxy*... as a *butterfly*."

Mark stopped.

Silence filled the room as he closed his notes, smiled at the class, and returned to his seat.

Jack walked to the front of the room and said, "Mark, our many thanks." Laying his Bible on the lectern, pausing for a moment to allow the silence to linger, Jack smiled then said, "Dee Dee established that *internally within* man there is and has been a spiritual incompleteness. Mark established that *externally to* man there is and has been a supreme designer. Our question then becomes... to whom does man look to assuage the incompleteness... and to whom does he look to ascribe the design?

"History's answer is that *prior* to Christ's coming—except for the children of Israel beginning in the 13th century BC—man has looked to numerous gods. *Since* his coming, man has looked to a single god: God.

"And *that* brings us to today's question, "*Who is God*?"

Jack said, "Trying to answer that question in a few words and in a few minutes is difficult for most, impossible for me. If I were to attempt it, I would say that God is one in three persons: Father... Son... Spirit. I would elaborate by describing his actions, such as by saying he creates... he loves... he forgives. I would add that he is omnipotent, omnipresent, eternal. I would include that he has emotions and that he can be angry, happy, hoping.

"But frankly, though those are true, I would soon feel at a loss. I would soon feel that those are just cold descriptions. I would soon find that I could no more answer the question of *Who is God?* than I could answer the question of *Why am I here*?

"So, I've picked a source other than myself to answer the question. I've looked at several and found one that I believe is *credible* enough in the qualifications of its contributors, *rigorous* enough in its endeavor to answer, and *articulate* enough in its ability to communicate to us lay believers.

"The source I've chosen is known within theological circles as *The Westminster Assembly*. A synopsis of the Assembly's history is this: In the mid-seventeenth century, the governments and clerics of England and Scotland were searching for unifying grounds between the Church of England and the Church of Scotland. To that end, a major conclave of spiritual leaders was held. It was major as measured by time—the endeavor took place between 1643 and 1647. And it was major as measured by the number of participants—representing the English were 120 ministers, 20 members of parliament, and 10 members of the House of Lords. Representing the Scottish were five ministers and three elders. And oddly, while the attendees to the Assembly were predominantly English, one source says the purpose of the Assembly was to bring the Church of England into greater conformity with the Church of Scotland.

"This large body of believers produced a large body of writing on worship, doctrine, church governance, and similar matters. Their written work is generally known as the Westminster *Confessions of Faith*. It is long and exhaustive. It includes what are called the *Westminster Larger Catechism* and the *Westminster Shorter Catechism*.

"The *Shorter Catechism* is formatted as a series of brief questions and answers. For our purposes this morning, the answer to their question number four is the answer to our question of the day, Who is God?

God is a Spirit... infinite... eternal... and unchangeable,
In His being... wisdom... power... holiness... justice... goodness... and truth."[6]

Jack paused, then said, "I can add nothing. I can take us back to what Dee Dee said about how we have *tried* to express ourselves to God, and to what Mark said about how God has *tried* to reveal himself to us. I'll now speak of how this book, this Bible, *tries* to enable us to do the former and enable God to do the latter. I say 'tries to' because we can no more see the whole of God through the Bible than we can see the whole of space through the Hubble. We can get a glimpse of him. But it's important that we recognize that it's only that—a glimpse.

"In that glimpse we see the essence of him.

"We see, as an example in 1John 4:8," he said as he erased then wrote on the board:

God is LOVE.

"I must tell you," he said as he turned back to the class, "that I think that this most famous of verses—though intended to be a concise statement defining God—is inadequate.

"I think that because I believe this is only part of it. The other part is...", he said as he again turned and wrote on the board:

God is LOVE.

God is GRACE.

Laying the marker back in the tray, he stepped to the center of the class and said, "*Grace* is love in action. *Grace* is to love as charity is to empathy… as benevolence is to sympathy… as forgiveness is to compassion. It was *grace* that led him to clothe Adam and Eve as they were driven from the Garden of Eden, *grace* that led him to send his son as a sacrifice, and *grace* that allowed me to be redeemed by that sacrifice.

"We get thousands of other glimpses of him, both those that define his perspective toward us and ours toward him. As examples of the latter, in Numbers 14:28 we see the *trust* he demands of us, in Matthew 25:28 the *work,* and in John 3:16 the *faith.* But these are only sketches, drawn on the canvas of history. God is dynamic, moving in lives with plans so complex, using means so unimaginable, that the few codified pages in this small inspired book cannot contain him. And, particularly, it cannot tell the whole of the purpose he has for you, the way that purpose fits into his larger plan, nor the means he's going to use to enable you to do your part. Those revelations are for you personally, revealed moment by moment, sometimes with great clarity, sometimes through unexpected circumstances, but always with *grace*… with his *love* in action."

Jack asked Beverly to pass out the work sheets, then said to the class, "Today's question is personal… what you write will not be discussed… when we're through I'll ask you to fold them and take them home. Turn your papers to the back side and answer this:

What would you ask God to reveal to you?

After a few minutes, Jack stepped to the lectern, again expressed thanks to Dee Dee and Mark, and said, "I want to leave you with this closing thought: A few weeks ago I talked about the importance of early, daily, fellowship with God. Today's lesson is a part of this time for me. I begin by reminding myself—as clearly as I can—of who it is I'm approaching. This reminding helps me to focus, helps me to listen, helps me to pray. And this reminding often takes the shape of simply whispering these two phrases slowly, thoughtfully, silently…

"God is love,

"God is grace.

"This week, I encourage you to open your quiet times with the same phrases. I encourage you to pace them with your breathing. And I encourage you to repeat the phrases at least seven times, like this:

"With the first exhale, *'God is love.'*

"With the next exhale, *'God is grace.'*

"Then, *'God is love.'*

"Then, *'God is grace.'*

"*God is love.*

"*God is grace.*

"*God is love*."

Jack paused and said, "I hope this brief practice, this almost brief prayer, blesses you as much as it does me."

Wanting nothing else to distract from this moment, he said, "Next week, lesson four in this series: Who is Christ."

Then, "Bev, please close us."

###

Your Takeaways and Action Items from this Chapter

Takeaway 1

(page__)

Takeaway 2

(page__)

Takeaway 3

(page__)

Your Takeaways and Action Items from this Chapter (cont.)

Action Item 1

(page__)

Action Item 2

(page__)

Action Item 3

(page__)

Who Is Christ?

Chapter 8 - Sunday, June 26

With announcements, prayer requests, and prayer time completed, Jack walked to the music stand, smiled as he placed teaching notes and three small books on the lectern, looked at the class, and said, "Good morning. Today is part four of our six-part series and the one in which we address the question: 'Who is *Christ*?

"We'll begin with this definition of the word, which is *Christ* in English, *Christos* in Greek, and *Messiah* in Hebrew, all of which have the same meaning: *the anointed one*.

"And we'll begin with what will seem like the second half of Mark's lesson from last week. It will seem so for three reasons. First, because I want to recommend to you another book by Lee Strobel, this one called *The Case for Christ*." Holding up the book, he said, "I recommend this because there is far more to the question than can be covered in our few minutes together, and because Strobel does such a superb job of examining this question from historical and archeological as well as Biblical perspectives."

Picking up another book, he said, "I also strongly recommend *Mere Christianity* by C.S. Lewis, as you know, another former atheist-turned-Christian and extraordinary writer.

"Finally," he continued as he laid the books on the stand, turned to the whiteboard and said as he wrote, "this will seem like the second half of Mark's class because of the questions he put before us."

> If God revealed himself, how would He do it?

Laying the marker down, Jack turned back to the class, smiled again, and said, "On several occasions I have said that I am sharing *personal* impressions with you, and I warn you now that I am about to do it again… this time revisiting an opinion I shared with you a few weeks ago."

Stepping to the side of the stand, he said, "It seems to me that the principal theme running through the entire Bible is that of God's effort to reveal himself to man. It seems to me that most Scripture—whether Old or New Testament, whether dealing with characters or events—is focused on this primary issue. And it seems, as I've said before, that all of Scripture can be broadly divided into his four core efforts: First, his attempt to reveal himself through a *couple*… Adam and Eve. Then his effort to do so through a *family*… Abraham's. Then through a *nation*… Israel. And then, finally… *I'll go myself.*"

Jack stood quietly for a moment, hoping that this picture of the creator's *progression* in—the creator's *obsession* with—revealing himself to his created would be clear. He then said, "This last act… this coming himself… reminds me of Paul Harvey's great Christmas story that goes something like this:

> *There was a family—father, mother, and children—that lived on a farm. One Christmas Eve, mother and children tried but failed to persuade their spiritually-skeptical father to join them at their small church in town for a midnight service.*
>
> *The hours passed and the father—alone at the farm—finished his chores as evening became night, as the clear night turned dark, and as a snowstorm moved in. Knowing his family would be safe with friends in town, he stood at the kitchen window and watched the snow fall, gently at first, in large flakes. He continued to watch as the wind strengthened, the storm intensified, and with surprising speed shrubs and fences and equipment banked into unrecognizable mounds and knolls and hillocks.*
>
> *And with growing concern he watched a small flock of tiny birds as they fluttered and floundered, fighting gusts that were stronger than their elfin wings, trying to find shelter. After watching their futile attempts for some time, the farmer pulled on coat and boots and hat and gloves and stepped into the biting cold and blinding wind. He walked through the swirling whiteness that stung like blowing sand to the barn… and opened the doors.*
>
> *When the birds did not respond to the open shelter, he bent forward against the wind, trudged to where they were struggling and tried to shoo them toward the doors.*
>
> *When the birds would not be driven in, he returned to the barn and turned on inside lights thinking it would draw them in.*
>
> *When the birds were not drawn, he stood in the storm, considering alternatives.*
>
> *Finally, when they would not be attracted, driven, or drawn in, he thought 'if only I could be a bird for a moment, I could lead them in'—and, instantly, the spark of insight burst into an explosion of understanding of who Christ was and why he came."*

Jack paused for a moment, letting Harvey's story linger in mind and imagination, then returned to describing the outline of the morning's lesson. With a growing smile, he said, "The third reason this will feel like a continuation of last week's class is because we're going to do now what we did then… we are going to *team* teach."

Still smiling—loving what was coming—he said, "Today will be different in only this respect: *you* will be part of the teaching team. Today and today only we are going to use the Socratic method, one based on teaching through questions. But there will be a switch from the traditional Socratic format because it will be you—the *class*—asking the questions, and it will be me—the *teacher*—attempting to answer them.

"Our purpose will be to explore the generally unexplored. Translated, that means your question must be one that does not have a pat answer. It must be one that makes us *think.*

"…and so… we begin."

The room was silent for 15 seconds… 20… 30. As Jack waited he thought, *come on guys… what have you wanted to ask?*

Then Doug White raised his hand and said, "I've been a Christian since I was eight years old and have been out of college, in the adult world, for about 15 years. As the years have gone by and my responsibilities have increased, I have attempted to find an example—a model—in Jesus for how to be a husband, a parent, a breadwinner… for how to make small decisions such as picking a vacation site or buying a car… and large decisions such as accepting a job offer in another city or and buying a home in a neighborhood based on its schools. I don't think I'm going over the top when I say I think he *should* be, *wants* to be, involved in these decisions because—among other things—they determine the lives we'll touch and those who'll touch ours… guide our stewardship of finances and talents… and—maybe most importantly—reflect our commitment, our dependence, our trust in his leadership. I've been disappointed in what I've found—what I've *not* found—in Scripture because he was never any of those things… husband, father, provider… never faced any of those very real, very serious, often very difficult choices. I know most of the answer, but I'd like to hear your thoughts on it."

Jack answered, "I wrestled with the same question at about your age, Doug. Here are the three things I discovered.

"First, God's *primary* role for Jesus—besides payment for our sins—was to show us the father. Jesus even said that... *if you have seen me, you have seen the Father.*[1]

"Second, God *did* assign the role of models on how to live to someone, and that someone is *you* and *me.*

"This assignment of dual roles—one to Christ, one to us—again displays God's genius. God does *not* change, so there only needed to be a *one-time* revelation of himself to man.

"However, man *does* change as his *culture* changes, so there needed to be a streaming revelation of how man is to live in an ever-evolving environment.

"For evidence, think of our own brief lifespans. Think of the ways our culture has changed... think of the sex in music videos, violence in video games, body-function commercials on television, obscene language in movies.

"Then think of how our culture has changed in response, how it accepts as decent that which was once indecent… moral that which was once immoral… ethical that which was once unethical. Think of how *we* have changed in response to those *cultural* changes. And that's just in a few decades.

"Now think of the broader picture. Think of the 2,000 years since Christ was here, how man's *economy* has changed from agrarian to industrial… his *lifestyle* from survival to abundance… his *governance* from kingdom to republic… his *entertainment* from roaming minstrels to virtual reality… his *creativity* from wood carving to human cloning… his information *dissemination* from the speed of a horse to the speed of light… his information *production* from Gutenberg to Google… his information *source* from balladeer to blogger… his dominate means of *communication* from face-to-face to phone-to-phone."

Pausing for a moment as a thought darted through his mind, Jack opened his teaching binder to the back and pulled a Xerox copy of a quote from the materials he was collecting for another book. Holding the paper and looking up at the class, he said, "I just remembered this article by Francis Schaeffer, an agnostic who became a Christian and who, some say, was, after C. S. Lewis, one of the most influential writers of the mid-twentieth century. Schaeffer began as a preacher in churches in Missouri and Pennsylvania, traveled in Switzerland with the American Council of Christian Churches, and there saw such a need among the country's youth that in 1948, in Lausanne, he founded Children for Christ ministry. He continued to lecture and travel, and in 1955 opened his home, his chalet, l'Abri, as a discussion and teaching site for those disillusioned with traditional churches.

"In 1968 he wrote the first of many books, two of the most notable being *How Should We Then Live?* following the 1973 Roe vs. Wade decision, and later, with former Surgeon General C. Everett Koop, *Whatever Happened to The Human Race?* Schaeffer was a long-haired purveyor of essential Christian values. When he died of cancer in 1984, President Reagan said: *It can rarely be said of an individual that his life touched many others and affected them for the better; it will be said of Dr. Francis Schaeffer that his life touched millions of souls and brought them to the truth of their Creator.*

"I want to read to you a small paragraph in Chapter 1 of the book he co-authored and published in 1979 with Dr. Koop, *Whatever Happened to the Human Race?,* in which he talks about the cultural slippery slope in which we constantly live:

> *The thinkables of the eighties and nineties will certainly include things which most people today find unthinkable and immoral, even unimaginable and too extreme to suggest. Yet—since they do not have some overriding principle that takes them beyond relativistic thinking—when these become thinkable and acceptable in the eighties and nineties, most people will not even remember that they were unthinkable in the seventies. They will slide into each new thinkable without a jolt."*[2]

Returning the copy to the back-cover pocket, Jack continued, "I could go on, but the point is clear: Socially, technologically, economically, industrially, demographically, and politically, man's world has changed... will continue to change... and therefore must have contemporary role models in a constantly *changing* culture to reveal God's *unchanging* message, relevance, and standards. And how better to do that than by instilling in people in that culture the same agent that was first instilled in Christ—the Holy Spirit.

"Third, having said all of that, I must say this: Jesus *did* provide us with an essential example of how to prepare for the common and uncommon exigencies of life, and that is found in Mark 1:35 ...*Very early in the morning, while it was still dark, Jesus got up, left the house and went off to a solitary place, where he prayed.*[3] You have heard me say before and I will say it again now, anyone serious about developing a relationship with God that permeates all thought, all choices, all decisions, start with this: every morning get up as early as you would if you were meeting your most trusted friend or coach or relative for coffee... and then in the silence and the dark and the moment, talk to God as you would talk to that person. Start there: e*very day—talk—and listen.*

"Finally, I must add that—not only did God ingeniously assign to man this task, equip him with the Holy Spirit, and present him with Jesus' example of early daily prayer—he also gave us the church, this marvelous entity of believers where we could *see others* dealing with the complications of life and *others could see us* dealing with the same complications... where we could teach and be taught... encourage and be encouraged... love and be loved, and then, prepared, go out into the world as role models."

Looking again at the questioner, Jack said, "Excellent question, Doug. I hope that helps."

Looking at the class, he said, "Next?"

Again, the room was silent... 10 seconds... 20.... Then Teresa Ortego said, "I'd like to ask a follow-up to Doug's question: What do you do when you don't find specific directions to specific questions in the Bible?"

Jack answered, "I take the position Robert Bork did in 1987 when questioned by the Senate during his Supreme Court confirmation hearing. When asked a similar question about the Constitution, he said he looked to the *original intent* of the framers. I do the same thing: When in doubt, I ask myself what I think God's original intent was. With that—his original intent—as my magnetic north it makes finding direction, staying on course, making decisions when there are no specifics, pretty easy.

"Further, specifics don't work. We know. God tried it. Spend a couple of hours reading Deuteronomy. Then spend a couple of minutes reading Matthew 23. You will see how over the centuries the minutia of Deuteronomy had become law, how the law had become the North Star of the Pharisees, and how Jesus condemned them for the manner in which they used the law to subjugate, dominate, oppress the very ones they were to lead to serve… to love.

"Teresa, that's a terribly brief answer to one of the most important questions any of us could ever ask. I don't know if I could answer it more succinctly than by saying this matter of being free of specifics—this matter of being free from the law—is a point central to Jesus' coming.

"So, when in doubt, I look to original intent."

Jack said, "Next?"

As the stillness extended, Jack said, "While you're thinking of the next question, I'll share with you one more observation about Doug's question and the role assigned to us. And I will do it by asking this: Do you remember the moment when you not only knew your dad *loved* you, but that he *trusted* you? For many of us, it was at age 16 when he placed the keys to the family car in our young hands. What a moment. You knew your dad loved you. But, now… to be trusted!… this was whole new dimension.

"Our relationship with our heavenly Father is the same. You know he *loves* you. But what joy when you realize he also *trusts* you. You see that trust all around you: He entrusts to you stewardship of your body, your family, your job, your assets, your relationships, your ministries, your time. And he expects back from us but three things: that we seek his will, that we act responsibly, and that we trust *him*.

"One of the questions to naturally come up is about the first of these three… seeking his will. As I said a moment ago, it begins with setting aside the first part of every day for prayer. The question is 'how should I pray? And part of the answer is found in a passage I mentioned several weeks ago, in Romans 8:26 and 27: *…the Spirit helps us with our weakness. We do not know how to pray as we should. But the Spirit Himself speaks to God for us—even begs God for us—with deep feelings that words cannot explain.*[4]

"With regard to the second of these… acting responsibly… you have heard me say before that your only responsibility is to act responsibly, and to leave the result of that action to God.

"Finally, with regard to the last… that we trust him… you have heard me quote Psalm 33:21: *Our hearts shall rejoice for we have trusted in His holy name.* And you know Proverbs 3:5 and 6: *Trust in the Lord with all your heart, lean not on your own understanding, in all your ways acknowledge Him and He will direct your path.*[5]

"In summary: He has assigned us a role and has provided us with the resources to fulfill it."

Jack paused, waiting for the next question. Bill Waller raised a hand and said, "Two questions. Within the covers of the Bible, who do you admire the most, and what is the most untaught lesson?"

Jack smiled and without hesitation said, "One of those I admire most is Mary, mother of Jesus, because of her unwavering faith in God's word. Here's why I say that: As a young girl, she is told by the angel Gabriel that she is favored by God… that the Holy Ghost will come upon her…that she will conceive and give birth to a son… that he will be called the son of the Most High… that God will give him the throne of David… that he will reign over the house of Jacob throughout the ages… and that of his reign there will be no end.

"Fast forward 33 years: Now we see her on a hill. She is at the foot of a cross. Impaled on the cross is her son. As wrenching as the dying of her *son* above her should have been the dying of her *faith* within her. Everything… *everything!*… she believed about the *power* of God, the *veracity* of God, the *love* of God should have been shattered. And you'd think we'd see *Mary*… not just Jesus… but *Mary* saying, *My God, My God, why have you forsaken me.*

"But we don't! In Acts 1:13 and 14—in the very *first* chapter of the very *first* book that follows the Gospels' report of his execution—we find this simple, profound, pre-Pentecost statement:

> *And when they had entered, they went up into the upper room where they were staying: Peter, James, John, and Andrew; Phillip and Thomas Bartholomew and Matthew; James the son of Alphaeus and Simon the Zealot; and Judas the son of James. These all continued with one accord in prayer and supplication, with the women, and Mary, the mother of Jesus…."*[6]

Jack stopped, looked over the class, into the eyes of the mothers, and said, "You've felt it, haven't you? You've felt betrayed. You've prayed for a child then felt their pain when they've been ignored by friends, or been dateless on prom night, or not made the team. May I ask that you *not* feel betrayed… that you *not* feel God has abandoned you or your child… that you—in that most important of moments—*not* abandon God. I don't have an answer for why these things happen. Nor do I have an answer for the more serious issues: of why they have this illness, or not gotten the job, or miscarried a newborn. While I don't have an answer, I do encourage you to think about and pray about this model of *faith*, this model of *hope*, this model of *acceptance*—this Mary."

Jack again stood silently… knowing his words were inadequate… knowing fathers felt the same betrayal… and knowing that God alone understood the why of it, that God alone could bring peace in the worst of it, and that God alone foresaw our need for this story about the mother of his son.

After another moment, Jack looked over the class, found his friend, then said, "Bill, your next question was my opinion of the most untaught lesson. That would be this: God wants *your* mind and *his* mind to merge. I'm going to say that again and elaborate on it a little, because it is so astounding: God wants to fill *your* mind with *his* thoughts so that you make decisions as he would make them… so that you make choices consistent with his will… so that you exercise judgment that trumps emotions, intellect, or circumstances. This he calls wisdom. And he wants you to *pursue* wisdom, you to *have* wisdom, you to *exercise* wisdom so badly that he inspired an entire book in the Bible dedicated to it: Proverbs."

Looking back at the class, Jack said, "Next question."

Dianne Downing, sitting on the third row, said, "Jack, as you know, I'm a new Christian. Sandra and this class have been an enormous help in my finding this new life. I need, however, to find more of it on my own… through quiet time… prayer… reading the Bible. It's this last, this time in the Bible, I want more of and finding it more difficult than I expected. I think it's difficult because the book is so big, there are so many places to start, it deals with so many things. What I need most… *want* most… are simple directions to two or three books which will solidly ground me in the fundamentals. What would you recommend?"

Jack replied, "That's a great question, Dianne… a question many of us—probably most of us—wish we'd asked at our own beginnings.

"I'll give you my recommendation in three parts, starting first with the *type* of Bible translation. There are two dominate types: one called 'literal' and the other called 'dynamic equivalence.' The former attempts to literally translate *word-for-word* the original Greek and Hebrew into English words. The latter attempts to translate *sense-for-sense*. Neither is particularly better… in fact, one of my most-used translations is the New International Version, the NIV, which is a sense-for-sense.

"Though I use it, I'd not recommend it for your purpose. Instead, I'd recommend the word-for-word, and three of the most popular are the English Standard Version (ESV), the Revised Standard Version (RSV), and the New King James Version (NKJV). I could confidently recommend any one of the three because you'd be starting with man's best… *scholar's* best… attempt at an accurate translation in grammar, syntax, and idiom between the original languages and the current English. You can always go to others, but best to start with a word-for-word.

"Second, each of these three... the ESV, RSV and NKJV... has a 'Study Bible' edition. This is an important distinction: A *standard* Bible has Scripture only, and a *study* Bible has Scripture *plus* supplemental information. That additional information helps to understand Scripture by giving you the broad context of *who* wrote the book as well as *why* and *when*... study notes on key verses, key people, and key places... and overarching material such as historical timelines, regional maps, and references to related passages in other books.

"My suggestion would be to look at all three translations in Study Bible form, and to pay particular attention to the ESV. This suggestion in part is because of the ESV's wide endorsement by so many prominent evangelical pastors and theologians... in part because it received the ECPA—the Evangelical Christian Publishers Association—Christian Book Award for 2009, the first time a Study Bible had ever received this recognition... and because our pastor uses it in his sermons.

"Finally, once you've chosen a Bible version in its Study Bible format, do these three things ...these three steps which constitute a *process*.

"First, plan on several weeks in the process. Stated another way, *do not rush*. Don't because, through the process, you'll be covering the *fundamentals upon which your life will be based*. So, don't rush... take your time... absorb each part, thoroughly.

"Second, follow the process through three New Testament books: *John, Romans,* and *1st Peter*. Start with *John*, then *Romans*, then *1st Peter*, in that order. The basics covered here are also covered in other books, but this is a sound place to start if we limit it to three.

"Third, read all of one or two *pages* per day.

"And I mean *all*. Carefully read the Scripture *and* the supplemental information on the lower half of each page, including *all* of the notes... footnotes... cross-references... megathemes... maps... timelines... and story blueprints. Read the biographical descriptions of main characters and summaries of their strengths, accomplishments, weaknesses, and mistakes. Read of their lessons for life.

"Some days, when there is much information to be processed, cover only one page, but never more than two. The reason for two pages max is that this is not a sprint, but a marathon. Limiting yourself to no more than two helps you focus... consider... think."

With a smile, Jack said, "Dianne, that's it. I applaud your question and recommend these steps with heartfelt hope you'll follow them. This will not be the end of your learning, but a solid beginning. I envy you in what you're about to discover for there are few things as enriching as learning, or as gratifying as knowing you're growing... and doing both in this dimension of life."

Turning to the class, Jack said, "Next?"

After a moment, from somewhere someone asked, "Have you ever had an epiphany?"

"No," Jack answered, "but I've recently had a memorable dream. In it, Kelli and I have died ...happily at the same time. With her hand in mine, we are entering heaven. There to meet us is not Saint Peter, but Jesus. I should not be surprised at this, but I am. As Kelli and I stand there, still hand in hand, he approaches. He is smiling at us. We are smiling at him. I suppose because of so many first meetings with others that Kelli and I have had over our married years, I take the lead, look at Kelli, and quietly with pride, say, 'Jesus, this is Kelli.' And he—without taking his eyes off her, without changing the look of joy on his face, and without a hint of reproof in his voice for my presuming the need for an introduction—replies to me, 'I know, Jack. Kelli and I have known each other for a very, very long time.' He embraces her and says, 'Welcome home, Kelli.' I am happily watching this when he turns to me, and with the same unmitigated joy, hugs me and says, 'Welcome home, Jack.' He then puts his two arms around our shoulders and with a sense of happiness that matches ours, says, 'I want to show you your place—and get you to your family and friends that have been waiting for you.'"

Off we go.

"For some reason, I always thought this moment would be rather formal—happy—but reserved… almost courtly, as one coming into the presence of an Earthly king or dignitary. Choirs? Celebration? Homecoming? Yes. Yes. Yes. But all rather subdued, with 'proper' behavior. Instead, I see the three of us and am reminded of that old *Singing in The Rain* poster—with Kelli/Jesus/me as Debbie/Gene/Donald—headed to the place he has prepared with a spring in our step, a song in our hearts, and eternity before us.

"I am humbled and awed at this personal attention when there must be hundreds of thousands of others entering heaven at the same time. I tell myself that he is somehow with them, even at this instant, as he is with us. And I tell myself that this is a moment of personal fulfillment for *him* as well as for *us*… for him, a moment *he* guaranteed at the personal unspeakable price… for us, a moment *we* guaranteed when we accepted his sacrifice with the two simple words, 'I believe.'"

Jack smiled, stopped, glanced at the clock, and said, "Okay, time for one more."

Marilyn Brewer, a former programmer now building a small dotcom business, raised her hand and asked, "Why did he come when he did? Why not now when it could be covered on dozens of 24-hour newscasts and scores of social media sites. All of which would have made spreading of his word so much easier… so much quicker?"

"Good question, Marilyn. I'll give you my CliffsNotes personal opinion.

"First, he came at the time God had planned. My ESV says it this way in Galatians 4:4: *But when the fullness of time had come, God sent forth his Son….*

"Second, I think this time was the first *best* opportunity. By that, I mean he came at the first occasion when, throughout most of the known world, two essential elements were in place: a common *government* and a common *language*. Though those two elements could have appeared earlier in large empires—Persia and Greece come to mind—but they didn't. Why then Rome… which was a country only a little larger… and at a time only a little later?

"Maybe because Latin and Greek were its *dominant* languages, essentially giving it a *common* language.

"Or maybe because no other country had Rome's form of *government*… its decentralized administrative system, *plus* its military, its Legions, to protect and enforce that system. It was a system which stretched from the Black Sea in the east to the Atlantic in the west… from Britannia in the north to Africa in the south… whose power and presence controlled every country in between. Under its control were today's England, Scotland, Belgium, Germany, the Netherlands, France, Spain, Portugal, Italy, Switzerland, Greece, Turkey, Palestine, Israel, Syria, Iraq, and dozens of smaller countries like Malta and Macedonia, plus all countries on the northern rim of the African continent including Egypt, Libya, and Morocco. Remove the common language and common governance and you have pockets of tribes and kingdoms speaking local languages and dialects, making wide-spread dissemination of the news problematic.

"Maybe it was because Rome would reign 200-plus years longer than Persia or Greece.

"Maybe it was because the Jews' expectation of the Messiah was high.

"Or repeating Galatians 4:4, this from my NIV, because:*…the set time had fully come…."*

Pausing, Jack looked at the floor, gathered fragments of another thought, then said, "It is interesting to think about what it would be like if he had come now. As an example, he would probably have been a carpenter… maybe a framer for a custom home builder in Jerusalem. And he would probably have taught with parables based on tools of his trade.

"One evening, with work over but still at the worksite with his crew—his twelve—around him, I can see him pulling a common wooden level from the back of his pickup and saying something like this, as he did in John 14:

…when I go, I will send the Comforter. He will reside in you as this bubble resides in this level. He will not be the level… for that is you. But he will reside in the level… reside in you.

His purpose will be to make God aware of your needs, to make you aware of God's presence, and to give you God's direction in fulfilling His purpose—particularly, as it relates to service. When the level is held vertically and the bubble is in the center, you know your service to your Heavenly Father is as it should be. When the level is held horizontally and the bubble is in the center, you know your service to your fellow man is as it should be. Therefore, at all times, whether here on the job with your coworkers, at home with your family, or at soccer games with your friends… be conscious of the bubble. Even as Jabez prayed that he would be conscious of My hand upon him, so you pray that you will be conscious of the Holy Spirit within you.'

Jesus stops talking for a moment, turning the level in his hands, considering its length and form, then, looking again at the twelve, continues, 'Levels come in all sizes and materials. Some are three inches long, some are three feet. Some are made of wood, some of aluminum. Irrespective of the size and the material, embedded in each is this bubble. Without this bubble, they are not levels—they are just pieces of wood or aluminum. So it is with people… so it will be with you. It will be your believing in Me and the Comforter embedded in you that will make you a follower of Me, that will make you what will be called a Christian. Some will believe that being good, or going to church, or believing that there is a God will make them Christians. They will be wrong. They will no more be Christians than a piece of wood is a level simply because it is well formed, or in a dedicated toolbox, or believes there is a higher power called a Framer.

'It must have the bubble.

'However, there will be a difference, and that will be this: The bubble in a level is visible, the Holy Spirit in a person will be invisible. The only outward sign that a person is embedded with the Holy Spirit will be their actions… their humility, peace, charity, ethics, kindness, love, grace, gentleness, self-control. And for them to do that, this level must be right with God—meaning bubble centered vertically, and be right with man—meaning bubble centered horizontally, simultaneously.'

'How can this be?', the twelve ask. 'If each of us is only one level, how can we be pointing in two directions at the same time?'

In answer, Jesus takes another wooden level from the back of the pickup, holds them together at right angles—one vertically, one horizontally so that they make to the followers what appears to be a plus sign or a cross—smiles and says, 'Don't worry. It's not up to you. It's up to Me… and the bubble. In fact—and I tell you the truth—it is good for you that I go. Otherwise, the bubble will not come to you… will not convert you from being wood to being a level… will not change you from being builders of buildings to builders of men.'"

Jack stood quietly for a moment, letting the allegory linger.

Then glancing at the clock and seeing there was time, he said, "To this question of who is Christ, I want to add one more thought… actually the merger of two thoughts. As I've said, I occasionally write a poem in quiet time in an attempt to capture a deeper feeling, and I did it again in this case.

"The first thought is of a pretty common occurrence: that which you've done when you've *voluntarily* given up something for the benefit of someone else. As simple examples, guys, you've done it when waiting for a table in a packed restaurant you've given up your seat for a lady. Mothers, you've done it when you've given up a new outfit for your child's special birthday party.

"Now hold that while I add the second, one held by many, myself included. That thought is this: Hell is the absence of God.

"In my quiet time I began to see that that is exactly what Christ did for me: He *voluntarily* and—according to John 15:11—*joyfully* removed himself from God's presence.

"Stated another, clearer, unequivocal way: He gave up God for me.

"*How* could he do such a thing? *Why* would he do such a thing? To intentionally close himself off from God is simply *unthinkable*.

"But he did.

"And with those two merged thoughts, I wrote this. I call it *He Gave up God for Me:*

If I were separated
For just a single day
From God's good grace and presence
From His guiding ways
From His hope and purpose
From His love for me
From His filling Spirit
Would I start to see
What it was that Christ gave up
So I would never be
In hell without a hope or prayer
For eternity
Somehow I think that's what He did
For three days did he suffer
As He gave up God for me
And paid the price to cover
My sins, my faults, my failings
In love and full redemption
He gave up God so I'd not know
Eternal separation."

Jack stopped, stood silently, then said, "Our question is *Who is Christ?* The answer—simply… clearly… profoundly—is this: *Our redeemer*."

After a moment, he said, "No Q&A sheets today. Bev, please close us."

###

Your Takeaways and Action Items from this Chapter

Takeaway 1

(page__)

Takeaway 2

(page__)

Takeaway 3

(page__)

Your Takeaways and Action Items from this Chapter (cont.)

Action Item 1

(page__)

Action Item 2

(page__)

Action Item 3

(page__)

Who Is Satan?

Chapter 9 - Sunday, July 10

As Jack watched Beverly open the morning, he was reminded of last weekend—of the trip to be with the kids for the July 4th holiday, of the parade of decorated bikes and polished convertibles, of the snapping flags and happy grandsons—then smiled and thought, *Summers... you gotta' love 'em.*

Jack was happy for the momentary memory, the needed break in thought, as he approached the lectern less gregariously than normally. He laid teaching notes on the stand, added his greetings to Beverly's, and said, "This morning we continue our six-lesson series with the question: *Who is Satan?*" He paused, then added, "And again I begin with this warning: what you will hear is *my* opinion, based on *my* study, based on *my* interpretation of Scripture."

With that, Jack stepped to the side of the lectern and said, "Preparing this lesson, to a depth I've not done before, has been one of the most unsettling experiences in my long years of teaching. It has been because to teach, one must examine. To examine, one must draw close. And to draw close... to this... even academically... is to be immersed in the stench of evil.

"Satan is his common name, a name that has become sanitized through playful humor on *Saturday Night Live*... through tiny, beguiling images of red cartoon characters with horns, tails, and pitchforks on small cans of processed meat... even through Darth Vader who subliminally advances the notion that even in an evil-being of galactic proportion there can be found an atom of redemption.

"Satan is the Hebrew word for *adversary*, a most appropriate but misleadingly placid translation because it lacks the force of words like *power* and *lethal*. He is a fallen angel, the explanation for his *power*. And though he is not God's equal in power, his sole adversary is God which to you and me makes him *lethal*.

"*Why* and *how* and *when* he fell is another study for another time. We read of him in the *beginning* of the Bible, in Genesis 3, in the Garden of Eden, where he takes the form of a snake and says to Eve, *you will not surely die.*[1]

"We read of him in the *end* of the Bible where he takes the form of a dragon in Revelation 12:3-4, *And another sign appeared in heaven: and behold, a great red dragon having seven heads and ten horns, and on his heads were seven diadems. And his tail swept away a third of the stars of heaven, and threw them to the earth....*[2]

"And we read of him between the beginning and the end, as in Matthew 4:1 where... *Jesus was led up to the wilderness by the Spirit, to be tempted by the Devil,*[3] and in Mark 3:23 when Jesus *called them to Himself and began speaking to them in parables, How can Satan cast out Satan? And if a kingdom be divided against itself, that kingdom cannot stand.*[4]

"Even with Biblical descriptions here and in other places, we do not understand him. One of our biggest misunderstandings is to think that he is a magnetic south to God's magnetic north, pulling us to him with the same passion that God pulls us to him.

"That is wrong.

"And it is wrong because Satan doesn't *want* us. Did you hear me? He does not *want* us... he simply *does not want God* to have us.

"I once heard that the most heinous kind of leader... parent, president, or any other... was one who exercised his power with 'intolerant indifference.' This is the parent who disciplines a child for an act about which the parent cares nothing, or the employer who humiliates an employee for a deed which is of no consequence. Their only motivation is to demonstrate that they can. Their only inspiration is pride... the kind of pride C. S. Lewis talked about and we discussed several weeks ago. In one of his examples, Lewis spoke of the guy wanting the girl simply to keep another guy from having her. *That*, my friends, is Satan. He doesn't want *you*—he just doesn't want *God* to have you.

"Call it '*possessive* indifference.' In its most common and most innocent form, we see it in a child keeping a toy from a sibling. He doesn't *want* the toy. He doesn't *like* the toy. He simply wants to see his brother—to whom it belongs and who wants it so much—cry.

"Satan's principal tool to keep us from God is *deception*, and his primary instrument for deception is *humanism*. Humanists' believe that there is no God... no higher authority... no creator. In a word, they believe there is no being superior to themselves."

Jack paused, letting their premise filter through the room, then quietly continued, "I want to be careful in what I'm about to say because I don't want to sound sarcastic or demeaning or dismissing... but I'd say that—while it's commendable to have that level of confidence in one's self—I would be cautious in believing human brains are capable of such *spiritual* perspectives if one also believes that human brains are no more than the current evolutionary state of that which began as the seaborne blue-green-algae *cyanobacteria*... that from this multicellular life developed amphibious crawling fish called tetrapods... and from these tetrapods, eventually, came Darwinian monkeys.

"I have, as you no doubt have, humanistic friends, and I'm only speaking of the spiritual views to which they are asked to subscribe. Here is the full definition of humanism as posted on the American Humanist Association's website", he said as he wrote on the whiteboard:

Humanism

A progressive philosophy of life that, without theism and other supernatural beliefs, affirms our ability and responsibility to lead ethical lives of personal fulfillment that aspire to the greater good of humanity.[5]

Turning back to the class, he said, "Though it had been around for some time, the first time I heard this word—humanism—was in the mid-1970s. It was during an intense period of the Cold War with Russia, and a time when global attention was being given to a controversial Pulitzer Prize winning Russian named Alexander Solzhenitsyn who had, after years of imprisonment, been exiled by Russia for his inflammatory political writings and who had, after a brief stay in Switzerland, immigrated to a small town here, in Vermont. I don't remember how I first saw or heard the word... whether it was in our morning newspaper or on the evening news. I only remember that the source was credible, and its referring to a thing called humanism in a hard-news context was surprising. Equally surprising to me was that Solzhenitsyn, a man of such political prominence and a man with such a global perspective, would speak of something which had such spiritual overtones.

"Later I read part of his speech delivered at the Harvard Class Day Afternoon Exercises in June 1978. I want you to read a portion of it now," and he handed Bev copied material to distribute to the class. For the next several minutes the room was silent as they read:

> *The split in today's world is perceptible even to a hasty glance. Any of our contemporaries readily identifies two world powers, each of them already capable of entirely destroying the other. However, understanding of the split often is limited to this political conception, to the illusion that danger may be abolished through successful diplomatic negotiations or by achieving a balance of armed forces. The truth is that the split is a much profounder and a more alienating one, that the rifts are more than one can see at first glance. This deep manifold split bears the danger of manifold disaster for all of us, in accordance with the ancient truth that a Kingdom -- in this case, our Earth -- divided against itself cannot stand....*
>
> *How has this unfavorable relation of forces come about? How did the West decline from its triumphal march to its present sickness? Have there been fatal turns and losses of direction in its development? It does not seem so. The West kept advancing socially in accordance with its proclaimed intentions, with the help of brilliant technological progress. And all of a sudden it found itself in its present state of weakness.*
>
> *This means that the mistake must be at the root, at the very basis of human thinking in the past centuries. I refer to the prevailing Western view of the world which was first born during the Renaissance and found its political expression from the period of the Enlightenment. It became the basis for government and social science and could be defined as rationalistic humanism or humanistic autonomy: the proclaimed and enforced autonomy of man from any higher force above him. It could also be called anthropocentricity, with man seen as the center of everything that exists.*
>
> *The turn introduced by the Renaissance evidently was inevitable historically. The Middle Ages had come to a natural end by exhaustion, becoming an intolerable despotic repression of man's physical nature in favor of the spiritual one. Then, however, we turned our backs upon the Spirit and embraced all that is material with excessive and unwarranted zeal. This new way of thinking, which had imposed on us its guidance, did not admit the existence of intrinsic evil in man nor did it see any higher task than the attainment of happiness on earth. It based modern Western civilization on the dangerous trend to worship man and his material needs. Everything beyond physical well-being and accumulation of material goods, all other human requirements and characteristics of a subtler and higher nature, were left outside the area of attention of state and social systems, as if human life did not have any superior sense. That provided access for evil, of which in our days there is a free and constant flow. Merely freedom does not in the least solve all the problems of human life and it even adds a number of new ones.*
>
> *However, in early democracies, as in American democracy at the time of its birth, all individual human rights were granted because man is God's creature. That is, freedom was given to the individual conditionally, in the assumption of his constant religious responsibility. Such was the heritage of the preceding thousand years. Two hundred or even fifty years ago, it would have seemed quite impossible, in America, that an individual could be granted boundless*

freedom simply for the satisfaction of his instincts or whims. Subsequently, however, all such limitations were discarded everywhere in the West; a total liberation occurred from the moral heritage of Christian centuries with their great reserves of mercy and sacrifice. State systems were becoming increasingly and totally materialistic. The West ended up by truly enforcing human rights, sometimes even excessively, but man's sense of responsibility to God and society grew dimmer and dimmer. In the past decades, the legalistically selfish aspect of Western approach and thinking has reached its final dimension and the world wound up in a harsh spiritual crisis and a political impasse. All the glorified technological achievements of Progress, including the conquest of outer space, do not redeem the Twentieth century's moral poverty which no one could imagine even as late as in the Nineteenth Century.

As humanism in its development became more and more materialistic, it made itself increasingly accessible to speculation and manipulation at first by socialism and then by communism. So that Karl Marx was able to say in 1844 that "communism is naturalized humanism."

This statement turned out not to be entirely senseless. One does see the same stones in the foundations of a despiritualized humanism and of any type of socialism: endless materialism; freedom from religion and religious responsibility, which under communist regimes reach the stage of anti-religious dictatorship; concentration on social structures with a seemingly scientific approach. (This is typical of the Enlightenment in the Eighteenth Century and of Marxism). Not by coincidence all of communism's meaningless pledges and oaths are about Man, with a capital M, and his earthly happiness. At first glance it seems an ugly parallel: common traits in the thinking and way of life of today's West and today's East? But such is the logic of materialistic development.

The interrelationship is such, too, that the current of materialism which is most to the left always ends up by being stronger, more attractive and victorious, because it is more consistent. Humanism without its Christian heritage cannot resist such competition. We watch this process in the past centuries and especially in the past decades, on a world scale as the situation becomes increasingly dramatic. Liberalism was inevitably displaced by radicalism, radicalism had to surrender to socialism and socialism could never resist communism. The communist regime in the East could stand and grow due to the enthusiastic support from an enormous number of Western intellectuals who felt a kinship and refused to see communism's crimes. When they no longer could do so, they tried to justify them. In our Eastern countries, communism has suffered a complete ideological defeat; it is zero and less than zero. But Western intellectuals still look at it with interest and with empathy, and this is precisely what makes it so immensely difficult for the West to withstand the East.

I am not examining here the case of a world war disaster and the changes which it would produce in society. As long as we wake up every morning under a peaceful sun, we have to lead an everyday life. There is a disaster, however, which has already been under way for quite some time. I am referring to the calamity of a despiritualized and irreligious humanistic consciousness.

To such consciousness, man is the touchstone in judging and evaluating everything on earth. Imperfect man, who is never free of pride, self-interest, envy, vanity, and dozens of other defects. We are now experiencing the consequences of mistakes which had not been noticed at the beginning of the journey. On the way from the Renaissance to our days we have enriched our experience, but we have lost the concept of a Supreme Complete Entity which used to restrain our passions and our irresponsibility. We have placed too much hope in political and social reforms, only to find out that we were being deprived of our most precious boundless possession: our spiritual life. In the East, it is destroyed by the dealings and machinations of the ruling party. In the West, commercial interests tend to suffocate it. This is the real crisis. The split in the world is less terrible than the similarity of the disease plaguing its main sections.

If humanism were right in declaring that man is born to be happy, he would not be born to die. Since his body is doomed to die, his task on earth evidently must be of a more spiritual nature. It cannot have unrestrained enjoyment of everyday life. It cannot be the search for the best ways to obtain material goods and then cheerfully get the most out of them. It has to be the fulfillment of a permanent, earnest duty so that one's life journey may become an experience of moral growth, so that one may leave life a better human being than one started it. It is imperative to review the table of widespread human values. Its present incorrectness is astounding. It is not possible that assessment of the President's performance be reduced to the question of how much money one makes or of unlimited availability of gasoline. Only voluntary, inspired self-restraint can raise man above the world stream of materialism.

It would be retrogression to attach oneself today to the ossified formulas of the Enlightenment. Social dogmatism leaves us completely helpless in front of the trials of our times.

Even if we are spared destruction by war, our lives will have to change if we want to save life from self-destruction. We cannot avoid revising the fundamental definitions of human life and human society. Is it true that man is above everything? Is there no Superior Spirit above him? Is it right that man's life and society's activities have to be determined by material expansion in the first place? Is it permissible to promote such expansion to the detriment of our spiritual integrity?

If the world has not come to its end, it has approached a major turn in history, equal in importance to the turn from the Middle Ages to the Renaissance. It will exact from us a spiritual upsurge, we shall have to rise to a new height of vision, to a new level of life where our physical nature will not be cursed as in the Middle Ages, but, even more importantly, our spiritual being will not be trampled upon as in the Modern era.

This ascension will be similar to climbing onto the next anthropologic stage. No one on earth has any other way left but -- upward.[6]

Jack watched the class. When it appeared that they were through reading, he said, "To those of you who wonder if I made a mistake… if I pulled the article from a current newspaper… the answer is 'no', I did not. As noted, the speech was delivered in 1978. If you want to learn more about this remarkable man, I suggest you visit any number of sites by Googling 'Alexander Solzhenitsyn.'

"And if you're feeling that I'm spending much of our class time on this concept called humanism, you're right. I am because it is so subtle, so natural, and so pervasive that I believe it is the single greatest threat to our finding what God wants most, and that is our living a *faith-based* rather than a *self-based* life."

Stepping to the side of the lectern, he said, "Often, the clearest way to define a concept is by identifying people who manifest it. As examples, if I were to define the concept of leadership, I might point to Winston Churchill and Abraham Lincoln… or compassion, I might point to Mother Teresa and Florence Nightingale… or entrepreneurship, Henry Ford and Michael Dell.

"If we were to apply that same idea to humanists, two people—each of whom are listed on the American Humanist Association's website as recipients of their Humanist of the Year Award—are Margaret Sanger, founder of Planned Parenthood and Abraham Maslow, author of Maslow's Hierarchy.[7] I will leave to you your opinion of the first, but will tell you I was once intrigued with the second... and that my attraction as a *mature believer* to Maslow's theory is testimony to how deceiving and beguiling and captivating humanism can be.

"Dr. Maslow was one of the best known—and most controversial—American psychologists of the 20th century. And though he died in 1970, his tenets remain a 21st century topic of discussion as evidenced by articles in *Forbes*, *The Economist*, and the *New York Times*. He was born in Brooklyn in 1908, the son of Jewish Russian immigrants. He earned a BA, an MA, and his PhD in 1930, 1931, and 1934—all in psychology, and all from the University of Wisconsin. In about 1935 he returned to New York where he began teaching at Brooklyn College. There he became interested in research in human sexuality, where he became acquainted with several immigrating intellectuals from Europe who had been influenced by Gestalt and Freud, and where he met a Mr. Goldstein who had conceptualized a hierarchy of human needs… a man who put him on the path to development of what became known as Maslow's Hierarchy.

"Maslow asserted that the key to understanding human behavior was understanding human *motivation*… that this motivation could be segmented into five basic *needs*… that these were *hierarchical*, each becoming critical only after the lower need was met… and that the highest of these needs was *self-actualization*. If you Googled self-actualization, you would find several definitions and explanations by several psychiatrists and psychologists. My simple description is that the highest motivation is—in words of the old Army ads—*to be all you can be.*

"I could elaborate and explain why I was personally… as a young, achievement-oriented person …attracted to Maslow's theory. However, several months ago I found in Dee Dee Devonshire's doctoral dissertation on the architecture of man's faith such an eloquent examination of humanism in the context of man's highest calling that I have asked her to join us again to share with you some of her observations. Dee Dee…."

She stood, walked to the lectern with ease and elegance, smiled and said, "Good morning. It is again my pleasure to speak with you.

"After Jack called me, and as I thought about my portion of today's lesson, I considered reading the section of my dissertation to which he referred, then decided I could focus more specifically on today's subject of 'Who Is Satan' if I simply talked with you.

"I will begin by saying that there are those throughout history who *conspicuously* manifest man's nature at his *worst*. Four who immediately come to mind are Ivan the Terrible in the 1500s; Hitler in the 1940s; Hussein in the 1970s; and, more recently, Assad. I choose the word 'conspicuously' carefully for it is from the Latin cōnspicere, meaning *to observe*, and has the English meanings of 'easy to notice' and 'obvious.' Evil wrought by men such as those just mentioned is clearly *apparent*, visibly *appalling*, and thus *easier* to see and to deliberately avoid.

"Less conspicuously—and thus more dangerous, frequently more lethal, and too often more eternal—is the evil wrought by *stealth* agents of destruction. This because stealth agents are those whose core tactic is *deception*. The word 'deception' is from the Middle English word *decepcioun,* meaning to betray, to mislead, to beguile another into danger, thus making it *more difficult to see* and to deliberately avoid.

"Sometimes, stealth agents themselves are *unwitting* agents—I'll say that again: sometimes they are *unintentional* agents, leading others astray, but not knowing it. It is not uncommon to see this in religious organizations and in personal philosophies. That may have been the case with our Dr. Maslow. It may have been that he was trying to make some sense out of the world, out of life, and out of man's role in it, that led him to embrace a model framed by a colleague, Kurt Goldstein. It may have been that *he* was not evil but an *agent* of evil. To Satan, it matters not. To Satan, it only matters that many have been… and will be… kept from a life of *spiritual*-actualization because they are convinced their highest calling is to *self*-actualization.

"And the frightening thing is that there is just enough logic in the *foundation* of Maslow's theory to be persuaded that an *extension* of that logic makes sense. Listen to his definition of self-actualization from an article he wrote titled *A Theory of Human Motivation* originally published in 1943 in *Psychological Review*: *A musician must make music, an artist must paint, a poet must write, if he is to be ultimately happy. What a man can be, he must be. This need we may call self-actualization.*

"In other words, your highest calling is to serve this inner drive for self-fulfillment."

She turned, drew and wrote on the board as she said, "Maslow's Hierarchy is usually presented as a triangle—something like this—in which his five needs are stacked, with the most basic at the bottom and each becoming critical only after the lower need is met. If you do a web search, you'll find scores of detailed illustrations."

Pausing, Dee Dee considered whether to interject a personal note, glanced at the clock, saw there was time, then smiled again and said, "At the seminary, when a professor during a lecture took off on a tangent to touch on something that was interesting, but not particularly relevant, it was said that he was 'chasing a rabbit.' Stay with me while I chase one.

"As you will recall from my comments a few weeks ago, my spiritual awakening began at age twelve, in Giza, on the west bank of the Nile, halfway up a climb on one of the great pyramids, when our guide said *according to many scholars, the pyramids were shaped as they were to help the soul of the king climb to the sky and join the gods.* You might then imagine the irony I saw when I first held a diagram of Maslow's similar shape, saw that the pinnacle of his triangle was also fulfillment, but saw that his fulfillment was not embodied in a higher power, but in self… *self!* I could not imagine any thinking person—particularly given the hard-archeological evidence of stone circles and temples and cathedrals that document the fact that man has *always* deemed himself to be imperfect and inadequate and in need of the favor of a superior being—would be so vain or naïve or vulnerable to Satan's gentle nudging as to deem self... *self!*... as the zenith of worship."

Pausing, glancing again at the clock, then looking back at the class, Dee Dee smiled and said, "I fear my rabbit has eaten more time than I expected."

Smiling again, she continued, "Merriam-Webster includes this phrase in their online dictionary under the definition of god: *one controlling a particular aspect or part of reality.* I like that, but I think there's more to it. I think they miss the element of *expectation.* That's why I like my definition a little better. I think a god is *any person or thing which we expect or hope can influence or enable beyond our ability to do so.* To that person or thing, we typically—usually secretly, quietly, even unconsciously—place *trust*, pay *homage*, lift up *worship*."

Tapping the tip of the triangle with a small black pen, Dee Dee continued, "The significance of what I am saying is that a God-substitute need not only be at the *top* of this hierarchy. The threat exists all the way down this triangle. Wherever there is a need… for food, safety, companionship, or anything else… Satan—the deceiver—will use whatever it is that we *think*, that we *expect*, that we *hope* will meet that need as a God-substitute.

"These can be *things* as well as *people.*

"If they are *things*, we call them cars, boats, homes, assets.

"If they are *people,* we call them bosses, parents, spouses, friends.

"And if they are *any* form of God-substitute, Satan calls them blessed."

Closing her notes, smiling at Jack, she stepped back from the lectern and walked to her seat. Jack, taking the cue, rose from his, and moved to the music stand. He looked at her and said, "Dee Dee, thank you, again."

Turning to the class, he said, "Dee Dee just spoke of names. The one we have talked about this morning takes many forms, has but a single purpose, and should—hereafter—be known to you, not by 'Satan' or other names that have become comfortable because of familiarity, or cute because of illustrations, or comic because of late night television—but by that name that reflects his true repugnant, repulsive, repelling nature: *Stench.*"

Jack stood quietly for a moment, letting the name linger in thought as smoke lingers over fire. He then pulled a small book from the stack it seemed he was always carrying, stepped to the side of the lectern to signal a change in subject, said, "I want—reluctant as I am to speak of personal spiritual experiences—to tell you of one I had this past Friday morning. But first I want to reintroduce you to this… one of the most profound, most insightful, most disturbing books ever written on the cleverness, the subtly, and the tactics of this deceiver. The book is C. S. Lewis' *The_Screwtape Letters.* It is written in a satirical fashion.

"The structure of Lewis' story is the mythical discovery of a collection of about 30 letters written by Screwtape to his nephew, Wormwood. Screwtape is an 'experienced tempter.' He is writing from hell to Wormwood on the surface of Earth. His purpose is to advise the young inexperienced 'junior tempter' on his first assignment who is a young man with an aging mother, a new girlfriend, and financial aspirations.

"In the book's first letter, we see the uncle's response to a situation the nephew described in an earlier correspondence about an incident in his assignee's movement toward Christianity—and we see Screwtape's recommended tactic to thwart such movement.

> *My Dear Wormwood:*
>
> *I note what you say about guiding your patient's reading and taking care that he sees a good deal of his materialistic friend. But are you not a trifle naïve? It sounds as you supposed that argument was the way to keep him out of the Enemy's clutches….*
>
> *I once had a patient, a sound atheist, who used to read in the British Museum. One day, as he sat reading, I saw a train of thought in his mind beginning to go the wrong way. The*

Enemy, of course, was at his elbow in the moment. Before I knew where I was I saw my twenty years' work beginning to totter. If I had lost my head and begun to attempt a defense by argument I should have been undone. But I was not such a fool. I struck instantly at the part of the man which I had best under my control and suggested that it was just about time he had some lunch. The Enemy presumably made the counter-suggestion that this was more important than lunch. At least I think that must have been His line for when I said, 'Quite. In fact, much too important to tackle at the end of a morning', the patient brightened up considerably; and by the time I had added 'Much better to come back after lunch and go into it with a fresh mind,' he was already half way to the door. Once he was on the street the battle was won....

Do remember you are there to fuddle him...."[8]

Closing the book, Jack said, "Okay… now, here's my Friday morning experience. I was in prayer and into my mind popped a picture of the *deck* I *may* want to build on the house we *may* want to buy!" The class laughed. Jack smiled. Pausing for a moment, looking at the floor, then up at the class, he said, "Being that we're good friends, I believe it would be all right for me to tell you that—in addition to the deck—the *other* most frequent prayer-interrupting thought I'm having is of a new putter." The class laughed again.

"The point I want to make is that the thing Stench uses need not be dark and evil to interfere with our prayers. It can be anything that fuddles and distracts—it can be as innocent as lunch plans, as inoffensive as a deck, and as innocuous as a golf club. Therefore, when you pray the Lord's Prayer, the fourth part of the Jabez' prayer, or your personal prayer, ask for protection from *any* distractions… evil or otherwise."

Then, holding the Lewis' book up, Jack said, "This, as you have heard me say before, is a great book… by one of the world's great writers… about the common and not-so-common moments and relationships and ambitions in our lives. Get it. Read it."

Nodding to Beverly, he laid the book on the stand and said, "Next Sunday, we complete the six-lesson series we started several weeks ago, and do so by discussing the question: What is Salvation?"

###

Your Takeaways and Action Items from this Chapter

Takeaway 1

(page__)

Takeaway 2

(page__)

Takeaway 3

(page__)

Your Takeaways and Action Items from this Chapter (cont.)

Action Item 1

(page__)

Action Item 2

(page__)

Action Item 3

(page__)

What Is Salvation?

Chapter 10 - Sunday, July 17

Kelli watched Jack as he spoke briefly with Ted Taylor, an old friend, a mountain of a man, and a former NFL offensive guard. He was known affectionately by his teammates, respectfully by his opponents, and now by the church where he was Director of Education by a single all-defining name, "Tug." They had talked several times over the last few weeks and, as she watched now, knew the subject and the pain it brought both of them. To her surprise, this time after they talked, Tug took a seat and stayed.

At the front, Beverly greeted guests, asked for requests, then led the group in prayer. As she finished, Jack walked to the lectern, laid stapled papers next to a Bose CD player he had plugged in earlier, and said, "Good morning.

"Today we conclude our six-part series with the question: 'What is Salvation?' As I've done in the past, this morning I will team-teach with guests… but today will be different in that I have virtual guests. Rather than being here in person, they are here in recorded and written forms and include Robert Velarde of *Focus on the Family*, C.S. Lewis, and Billy Graham. I've chosen this format and picked this team because, before you hear my views, you need to hear those of others, and few are more qualified and more articulate than these three. And before you hear any of us, we need to examine the answer to this question: What is '*salvation*'?

"The *Oxford Dictionary* defines salvation as *preservation or deliverance from harm, ruin, or loss. Zondervan's Bible Dictionary*—one of the resources you should buy and have in your personal library—dedicates almost a full page to the Old and New Testament meaning of the word. Summarized and simplified theologically, we may say that salvation is—through Christ—being saved from our sins and subsequently saved from hell.

"And while both Zondervan's definition and my summary are accurate, they are far too simple, too shallow, too glib for this most incomprehensible act of *one* man for the benefit of *another*. Now, you might think I would say 'the act of one man for the benefit of *mankind*', and while that's true, to do so would put it on a scale so large that the *personal* perspective—for you, for me—would be lost. And the *personal* perspective is this reality:

"He—for *you*—suffered the barbarity, viciousness, and atrocities of the bloody Passion.

"He—for *you*—suffered the emotional anguish of being forsaken by all, even God.

"He—for *you*—suffered the inexplicable horror of being separated from God.

"Further unequivocally confirming that it was very, very personal, Revelation 3:5 says: *…I will by no means blot out his name [your name] from the book of life, but I will acknowledge his [yours] before my Father and before His angels.*

"Robert Velarde also speaks to the personal nature of salvation, first about what it is not, then what it is. I want to read what he posted on the *Focus on the Family's* website.

What Salvation is Not

Before clarifying salvation in biblical terms, it will be helpful to look at ways of "salvation" that are not in line with Christian theology. Probably the most common approach is works-based. As the name suggests, this approach to salvation relies on human works and what we can do in order to save ourselves. But when it comes to salvation, Christianity is Savior-centered, not self-centered: "For it is by grace you have been saved, through faith—and this not from yourselves, it is the gift of God—not by works, so that no one can boast" (Ephesians 2:8-9 NIV). Good works are the natural outcome of following salvation through Christ.

Neither is salvation universal, meaning that not everyone will be saved. This does not mean that God does not love everyone. Indeed, He "wants all men to be saved and to come to a knowledge of the truth" (1 Timothy 2:4 NIV). But only Christ is "the way and the truth and the life" (John 14:6 NIV).

Salvation is not found in legalism, either. Strict adherence to a list of do's and don'ts is not what Christian salvation is about. Romans 3:20 reads, "no one will be declared righteous in his [God's] sight by observing the law; rather, through the law we become conscious of sin." We all "fall short of the glory of God" (Romans 3:23 NIV).

Some beliefs claim that salvation in a biblical sense is not required. Instead, terms such as "spiritual liberation" or "enlightenment" are used. Most of the time this is found in variations of Eastern worldviews such as pantheism. Usually the core idea is that human beings need only realize that they are perfect and divine, resulting in "salvation." But we are far from perfect and deep down everyone knows this fact. God exists, but He is not us and we are not Him.

Biblical Salvation

What then is biblical salvation? It's not by works, legalism enlightenment, and it's not universal. What, then, must we do to be saved? It's important to keep in mind that salvation encompasses what God has done for us, not what we can do for Him. God has taken the initiative in His plan of redemption, reaching out to us through Christ. Hence, the answer regarding the question of salvation as given by Paul and Silas is, "Believe in the Lord Jesus...." (Acts 16:31 NIV). The Greek word translated "believe" in the passage is pisteuo, meaning "to believe, put one's faith in, trust, with an implication that actions based on that trust may follow."

Belief, then, encompasses more than just knowing about Jesus. One must also act on this knowledge, combining faith and trust and acting on it.

Salvation also entails repentance—a sincere willingness to radically change our behavior (see, for instance Matthew 3:2; 4:17; Mark 6:12; Luke 13:3-5; Acts 2:38). There is a certain degree of humility that is also required on our part in order to submit to Christ and receive salvation. In the story of the jailer, for instance, we are told he "fell trembling before Paul and Silas" (Acts 16:29 NIV). He also addressed them as "Sirs," using a term of respect and acknowledging the authority of Paul and Silas in Christ. In other words, the roles are reversed. Rather than the Christian prisoners being under the authority of the jailer, it is the jailer who now humbly submits to them, sincerely seeking God's salvation."[1]

Jack set the paper aside and said, "C.S. Lewis, in his inimitable form, takes an interesting broad brush to the subject of what salvation is. Here's an excerpt in which he describes his views."

Tapping the play button on the Bose, Lewis began to speak:

And now, what was the purpose of it all? What did he come to do? Well, to teach, of course; but as soon as you look into the New Testament or any other Christian writing you will find they are constantly talking about something different—about His death and His coming to life again. It is obvious that Christians think the chief point of the story lies there. They think the main thing He came to earth to do was to suffer and be killed.

Now before I became a Christian I was under the impression that the first thing Christians had to believe was one particular theory as to what the point of this dying was. According to that theory God wanted to punish men for having deserted and joined the Great Rebel, but Christ volunteered to be punished instead, and so God let us off. Now I admit that even this theory does not seem to be quite so immoral and silly as it used to; but that is not the point I want to make. What I came to see later on was that neither this theory nor any other is Christianity. The central Christian belief is that Christ's death has somehow put us right with God and given us a fresh start. Theories as to how it did this are another matter. A good many different theories have been held as to how it works; what all Christians are agreed on is that it does work. I will tell you what I think it is like. All sensible people know that if you are tired and hungry a meal will do you good. But the modern theory of nourishment—all about the vitamins and proteins—is a different thing. People ate their dinners and felt better long before the theory of vitamin was ever heard of; and if the theory of vitamins is someday abandoned, they will go on eating their dinners just the same. Theories about Christ's death are not Christianity: they are explanations about how it works. Christians would not all agree as to how important those theories are. My own church—the Church of England—does not lay down any one of them as the right one. The Church of Rome goes a bit further. But I think they will all agree that the thing itself is infinitely more important than any explanations that theologians have produced. I think they would probably admit that no explanation will ever be quite adequate to the reality. But as I said in the preface to this book, I am only a layman, and at this point we are getting into deep water. I can only tell you, for what it is worth, how I, personally, look at the matter.

In my view the theories are not themselves the thing you are asked to accept. Many of you no doubt have read Jeans Eddington. What they do when they want to explain the atom, or something of that sort, is to give you a description out of which you can make a mental picture. But then they warn you that this picture is not what the scientists actually believe. What the scientists believe is a mathematical formula. The pictures are there only to help you to understand the formula. They are not really true in the way formula is; they do not give you the real thing but only something more or less like it. They are only meant to help, and if they do not help you can drop them. The thing itself cannot be pictured, it can only be expressed mathematically. We are in the same boat here. We believe that the death of Christ is just that point in history at which something absolutely unimaginable from outside shows through into our own world. And if we cannot picture even the atoms of which our own world is built, of course we are not going to be able to picture this. Indeed, if we found that we could fully understand it, that very fact would show it was not what it professes to be—the inconceivable, the uncreated, the thing from beyond nature, striking down into nature like lightning. You may ask what good it will be to us if we do not understand it. But that is easily answered. A man can eat his dinner without understanding exactly how food nourishes him. A man can accept what Christ has done without knowing how it works; indeed, he certainly would not know how it works until he accepted it.

We are told that Christ was killed for us, that His death has washed out our sins, and that by dying He disabled death itself. That is the formula. That is Christianity. That is what has to be believed. Any theories we build up as to how Christ's death did all this are, in my view, quite secondary: mere plans or diagrams to be left alone if they do not help us, and, even if they do help us, not to be confused with the thing itself. All the same, some of these theories are worth looking at.

The one most people have heard is the one I mentioned before—the one about our being let off because Christ has volunteered to bear a punishment instead of us. Now on the face of it that is a very silly theory. If God was prepared to let us off, why on earth did He not do so? And what possible point could there be in punishing an innocent person instead. None at all that I can see, if you are thinking of punishment in the police-court sense. On the other hand, if you think of a debt, there is plenty of point in a person who has some assets paying it on behalf of someone who has not. Or if you take 'paying the penalty', not in the sense of being punished, but in the more general sense of 'standing the racket' or 'footing the bill', then, of course, it is a matter of common experience that, when one person has got himself into a hole, the trouble of getting him out usually falls on a kind of friend.

Now what was the sort of 'hole' man had got himself into? He had tried to set up on his own, to behave as if he belonged to himself. In other words, fallen man is not simply an imperfect creature who needs improvement: he is a rebel who must lay down his arms. Laying down your arms, surrendering, saying you are sorry, realizing that you have been on the wrong track and getting ready to start life over again from the ground floor—that is the only way out of our 'hole.' This process of surrender—this movement full speed astern—is what Christians call repentance. Now repentance is no fun at all. It is something much harder than merely eating humble pie. It means unlearning all the self-conceit and self-will that we have been training ourselves into for thousands of years. It means killing part of yourself, undergoing a kind of death. In fact, it needs a good man to repent. And here comes the catch. Only a bad person needs to repent; only a good person can repent perfectly. The worse you are the more you need it and the less you can do it. The only person who could do it perfectly would be a perfect person—and he would not need it.

Remember, this repentance, this willing submission to humiliation and a kind of death, is not something God demands of you before He will take you back and which He could let you off if He chose: it is simply a description of what going back to him is like. If you ask God to take you back without it, you are really asking Him to let you go back without going back. It cannot happen. Very well, then, we must go through with it. But the same badness which makes us need it, makes us unable to do it. Can we do it if God helps us? Yes, but what do we mean when we talk of God helping us? We mean God putting into us a bit of Himself, so to speak. He lends us a little of His reasoning powers and that is how we think: he puts a little of His love into us and that is how we love one another. When you teach a child writing, you hold its hand while it forms the letters: that is, it forms the letters because you are forming them. We love and reason because God loves and reasons and holds our hand while we do it. Now if we had not fallen, that would be all plain sailing. But unfortunately, we now need God's help in order to do something which God, in His own nature, never does at all—to surrender, to suffer, to submit, to die. Nothing in God's nature corresponds to this process at all. So that the one road for which we now need God's leadership most of all is a road God, in His own in order to do something which God, in His own nature, never does at all—to surrender, to nature, has never walked. God can share only what He has: this thing, in His own nature, He has not.

But suppose God became a man—suppose our human nature which can suffer and die was amalgamated with God's nature in one person—then that person could help us. He could surrender His will, and suffer and die, because He was a man; and He could do it perfectly because he was God. You and I can go through this process only if God does it in us; but God can do it only if He becomes man. Our attempts at this dying will succeed only if we men share in God's dying, just as our thinking can succeed only because it is a drop out of the ocean of His intelligence: but we cannot share God's dying unless God dies; and He cannot die except by being a man. That is the sense in which He pays our debt and suffers for us what He Himself need not suffer at all.

I have heard some people complain that if Jesus was God as well as man, then His sufferings and death lose all value in their eyes, 'because it must have been so easy for Him.' Others (very rightly) rebuke the ingratitude and ungraciousness of this objection; what staggers me is the misunderstanding it betrays. In one sense, of course, those who make it are right. They have even understated their own case. The perfect submission, the perfect suffering, the perfect death were not only easier to Jesus because He was God, but were possible only because He was God. But surely that is a very odd reason for not accepting them? The teacher is able to form the letters for the child because the teacher is grown-up and knows how to write. That, of course, makes it easier for the teacher; and only because it is easier for him can he help the child. If it rejected him because 'it's easy for grown-ups' and waited to learn writing from another child who could not write itself (and so had no 'unfair' advantage), it would not get on very quickly. If I am drowning in a rapid river, a man who still has one foot on the bank may give me a hand which saves my life. Ought I to shout back (between my gasps), 'No, it's not fair! You have an advantage! You're keeping one foot on the bank'? That advantage—call it 'unfair' if you like—is the only reason why he can be of any use to me. To what will you look for help if you will not look to that which is stronger than yourself?

Such is my own way of looking at what Christians call the Atonement. But remember this is only one more picture. Do not mistake it for the thing itself: and if it does not help you, drop it.[2]

Jack tapped the *stop* button and said, "Lewis uses an interesting word here, *atonement*, which appears in Romans 5:11 and is styled *reconciliation* in other New Testament passages. Both refer to the core message of the Bible: *God wants reconciliation with man*. In the Old Testament, the word appears some 140 times as atonement was offered through animal sacrifices… as an example, in Leviticus 16:11, atonement was provided by an animal, a bullock, sacrificed as a sin offering. In the New Testament—and to the point that Lewis is making—that sacrifice is Christ."

Stepping back to the lectern, Jack picked up a book and said, "I now call on our third guest-teacher in this lesson and see another interesting word is used: *regeneration*. I want to read part of a chapter from this book I mentioned to you several weeks ago, and another of those I encourage you to buy and place in your personal library. It is Billy Graham's *The Holy Spirit."*

Opening the paperback to the last few pages of Chapter 4, a chapter entitled 'The Holy Spirit', Jack read,

"Along with repentance and faith, one of the works of the Spirit of God in the heart of man is regeneration. 'Regeneration' is another term for renewal or rebirth. 'He saved us, not

on the basis of deeds which we have done in righteousness, but according to His mercy, by the washing of regeneration and renewing by the Holy Spirit (Titus 3:5). Actually, the Greek word translated 'regeneration' here is a compound of two Greek words; it literally means 'birth again' or new birth.

This is a once-for-all change, though it has continuing effects. In John 3:3 the Bible speaks of one being 'born again', and the Amplified Version suggests 'born anew' or 'born from above' to clarify the meaning. The sinner in his natural state is spiritually dead in trespasses and sins. In regeneration that which was dead is made alive. He is justified by God from the guilt of a broken law, and he is forgiven of every sin. Further, by the new birth the justified sinner becomes a new creation—a new creature (2 Cor. 5:17; Gal. 6:15 RSV). Moreover, regeneration, like justification, is immediate and constitutes a one-time act of the Holy Spirit, though the person who is 'born again' might, or might not, be conscious of the exact time. Theologians have long debated exactly when regeneration actually takes place in a person's life. In spite of some disagreements, the central issue is clear: it is the Holy Spirit who regenerates us within.

The gift of new or divine life to the regenerated person comes to the soul from Christ through the Holy Spirit. Jesus said that the new birth is a 'mystery.' He uses the illustration of the wind blowing: We sense its effects but we cannot see where it comes from or where it is going. Thus regeneration is a hidden transaction in the same sense that it is something which takes place within the individual heart and may or may not be known to the one who receives it—and often is not immediately visible to people around him. The results that flow from the new birth are so incalculably significant that they deserve to be called a miracle—the greatest of all miracles! Even as unbelieving men did not know Jesus on earth, and failed to realize that God incarnate was standing before them, so it is possible the 'the new man' in Christ to go unrecognized for at least a while. Yet, known or unknown to the world, the new man exists within. Sooner or later the new birth will manifest itself in godly living. But the divine life, which will abide forever, is there, and the 'new man' who possesses the kingdom of God is there (2 Cor. 5:17)—a new creature.

This is not to deny the importance of personal faith and decision. We do not passively sit back and wait for the Spirit to do His work before we come to Christ. We are commanded to 'Ask, and it shall be given to you; seek, and you shall find; knock, and it shall be opened to you' (Matt. 7:7). We have the promise of God: 'And you will seek Me and find Me, when you search for Me with all your heart (Jer. 29:13). Furthermore, the Scripture tells us that even faith itself is a gift of God's grace: 'Because of his kindness you have been saved through trusting Christ. And even trusting is not of yourselves; it too is a gift from God' (Eph. 2:8 LB). We therefore have everything we need to decide for Christ, but we still have a responsibility to respond to the call and conviction of the Holy Spirit.

When a person is born again, the process is uncomplicated from the divine perspective. The Spirit of God takes the Word of God and makes the child of God. We are born again through the operation of the Holy Spirit, who in turn uses the divinely inspired word of God. God's Spirit brings life to men. At this point the Holy Spirit indwells a person for life. He receives eternal life.... The new birth will bring about a change in your relationship with God, a change in your relationship with your family, a change in your relationship with yourself, a change in your relationship with your neighbors. Gradually, if you are an obedient believer, it will bring about a change in disposition, affection, aims, principles and dimensions."[3]

As he finished, Jack closed and set aside the book. He stood quietly. He seemed to be resolving to continue. After a moment he said, "I'm about to take you where I've never taken a class before. I've touched on this subject dozens of times over the years, but never like I'm about to now. Never with the soul-searching I'm about to ask of you. Never with this degree of disclosure of my own view of salvation.

"We've seen three descriptions of salvation. Rather than focus on what it's like, I'm going to speak to the more critical matter of how to get there. These are, as I've said so many times in these lessons, my personal views. However, they are not based on personal opinion, but what I think Scripture says, albeit in ways you may not have heard or seen before.

"To that end I'm going to take you through five steps—five questions—which frame my view, and which will lead you to think and write, at least a note, about your view. This will be confidential… we'll not discuss your responses. In fact, the rest of the morning will be rather quiet as we'll not have any discussions, and rather slow as I want you to dwell on your answers. Further, there'll be a time and place for discussion, but not here and not now, for this room is far too public a place and this subject far too personal a matter. I'll say more about that at the close of our class."

Turning to the end of the first row he said, "Bev, please pass out the sheets."

Jack watched as Bev passed out paper and pens. When all was ready, he said, "You are about to profile your own view of salvation. To that end, on the blank sheets you'll write your answer to five simple questions. Each question requires a short one-word answer: '*Yes*', '*No*', or '*Unsure.*' Though brief, this exercise may be more personal and telling than you wish to share, so, again, you may want to keep your responses confidential."

Jack turned to the board and wrote as he said, "Question one:"

> **Do you believe that:**
>
> **1. There is life after death?**

Turning back to the class, Jack said, "*Do you believe that there is life after death?* This very brief question touches a very large issue. The question means that—irrespective of whether as a resurrected body, soul, or some other form—do you believe you will continue to exist, even after your death? Stated another way: Do you believe that there will never… *never... not* be a you?"

Jack stood quietly as they considered and wrote their answers, then wrote question two on the board:

> Do you believe that:
> 1. There is life after death?
> 2. That life will be spent in either heaven or hell?

"If your answer to question one is 'yes'," he said, "the second question, restated, is this: *Do you believe your eternity will be spent in only one of two places—heaven or hell?* We don't here need to deliberate definitions of heaven as a New Earth, or in the sky, or the presence of God… nor hell as a lake of fire, or the center of Earth, or the absence of God. The question is simply this: *Do you believe those are the only two options?*"

Jack sat down to indicate that there was no rush, that there was plenty of time to give the question the thought it was due. After a few moments, Jack stood and wrote question three.

> Do you believe that:
> 1. There is life after death?
> 2. That life will be spent in either heaven or hell?
> 3. It will be God's standard, not yours, that decides which?

"The third question, restated, is this: *Whose standard sets the bar for admission to Heaven… yours or God's?* On the surface this seems a silly question, but the sad reality is that many think *we* do. Many think our *goodness,* our *works,* or our absence of any *extreme sins* are the standards by which we will be judged and found acceptable… almost as if we're going to be graded on a curve, and the sole criteria is going to be my being better… or doing more good… than others.

"God, on the other hand, is clear that there is only *one* standard: *His*. And that standard is this: *perfection*. In Matthew 5:20 Jesus said, '*You are to be perfect, as your heavenly Father is perfect.'* His perfection does *not* mean a life without faults or mistakes or sin. It *does* mean a life that is covered by

Christ's sacrifice, making it in God's eyes *perfect.* I want to give you one of my favorite illustrations of this from one of my favorite Bible teachers. The guy is a retired neurologist in Austin, Texas who shared this personal mental image of Jesus' covering sins: He said he saw his sins, written in red, on a long list, nailed to the bottom of the cross. Then he saw Christ, nailed above the list, blood flowing down, red over red, covering the list, making each sin invisible."

Jack sat down.

After a few moments, he walked to the board and wrote question four.

> Do you believe that:
> 1. There is life after death?
> 2. That life will be spent in either heaven or hell?
> 3. It will be God's standard, not yours, that decides which?
> 4. You can make yourself perfect?

After another minute he said, "And that takes us to question four, '*Do you believe you can make yourself perfect?*

"Of course you can't—which makes this seem like another silly question—but it lies at the heart of this thing called salvation because if *you* can't… *who* can?... and *how*?

"In John 3:1-16, Jesus answered that question with a story:

> *There was a man of the Pharisees named Nicodemus, a ruler of the Jews. This man came to Jesus by night and said to Him, 'Rabbi, we know that You are a teacher come from God; for no one can do these signs that You do unless God is with him.' Jesus answered and said to him, 'Most assuredly, I say to you, unless one is born again, he cannot see the kingdom of God.' Nicodemus said to Him, 'How can a man be born when he is old? Can he enter a second time into his mother's womb and be born?' Jesus answered, 'Most assuredly, I say to you, unless one is born of water and the Spirit, he cannot enter the kingdom of God. That which is born of the flesh is flesh, and that which is born of the Spirit is spirit.'*
>
> *For God so loved the world that He gave His only begotten Son, that whoever believes in Him should not perish but have everlasting life."* [4]

Jack watched until it seemed all had finished question four and read as he wrote on the board, "This, then, becomes our fifth and final question: *Do you believe that you must be born again?"*

Do you believe that:

1. **There is life after death?**
2. **That life will be spent in either heaven or hell?**
3. **It will be God's standard, not yours, that decides which?**
4. **You can make yourself perfect?**
5. **You must be born again?**

Jack stayed at the board, waited for them to weigh and write their answers, then said, "We have seen that God's way is through Jesus, who—for no explicable reason other than unjustifiable love—willingly substituted himself for you, bearing the full measure of God's condemnation for your sins so that you would not have to… so that you would be sin-free… so that you would be perfect.

"It's baffling, I know, but it doesn't end there.

"It ends with *you*.

"It ends with *your* decision.

"It ends with *your* choice.

"Hear me clearly and see this plainly: *Rather than forcefully seizing you without your consent*—as a parent does in an intervention to save a drug-addicted child—*God gave you the liberty, gave you the freedom, gave you the autonomy to spend eternity where you choose*."

Jack stood quietly. He had said all he could say. There was left only this, "And he made choosing so very, *very* simple. If you choose eternity with him, all you have to do is *ask* for it… *pray* for it. That's all! And you may express that choice through any number of prayers you'll find online… or written by Billy Graham… or on the front of the card Bev is passing to you now… or one of your *own* you write on the back. It's all up to you. We're going to be quiet while you read—or pray—the one you're holding."

The class silently read:

> *Father, I acknowledge that I am of two distinct parts: one part physical which will perish at my death; the other part spiritual which will not. I believe my spirit—along with my body resurrected at Christ's second coming—will exist eternally with You in a place called heaven or eternally separated from You in a place called hell. I claim no qualification for heaven other than that which I have through Jesus' sacrificial act and Your merciful grace. I confess a life of innumerable misses of Your mark and ask Your forgiveness for those sins. I believe Your forgiveness of my sins, Your longing for my soul, and Your passion for my presence is an unearned, unjust, undeserved gift which—with profound humility, everlasting gratitude, and overwhelming joy—I accept.*
>
> *In Your Son's name. Amen.*

After several minutes, Jack stepped back to the front and said, "Tug, will you join me?"

As he came forward, Jack said, "Most of you know Tug, our Director of Education. He, for some in this room, may be the most important part of today's class. I'll let him tell you why."

Tug stood next to Jack and said, "Jack and I felt that some may have questions or simply want to talk privately about portions of this morning's lesson. We hope so. That's why my card is stapled to your sheets. See me after class or call me and we'll make plans to meet here, at a coffee shop, or anywhere else convenient for you."

Stepping to the side of the music stand to be nearer the class as Jack had so often done, Tug said, "There's another part to this lesson beyond what was said and the questions you may have about it, and that part is this: What does it mean for *tomorrow*? What does it mean for next *week,* next *month,* next *year*? What does it mean for *life*?

"The answer for some in here, if not careful, will be 'not much'... not in the long run. That's because if you don't take some clear, overt, intentional action steps over the next few *days*, it will fade. That it will fade, of course, is no surprise because we've all experienced it... we've all been there... we've all been attracted to something—reading the classics, learning a language, losing some weight—only to find that all too quickly the world has again pressed in and the *want*... the *conviction* ...the *vision* of a new dimension for the old you... is... just... *gone*!

"And the sad part is that—unlike the inspiration to read the classics, learn a language, or lose some weight—this moment... this confluence of spiritual information and motivation... this clarity of the connection between Earthly choices and eternal life... may never come again.

"So... what should you do?

"These three things. Write them down. These are your action steps.

"First, find a *coach* and find a *friend*. Recognize that it can be difficult to do this alone, so find a spiritual *coach* that can guide you, walk with you, influence you through this transition into a faith-based life. Coaches are there and available if you look. It may be someone on your church staff. It may be someone in something like Search Ministries if you're an adult or Fellowship of Christian Athletes if you're a student. Or it may be someone—if your circumstances are such—like a community-wide retirement or assisted-living chaplain, a college campus or house chaplain, a military chaplain, a prison chaplain, or... more and more... in the largest and smallest businesses... a workplace chaplain. You may find it helpful to take your notes and the five questions to that person for context on what has brought you to this moment. And find a spiritual *friend* who will make the walk with you. I once heard a friend defined as 'someone to whom you do not need to explain.' That would never be more true for you than right now. That friend could be the person in here that has gone through this lesson with you, or someone outside you've yet to engage in this walk.

"Second, recognize that this is not a sprint but a marathon, so be patient... stay focused... remember that it was 40 days for Jesus, three years for Paul, and 25 years for Abraham before the fullness of God's time.

"Third, get involved. Join a small Bible study group at church, or work, or neighborhood, or remotely via Zoom... or start one."

Tug stood silently for a moment, then sat down.

Jack paused, content that all that could be said had been, then announced, "Next week we begin a new four-part series that is a natural extension of the six-part we completed today:

"Next Sunday... *Christianity in the American Culture.*

"The following Sunday... *Christianity in the Family.*

"The next Sunday... *Christianity in the Workplace.*

"The fourth Sunday... *Christianity in the Church*."

Jack closed the class in prayer and visited with a few members while the room cleared. As he walked with the last to the classroom exit and started to turn off the lights, he remembered the board. When he turned to go back and erase it, he noticed some still sitting… silently… rereading the questions, reviewing their answers, rethinking the lesson:

> Do you believe that:
>
> 1.There is life after death?
>
> 2.That life will be spent in either heaven or hell?
>
> 3. It will be God's standard, not yours, that decides which?
>
> 4. You can make yourself perfect?
>
> 5. You must be born again?

Then, without comment or hesitation, Jack quietly stepped out, leaving the board untouched, and the lights on.

###

Your Takeaways and Action Items from this Chapter

Takeaway 1

(page__)

Takeaway 2

(page__)

Takeaway 3

(page__)

Your Takeaways and Action Items from this Chapter (cont.)

Action Item 1

(page__)

Action Item 2

(page__)

Action Item 3

(page__)

Where Is Christianity in the American Culture?

Chapter 11 - Sunday, July 24

Jack smiled as he watched Beverly acknowledge a birthday, take requests, and lead them in prayer. He then walked to the music stand, laid his binder and a small book on it, and added his good morning to Beverly's.

"Over the past six weeks," Jack said, "we've completed a series of studies on Who is the Holy Spirit?... Who is God?... Who is Christ?... Who is Satan?... and What is Salvation?. Over the next four weeks I want to focus on how these elements fuse together to make life. Not just *living,* but *life... life* as a Christian, *life* as a servant, *life* as an adopted of God.

"And I want to begin by posing this question: Is *Christian* a noun or a verb? Most would say *noun* because, per Merriam-Webster, *A noun is a word that is the name of something such as a person, animal, place, thing, quality, idea, or action.* Others would say a *verb* because, per the same source, *verbs are words that show an action, occurrence, or state of being*. I would argue that it is the last—*state of being*—that God wants most for us. And it is on that we will concentrate as we examine it in four settings," he said as he read and wrote on the whiteboard.

> Today: Christianity in the <u>American Culture.</u>
>
> Next Sunday... Christianity in the <u>Family.</u>
>
> The following Sunday... Christianity in the <u>Workplace.</u>
>
> The fourth Sunday... Christianity in the <u>Church.</u>

Holding the marker and tapping the words *Christianity in the Family*, Jack said, "I'll give you a quick preview of next week's lesson. We will be applying our three key questions—*What* is being said? *Why* is it being said? *How* does it apply to my life?—to several Scriptures including Ephesians 5:21-25. Guys, you may want to get a jump on this by reading verse 25 because I will be asking you this question: What did Paul mean when he wrote... *Husbands, love your wives as Christ loved the church?"*

Jack paused for a moment, wanting the fullness of the question to be understood... wanting them to start formulating the answer that the Christ/church relationship is God's model for the husband/

wife relationship… that the standard for a husband's love for his wife is that of Jesus' love for *his* bride, the church… and that a husband's love for his wife—manifested in patience, selflessness, generosity, and fidelity—is to be resolute in spite of her real or imagined imperfections, just as Christ's love for his bride is resolute in spite of the church's 2000 years of very real and very well documented imperfections.

"We will also be talking about two kinds of extramarital relationships, but not the kinds you typically think about.

"For the first, read all of Proverbs 7 three times, then three more substituting the word *work* for *harlot, prostitute,* or *adulteress.* What I want you to see is that your work can be the most *seductive* and *destructive* force in your married life. It can consume your time, your attention, your creative energies, and your financial resources. It can offer you emotional fulfillment and social respect. And while family and friends will have no patience with your involvement with another woman—be her old girlfriend, office colleague, or euphemistic 'escort'—they will indulge… even approve… often encourage… your frequent liaisons with this easily accessible, publicly acceptable, and potentially destructive mistress. Read it and we'll talk about it next week.

"The second kind of extramarital relationship," he said as he pulled a newspaper clipping from the back of the binder, "is well stated in the title of this article by Carolyn Susman of the *Palm Beach Post*: *'You Don't Have to Take Your Clothes Off to Cheat.'*[1] The baseline for her story was the breakup of the marriage of movie icons Jennifer Aniston and Brad Pitt in which Aniston said in a *Vanity Fair* interview that she did not think her husband had sex with his co-star, but that he 'emotionally exited' the marriage months earlier when he met Angelina Jolie.

"The source for the point of Susman's story was a book by Miami Beach psychotherapist M. Gary Neuman called *Emotional Infidelity* in which he said:

> *When we think affair, we think sex. But an emotional affair can be just as dangerous to a marriage. When a spouse places his or her primary emotional needs in the hands of someone outside the marriage, it breaks the bond of marriage just as adultery does.* [2]

"This does not mean that a spouse places in someone outside the marriage *all* primary emotional needs. It means that:

"(a) if you have a relationship with someone other than your spouse—whether that person is a colleague, neighbor, old classmate, or chatroom stranger;

"(b) if in that relationship you share emotions—whether those emotions are dreams, concerns, frustrations, or fun;

"(c) if that sharing satisfies your need for a confidante—whether that satisfaction is in the form of companionship, reassurance, confirmation, or adulation; and

"(d) *if you do it in secret*—whether that form of secrecy is that you just don't tell your spouse about it, simply prefer that it not be brought up, or actually hide it—then

"(e) you have dishonored the marital bond, violated the nuptial union, and committed emotional infidelity.

"If you have *not* done it guys… or girls… you now know the litmus test—*secrecy*—so avoid it. If you *are* doing it guys… or girls… you have put your marriage at risk with an emotional affair, so walk, break it off, get out—now."

Jack returned the article to the binder, paused for a moment, glanced at the clock, saw that there was time, pulled a second sheet of paper from the back of the binder and said, "Dads, it may seem that I'm focusing on you as I talk about family, and that's probably true because of the subtle, powerful, indelible role you play in the lives of your children. I want to read to you part of a paper written by a young woman I admire. She sent it to me as an unedited 'brain dump' following a class I taught young adults a few years ago. I have kept it because I intend to use it in a book someday. I intend to use it because it so persuasively speaks to that extraordinary relationship that exists between father and daughter, and to how that relationship—when she is a child—forms her expectations... her standards... her confidence when she becomes a woman.

> *What all single women should have is this: A doting father. A father who tells you that you deserve to have doors opened for you. A father who tells you that he wants you to be a strong and independent woman, but never wants you to lose the softness that makes him your "Daddy" for life. She needs a father who shows the strength—and the gentleness—of what a man can be. He needs to model of what a trusting relationship is and what that looks like mutually. He should sit down with her when she's six years old and tell her that he wants her feedback on some age-appropriate matters he is concerned about. He needs to show her how she should be treated when going out to dinner and how it's a lot better conversation when the two of you are sitting side-by-side in a booth.*
>
> *He should find out from her what she wants to be and who she wants to be. Because when life happens to that little girl, a lot of that information gets mixed with hard life lessons and what started as the ONLY truth becomes a string in the fabric that creates her foundation. She will make wrong choices, she will get hurt, she will get treated poorly and she will question her value and worth to men and in this world. But, over time as she continues to grow into adulthood and she continues to learn about herself, the value and power of that single thread becomes the cornerstone for what she'll demand for herself. Though all the other experiences are there and are a part of who she is, that thread remains and its truth becomes too valuable and sacred to forget.*
>
> *And what she was taught by her father as a girl becomes a hope to the young woman and a requirement to the grown woman. As a woman she will claim for herself the fact that she is valuable to a man and to this world because of her individuality and beautiful uniqueness. She will find the man who wants to open her door, but wants her also to be independent and strong. She'll find the man who values her thoughts and ideas and who sits next to her at the booth because you can talk better. She'll hold out for the man who loves to watch her "put her foot down", and gets sheer joy from hearing her giggle like a little girl when she's excited about something.*
>
> *But, she only holds out for it because somewhere, when she was little, it was instilled in her by the most powerful man in her life as truth, and no matter what life brings—more than she trusts what she's seen or how she's been treated—she will go back to that truth because she trusts her "Daddy".*
>
> *The reality: Not every woman gets that from her father, so where does she learn to make these demands for herself? That's a tough one, I'm not sure I can answer, but I would have to say FIRST - look to your Heavenly Father.... He thinks you're AMAZING. He thinks you're worth dying for and He thinks you're worthy of all the treasures in heaven. He has saved a special seat for you with Him when you die. He has taken the time to create you uniquely, different from anyone else in the world. And when I say "uniquely", I mean, whether or not you had an earthly father to show you what you deserve, God did create you with desires for yourself. He created*

you with specific ways you want to be treated, specific languages that, when interpreted by your heart, mean "love." He's created you with a mind and emotions that come together to articulate to you what you wish you could find - listen to it, hang on to the fact that the desires of your heart and how you are to be treated are planted there by a God who wants you to have fulfillment and love in your life. He is a God of love and He wants His children loved in the right way. If you look to Him and ask Him to show you the person who, on this earth can provide it to you, then hold on to your seat and get ready for the biggest blessing of your life. Never downplay the value or rightness of the feelings of love that you need to receive from a mate. If you need to be hugged, then find a hugger, if you need someone to be gentle and loving with you - then ask for him in God's will and He'll provide. God can only create the best, He is not able to provide less."[3]

Jack returned the sheet to the back of the binder, smiled and said, "I know this young lady and I know her dad. And I agreed with him when he once said, 'In a Bud Light world, she's Dom Pérignon.'

"More on the family next week. This week, '*Where Is Christianity in the American Culture?*"

Jack paused. Stood quietly. The smile fading. Though he had spent hours preparing this lesson, he still felt unprepared. He still felt inadequate. He still felt the enormity of this subject called for several weeks of discussion. He looked at the floor, finally thought: *Nope... no change. We need to talk about this... here goes.*

He then stepped to the side of the lectern, smiled, and said, "If you're wondering why your teacher of a dozen years is standing up here acting as if he'd forgotten his notes, that's not the case. *Close*, but not the case. Close because I don't have *notes* that adequately cover... *answers* that adequately explain... *data* that adequately documents my thoughts on this subject of Christianity in the American culture.

"My principal thought is this: America is changing... and Christianity is changing with it. Or more accurately, *Christianity* isn't changing because the core beliefs have not changed, but America's *perception* of Christianity... of church... of faith is changing.

Jack paused, then said, "I think, in part, this is happening because America's perception of *all* institutions is changing... shifting... and for most, that shift is away from *trusting* to *distrusting.*

"Peggy Noonan—the 2017 Pulitzer Prize winner for Commentary who is a weekly contributor on the Opinion page of *The Wall Street Journal*... an author of several books on culture, politics, and faith... a frequent guest on Meet the Press, CBS, MSNBC, FOX, and other networks... said this in the *Journal* on June 2, 2018:

> *I have been thinking about trust. All the polls show and have for some time what you already know: America's trust in its leaders and institutions has been falling for four decades. Trust in the federal government has never been lower. In 1958, Pew Research found 73% trusted the government to do what is right "always" or "most of the time." That sounds healthy. As of 2017 that number was 18%. That's not. Other institutions have suffered, too—the church, the press, the professions."*

Jack continued, "As she said, distrust is not new. This is particularly true for those of us who are old enough to have witnessed monumental spikes of trust-abuse during the last century, spikes so large and so conspicuous that they became identified with single names like Vietnam and Watergate.

"There have been fewer such spikes, fewer tsunamis, fewer surprising great waves of distressing news identified by single iconic names... news that overwhelms, then ebbs. It's been more like constant rain that floods, but never ebbs. A flood that seems to continue to rise. A flood that reminds us of the story of the frog in a pan who endured gradually hotter water until it boiled him... with the temperature of our water slowly increasing and our minds slowly becoming accustomed to it... or unconscious of it... or cynical about it.

"Then, in the middle of a rising flood with which we were uncomfortably but gradually becoming acclimated, we were hit, multiple times, by a staggering series of events. First, we were hit by the Coronavirus with the surprise of a Pearl Harbor and the scope of a Black Plague. Then hit by the death of a Black man at the hands of police which spotlighted racial divides at an intensity rarely seen since the Civil War. Then hit by the virus-banning of public gatherings—in restaurants and schools, at sporting events and churches, even of families at Christmas and Thanksgiving—causing businesses to close at the rate of more than 1,000 a day and the loss of 22 million jobs. Then hit by a bitterly contested election, a presidential impeachment, and in a moment not experienced since the British in the War of 1812, the storming of our Capital. Then hit by confusion and anxiety over where and when we could be vaccinated. Then—for *tens of thousands*—hit by the passing away of a loved one... *alone*... in a nursing home, hospital room, or ICU... without family, without goodbyes, without touching... with only a remarkable —*remarkable*—nurse, there, quietly holding a hand, whispering assurance, saying goodbye. Then hit by the *number* of Americans who died from the virus during the first 12 months... 500,000... with the number growing as variants appeared. And finally—I fear for far too many of us—hit by the loss of hope."

Jack paused. Started to speak. Paused again, then said, "I was talking about the loss of trust. I would submit that the *depth* of our distrust has measurably *deepened*, and the *breadth* of our distrust materially *broadened*, to include virtually every element of our daily lives. Specifically, I submit our distrust has expanded to include our government... our press... our businesses... our educational systems... our financial institutions... our law enforcement agencies... our charities... our churches.

"With regard to *Christianity*, while some of the cultural shift in views of the church may be due to a shift in trust, it seems to be due to much, much more. Before we look at some of the reasons, I'd like to look at statistical confirmation that there is indeed a shift. To do that, I'd like for you to see a chart based on studies conducted and published in 2014 by Pew Research that tells us some of the story. By the way, while their corporate name suggests a theological focus, they're a leading researcher in a wide-ranging spectrum of social, opinion, and demographic trends for scores of non-religious groups."

As Jack turned to Bev and asked her to pass out summary sheets of the Pew study, he said, "Take a moment and look at this change in the percentage of our population affiliated with... and *not* affiliated with... any religious institution between 2007 and 2014."

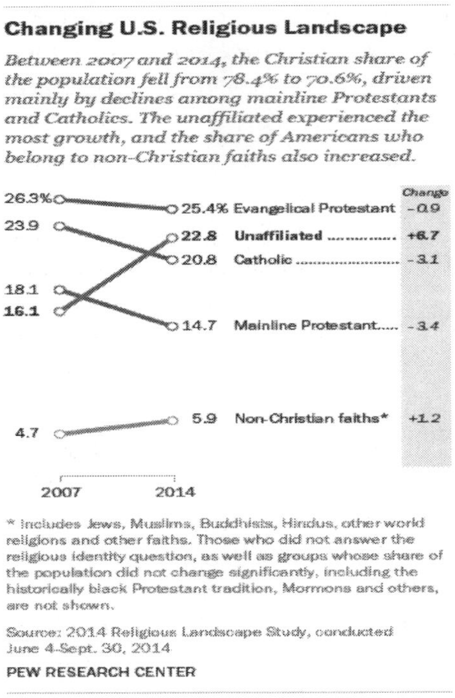

Jack continued, "While I don't have an updated chart, in an article published by the *Journal* in 2021, Pew reported a current survey in which it said, *Religious affiliation in the U.S. has continued to fall during the pandemic.* Statistically, it found that between 2007 and 2021 the percentage of U.S. adults who identified with Christianity fell from 78% to 63%, and the percentage who identified as No Religion increased from 16% to 29%. Charts and stats reflect *what* is happening, but not *why*. So I want to turn our attention to some reasons why as expressed by others who are more qualified to espouse theories than I am."

Then, smiling, he added, "But you're still going to get my opinion.

"Scores of books have been written on why affiliation with churches is declining. Two, in particular, which search for core reasons are Julia Duin's *Quitting Church* and David Kinnaman's *Unchristian*. I doubt that there's a pastor in America who doesn't have one of these or similar books on their desk. Interestingly, that's how I got these. A few years ago, I was asked by a Houston church to facilitate a strategic planning retreat and for my preparation the pastor gave me copies.

"At the time of her writing, Duin was the religious editor for the *Washington Times.* She holds a master's degree in religion and regularly wins awards for her national and international religion reporting. Though she quotes research—from Gallup, the National Opinion Research Center at the University of Chicago, and others, all of which essentially echo those of Pew's charts—much of her writing is anecdotal, based on her own experience and that of those she interviewed, little of which has metrics that can be measured. On page 50 she summarizes her views: *One of the top reasons people are giving for their leaving church is loneliness—especially in large congregations that no one knows or cares whether they are there.* Earlier she writes: *It's an odd pattern. Americans like small groups but prefer big churches.* I'll remain only for a moment longer on her writing and on what I think are—in today's culture—two of the most important words in Christendom: *small groups*.

"If Duin's *Quitting Church* proposes that some *outsiders want to be loved more*, Kinnaman's *Unchristian* proposes that other *outsiders want to be disliked less*. Kinnaman is more analytical than Duin's anecdotal approach, and principally deals with the general public's negative perceptions of Christians: That we are widely viewed by nonbelievers as being judgmental, hypocritical, and anti-everything, that we have become, as he says on page 26, *famous for what we oppose rather than what we are for."*

Jack stepped back behind the lectern and said, "I think that's enough thrashing of ourselves for perceived... and in some cases... actual failures. The truth is that we're *trying*... that we're *searching* ...that we're *not quitting*. I'll come back to this in a moment, but first I want to look at the environment in which we live, the flood-like forces over which we have little or no control, and the influence those forces have on us, our friends, our family, our church, our country.

"In a word, I want to look at our *culture*... specifically I want to look at seven reasons why I believe finding and living a faith-based life in this culture is so very, very, *very* difficult.

"The first reason is that in our culture the perception of heaven and hell is significantly different between Christians and non-Christians. This is most clearly reflected in Pew's *2014 Religious Landscape Study*. Pew reported that 72% of Americans believe in heaven and 58% believe in hell... where heaven is defined as a place *where people who have led good lives are enterally rewarded*... and hell as a place *where people have led bad lives and die without being sorry are eternally punished.*

"The second reason is that we tend to confuse *prosperity* with *righteousness*. We think that because America has such *abundance*, it has God's *approval*... and if we have his approval, why change how we live or think or believe.

"The third reason comes from the old saying that 'familiarity breeds contempt.' In this case it is not our familiarity, but our kind of assumed chumminess with God... and it's not contempt but our irreverence with, our disrespect for, our trivialization of the relationship we have with him. We see it all the time. We see it—and this is a very personal opinion—in politicians who end speeches with 'God Bless America' with no more spiritual intent than umpires begin games with 'play ball.' We see it in you and me as we toss 'bless you' to those sneezing during cold seasons with the no more spiritual thought than revelers who toss beads to flashers during Mardi Gras. And we see it as Christmas has become a season of buying with no more spiritual point than back-to-school shopping.

"The fourth reason is that so many of those who influence America's youth—actors and athletes, musicians and comedians, writers and directors—demean or disregard virtually anyone and anything that supports and promotes spirituality. There are clear exceptions to this, but they are that—exceptions—rather than the norm.

"The fifth reason—and among the most benign and thus the most dangerous—is distractions. This is our busyness. These are our elective activities that go well beyond those that refresh the mind and renew the body. These are those innocent time-consuming distractions that make us spiritual couch potatoes... that make our days feel full the way fillers make coffee seem pure... that are at our fingertips in the form of iPhones and iPads and Fitbits... Facebook and Pinterest and YouTube... streaming movies and satellite radio and fantasy football... *People* magazine and Kindle e-readers and VR headsets... and hobbies and naps and paperbacks. But the most pervasive, the most beguiling, and the most fruitless of all is *television*. Like a black hole in space, this black hole in our homes pulls us into itself, absorbs our attention, and consumes our hours with generally redundant news cycles, trivial talk shows, and sophomoric sitcoms... its vibrancy mesmerizing like a crackling wood fire... its enlightenment fleeting like embers of gas logs.

"The sixth reason is our inability to differentiate between mentally *acknowledging* that Jesus is the Son of God and spiritually *accepting* him as such. This difficulty is not unique to Americans, but it is so easy to mistake one for the other that we need to talk about it. And it is no more unusual today than it was 2000 years ago. As I said last week, this problem is so old that it could be called the Nicodemian Syndrome because it was the Pharisee Nicodemus who, as recorded in John 3:2, acknowledged who Jesus was by saying, *Rabbi, we know that You are a teacher come from God; for no one can do these signs that You do unless God is with Him.'*[4] Jesus told Nicodemus that acknowledging was not enough, that, *'...unless one is born again, he cannot see the kingdom of God.'*[5] To this Nicodemus naturally responded, *'How can a man be born when he is old. Surely he cannot enter a second time into his mother's womb to be born.'*[6] Then Jesus replied with this simple, confusing, essential declaration: *'I tell you the truth, no one can enter the kingdom of God unless he is born of water and the Spirit. Flesh gives birth to flesh, but the Spirit gives birth to spirit."*[7]

Pausing, thinking of ways to make this point clear and compelling, Jack said, "We must see this difference. We must see that just *acknowledging* Christ as the son of God is insufficient… inadequate… incomplete… for *salvation*. There is no clearer example of this than Satan himself when he *acknowledged* him in Matthew 4:3 as he rhetorically said, *If you are the Son of God, tell these stones to become bread....*[8] Satan acknowledged him again in 4:6 when he took him to the holy city and had him stand on the highest point of the temple and said, *'...Since you are the Son of God, throw yourself down, because it is written,' 'God will put his angels in charge of you,' and 'With their hands they will hold you up, so that you will never hit your foot against a rock.'*[9] And Satan acknowledged him a third time in 4:9 when he took Jesus to a high mountain, showed him all the kingdoms of the world and said, *'I will give you all these things if you will bow down and worship me.'*[10] But acknowledging that Jesus is the son of God will no more take me to heaven than acknowledging that Delta flies to Paris will take me to France. If I am to fly to Paris, a physical *transaction* is required in which I exchange my credit-card charge for their seat-assigned ticket. In accepting Christ as my savior, there is a spiritual *transaction* required in which I exchange my hope in *my* goodness for his promise of *his* grace."

"Jack," a woman's voice from the third row said, "My apologies for only now asking, but I'm a little confused about your first reason and this one because somewhere I read a verse that said if you persist in doing good you will have eternal life."

"You're right, Beth," Jack replied, "in Romans 2:7 Paul wrote, *To those who by persistence in doing good seek glory, honor and immortality, He will give eternal life.*[11] In saying that he was continuing to elaborate on his thought from the previous verse, 2:6, in which he was quoting Psalms 62:12 which said, *God will give to each person according to what he has done*[12]… and *that* was an elaboration of the point he was making that we are not to judge one another, and if we do so, don't think we are going to escape God's subsequent judgment of us. To make his point he, at the beginning of the section, said, *Now we know that God's judgment against those who do such things is based on truth. So when you, a mere man, pass judgment on them and yet do the same things, do you think you will escape God's judgment?*[13]

"It's an excellent question, Beth, and I'm glad you asked it. If we look at *all* of Paul's writings in *all* of his books—as well as this in Romans—we see that goodness has no more to do with becoming saved than honey has to becoming a bee. Goodness is important, as we see him say in Galatians 5. But it follows… never precedes. And that which precedes is this transaction of faith in Jesus. As examples, a couple of chapters later in Romans 5:20 he says, *God's law was given so that all people could see how sinful they were. But as people sinned more and more, God's wonderful grace became more.*[14] And in the next chapter, 6:23, he says the famous, *For the wages of sin is death, but the free gift of God is eternal life through Christ Jesus our Lord.*"[15]

Jack stopped to organize his thoughts, wanting to spend more time on the heart of this question. After a moment, he said, "There is no doubt several others who have asked themselves the same question or wondered about the role of works in salvation. There are but three problems with that view: the *cross*, *grace* and the *Messianic Strain.*

"Starting with the *cross*, we need to ask ourselves this question: If works are sufficient… if they are *sufficient*… why did Jesus have to die? Why did he have to suffer the pain and degradation of being stretched and nailed to a tree with all the contempt and triumph that a rancher would stretch and nail the carcass of a predator to a barn wall?

"Paul answers those questions and at the same time addresses the issue of *grace* with these simple sentences in Romans 3: *Everyone has sinned. No one measures up to God's glory. The free gift of God's grace makes all of us right with Him. Christ Jesus paid the price to set us free.*[16]

"The last—the Messianic Strain—is a term used by some Biblical scholars to describe a prophetic thread of a savior's coming running through the entire Old Testament. It weaves through more than a dozen books… through Genesis, Deuteronomy, Psalms, Isaiah, Jeremiah, Hosea, Joel, Amos, Micah, Habakkuk, Haggai, Zechariah, and Malachi. Jews called the expected one the Messiah... the *Anointed One*. And nowhere is their belief in a *Messiah*, and their expectation of his coming, more clearly demonstrated than on a raucous Sunday when with unrestrained joy they lined the streets of Jerusalem, waved palms of honor and exultation to a man riding a donkey, and shouted *...Hosanna! How blessed is the one who comes in the name of the Lord, the King of Israel!"*[17]

Stepping to the side of the lectern, eyes on the floor, searching for the right words, Jack looked up at the class. Finding the words, his eyes returned to the floor, his mind racing to decide whether to speak them. He looked back up at the class, a pall of sadness now starting to shadow him, and said, "If against this background I think my goodness is sufficient… if I think my *goodness* is enough… then here is what I, Jack Kirk, am saying to God:

"Uh... Big Guy... Jack here... with a decision about my salvation...

"I've been watching me and I've got to say, I'm pretty impressed.

"I see a good heart that wants to help others, quick hands that write checks for the needy, and no majors like murder that would deem me a sinner.

"So, I need to tell you that I may call on you from time to time during a crisis in my life, but, except for that, I've decided that my good heart, good works, and good karma are going to be sufficient.

"Further, I frankly find the prophecy stuff in Genesis, Isaiah, etc., a bit over the top.

"And your grace deal? Nice... but not necessary.

"And Jesus' crucifixion thing? Thanks... but not needed.

"There.

"Done.

"I'm surprised! Telling you this was easier than I thought it would be. I guess I still don't realize that you're leaving this decision entirely up to me. And I suppose that—as long as I'm on this honesty streak—I need to tell you that this wasn't my decision alone. I was influenced by a guy—actually, a heck of guy who was strikingly charismatic, understanding, even encouraging—who says he knows you...

"Says he also knows your son...

"Says to say hello...

"Says—with a laugh that seemed a little odd—to send his regrets...

"Says—instead of "Stench", he wished you'd use his real name—Lucifer."

Jack stood quietly. Ten seconds of silence ticked by. He stepped back to the lectern feeling that he had again failed to make this truth clear, hoping again that someday his words would make those who thought that goodness, or works, or crystals, or astrology, or numerology, or Ouija boards, or tea leaves, or aromatherapy, or Da Vinci Code, or Skywalker's force—or whatever the spiritual placebo *du jour* was—see the absurdity… the futility… the impudence… the contempt… the consequence of such thought.

After another few seconds of silence, eyes on binder, appearing to look at notes though actually allowing the sense of failure to dissipate, Jack glanced up at the clock, saw that there was time to finish, and returned to the original lesson plan saying, "I want to take us back to our theme and to look at the seventh and final reason I believe it is so difficult to be a Christian in America.

"And to do that, I want to take us back to a definition Dee Dee gave us several weeks ago. You will recall that she said that our god is that *person* in whom—or *thing* in which—we place our expectation for necessities of life, for fulfillment, for peace.

"I agree with her. I believe God agrees with her. And I believe that puts God the father in a very tough three-way contest with two very prominent, very convenient, and very obliging gods: business and government.

"These of course could be called by different names. Business could be called the gospel of self. Government could be called the gospel of entitlement. And each becomes bad only in the extreme, because business is good when it serves, and government is good when it enables. But too many of us have gone too far with both… too many of us have exploited both… too many of us have made gods of both.

"And for many of us—and this is the scary part—it is the *natural* thing to do. It is especially natural for those in America whose god is business. In our remaining moments, I want to swing our focus from our current culture to our genealogical past and to how the latter makes finding life… *life* as a Christian, *life* as a servant, *life* as an adopted child of God… so very, very difficult."

Pulling a sheet of paper from the back of the binder, Jack said, "So here I go, back to Plymouth, back to Jamestown, back to our beginnings. Several years ago I came across this short sentence in a book that spoke volumes about who we were in the beginning as immigrants… and from that… who many of us are today as Americans. The book was *Improbable Victories* by John P. John which, as you would guess from the title, reviewed battles in which the victor—outmanned and outgunned—defeated a superior opponent. This particular sentence came from his description of the Battle of Sun Falls in 1814 in which the British were defeated by a small group of Americans whom the author styled as being particularly tough because *'...there had immigrated to the United States the most independent and industrias.'*[18]

"Independent'… 'industrias.' In those two words he caught the American Spirit… he defined our DNA… he described the core characteristics of our matriarchs and patriarchs that have made you and me descendants of some of the most hearty, most self-sustaining, most ambitious men and women the world has ever known… men and women who would risk life on the seas and life in tenements and life on frontiers to begin anew… who would measure their worth—and the worth of their neighbors—by accomplishments… who would be driven by this single indelible belief: *If you worked for it, you deserved it.*

"I want you to see this *legacy.*

"I want you to see this *heritage.*

"I want you to see that you and I have been genetically altered and permanently hardwired by our immigrating *fore*fathers, by our constitutional *founding* fathers, and for many of us by our unrelenting *birth* fathers to be self-reliant, self-determining, and self-sufficient.

"This hardwiring would enable them to survive at Jamestown and Plymouth, to fight at Concord and Lexington, to win at Trenton and Yorktown… to push through starvation and epidemics, to clear wilderness and swamps, to convert streams into mills and bays into harbors… to build sod houses on prairies and blaze wagon trails to Oregon… to link a continent with rails and people with phones.

"This is not hardwiring in the remote, the impersonal, the abstract… this is hardwiring in you, now, today. I don't care if your patriarchs and matriarchs found themselves in America because of a potato famine in Ireland, or slave traders in Africa, or religious persecution in Europe, or poverty in Mexico, or colonization by mother England, you are here, in this room, in that chair, because someone chose… *chose*!... to survive. It may have only been *one* someone and it may have only been at *one* moment, but that someone overcame poverty, or faced down bigots, or became educated, or bet on a business… and in the process programmed *you*… pedigreed *you*… hardwired *you*... with the DNA of *independence*—and in so doing made dependence… *dependence*... on God so very, very difficult."

Jack stepped back behind the stand, smiled and said, "If that is the bad news, this is the good news: You have others in your genealogy… others who preceded the Santa Maria and the Mayflower …others who faced and overcame obstacles… others who have left you with an *option* of alternative wiring.

"One was a fellow who faced and overcame the demons of his own making… of disappointing someone he loved… of personal failure… fellow by the name of Peter.

"Another was a fellow who faced and overcame the distrust of others… the pain of stonings …the confinement of prison… fellow by the name of Paul

"A third was a fellow who faced and overcame the disillusionment of his students… the disappointment of a nation… the temptings by the Tempter… fellow by the name of Jesus.

"I used the word 'option' a moment ago and use it again now. Rewiring your DNA is your choice. As I say that, I am reminded of this statement by William James—a 19th century medical doctor who founded and led Harvard's Psychology Department and is generally considered the father of American psychology."

Jack turned and read as he wrote on the whiteboard:

- Be careful of your thoughts, for thoughts become actions.
- Be careful of your actions, for actions become habits.
- Be careful of your habits, for habits become character.
- Be careful of your character, for that is your destiny.[19]

William James

Laying the marker in the tray, turning back to the class, Jack said, "Thoughts to destiny. How easy is the first. How eternal is the last. How much control you have… *you* have… over both, and how clear is the option offered you."

Closing his binder, he turned to Beverly and ask her to pass out the Q/A sheets which asked the what, why, and how of John 3:2. For the next twenty minutes they addressed and discussed the decisive difference between acknowledging and accepting Christ as the Son of God.

Jack closed the discussion and prepared to close the class by saying, "A couple of decades ago there was a movie called the *Americanization of Emily*. Our focus this morning has been on the Americanization of Christianity. To counter this cultural saturation of mind and soul… to alter your DNA from dependence on self to dependence on God… you must be determined, and you must be well-informed. You may also think that you need to be 'strong', but you don't because this has nothing to do with personal strength. It, however, has everything to do with personal self-discipline.

"You must have the self-discipline to *pray* for you cannot do it without prayer.

"You must have the self-discipline to *read* for you cannot do it without study.

"And you must have the self-discipline to *think* for you cannot do it without questioning.

"This questioning must be careful, thoughtful, analytical… it must be of that which you *feel*, that which you *hear*, and that which you are *taught*. The last... *taught*… is true irrespective of the source of that teaching… whether that source is direct teaching from me in this class, a pastor's message from a pulpit, or a song from a choir.

"Do you wonder about my including a choir? Teacher and preacher, yes, but a choir? Here's an example: In our worship service, we often sing a hymn or praise song which says, 'make me more Holy… make me more righteous.' In fact, we often find ourselves repeating and repeating the verse though it can be easily misleading.

"It can be misleading because there is no more chance of making *me*—the person, the being, the mortal—more Holy with pleas and petitions than there is of making a baby's bottle more nutritious with washings and scrubbings. One can boil, bake, scald, and steam the bottle and it will never become *more* nutritious, *more* wholesome, *more* healthful because it will never become more than it was created to be: a *container*. In like manner, I will never become more than I was created to be: a *vessel*. And as milk in the bottle is the *sole* source of nutrition, the Holy Spirit in me is the *sole* source of Holiness. That is why 1st Corinthians 15:44 says *If there is a physical body, there is also a spiritual body.*[20] That is why Galatians 5 says that... *the fruit of the spirit...* hear that clearly: The fruit of the Spirit, not of me… i*s love, joy, peace, longsuffering, gentleness, goodness, faith, meekness, and temperance.*[21] And that is why Jesus… even Jesus… said in John 14:10 *The words I speak unto you I speak not of myself, but the father that dwelleth in me, he doeth the work.*[22]

"Pressing this analogy one step further, as one sees the contents—the milk—when they look at a bottle, so should they see the Holy Spirit when they look at me. They will not, of course, see him , but they should sense his presence in my speech, attitude, action, bearing, confidence, gentleness, self-control… in what Galatians 5 promises as the fruit of the Spirit.

"And that's what it comes down to, this examination of *Christianity in the American Culture*…it comes down to an examination of *Christianity in Me*."

"Next week, '*Christianity in the Family.*'"

He paused, smiled again, looked at the class and said, "How odd that as I say that, I think of us—you and me—and our Family in Christianity."

Still smiling, he said, "Bev, would you close us…."

###

Your Takeaways and Action Items from this Chapter

Takeaway 1

(page__)

Takeaway 2

(page__)

Takeaway 3

(page__)

Your Takeaways and Action Items from this Chapter (cont.)

Action Item 1

(page__)

Action Item 2

(page__)

Action Item 3

(page__)

What Is Your Mini-Mission?

Chapter 12 - Sunday, July 31

Jack looked over the class as Beverly led the group in prayer. Though he looked, he did not see. He did not see because his mind was focused inwardly. Had he seen, he would have noticed that the room was overflowing, that extra chairs had been brought in, that many were standing along the back wall. And had he listened, he would have noticed that there was less chatter than normally. Inwardly, where his attention and emotions were concentrated, his thoughts were solely this: *It is better this way: quick... no long goodbyes... just go.* When she finished, he walked to the music stand, paused for a moment, and said, "Good morning."

Pausing again he said, "As you know, for some time Kelli and I have been moving toward that day when it would be, literally for us, moving day. Last Monday I received a call which has changed our schedule and we will be leaving much sooner than first planned. In fact, I left last Monday, returned last night, and leave again tomorrow. I'll return on weekends; Kelli will stay here until the house is sold."

As quiet filled the room, as they listened to confirmation of what they had heard earlier in the week, he continued, "This means that today is our last Sunday together as a class, and *that* means," he said, smiling, "that my lesson will be something of a summary… for many of you, a summary of what I've taught over the past 12 weeks, and for others, over the past 12 years."

Picking up and setting the music stand aside, he thought, smiling again, *I can do this.* Stepping closer to the class, into the spot where the lectern had been, he said, "In fact, I don't want to teach today… I just want to talk… about this that is happening to Kelli and me… about grandchildren… about friends… about life.

"I want to begin with this move… this leaving this place… after all these years and all our expectations that we would forever be part of this community, this church, this kinship. I want to begin here because I believe what Kelli and I are experiencing is no different from what others *have* experienced, others *will* experience, and God *wants* us to experience.

"Now, I don't mean by that that one must physically move from this house to that house, or this city to that city, to experience a move. I don't believe it because to *live* is to move… to move *chronologically* from infant to toddler, from teenager to young adult, from middle age to senior citizen. It means to move *socially* from grade school to high school, from new employee to old guard, from new acquaintance to trusted friend. It means to move in *responsibility* from student to teacher, from guest to host, from care-receiver to caregiver."

Jack paused again—so badly wanting to make this point about dreams and directions and service clear—then said, "I believe these *natural* moves that I just described are God-*intended,* and I believe the most *powerful* of these are God-*driven.*

"By God-driven, I mean that there is *something* at the core of each of us… *something* planted there by God… *something* essential to his Great Design. I believe that this something is so unique to *each* of us that if you and I *don't* cherish it… *don't* pursue it… *don't* do it, then that something he wants, *won't* get done … not by the one he intended… not by you… and not by me."

Jack took a few steps to the right, glancing down as he formed his next thoughts, then looking at the class, continued, "This is not about being the person who discovers a cure for cancer, eliminates world hunger, or establishes global peace. This is about *you and me*… where we are today, right now, this minute… where we are socially, financially, and professionally… where we are in terms of gender, age, and family… where we are philosophically, attitudinally, and spiritually.

"Sometimes we feel as if there is not a *great* calling, there is *no* calling. Sometimes we feel that if we are drawn to do the expected—to be a loving parent… to be a dependable tither… to be a conscientious employee—that that doesn't really count in God's Cosmic Plan. The truth is *it does* count… it *is* what he wants… it *is* part of his purpose for your life. And to that end, I believe he gave each of us special talents. I also believe a harsh judgement awaits us if we do not use those talents.

"Would someone turn to Matthew 25 and read verses 14 through 30?" For a few moments there was the sound of Bibles being opened and pages being turned, then the silence was broken as a man from the seventh row read from the New King James Version:

> *"For the kingdom of heaven is like a man traveling to a far country, who called his own servants and delivered his goods to them. And to one he gave five talents, to another two, and to another one, to each according to his own ability; and immediately he went on a journey.*
>
> *Then he who had received the five talents went and traded with them and made another five talents. And likewise, he who had received two gained two more also. But he who had received one went and dug in the ground and hid his lord's money. After a long time, the lord of those servants came and settled accounts with them.*
>
> *So he who had received five talents came and brought five other talents, saying, 'Lord, you delivered to me five talents; look, I have gained five more talents besides them.' His lord said to him, 'Well done, good and faithful servant; you were faithful over a few things, I will make you ruler over many things. Enter into the joy of your lord.'*
>
> *He also who had received two talents came and said, 'Lord, you delivered to me two talents; look, I have gained two more talents besides them.' His lord said to him, 'Well done, good and faithful servant; you have been faithful over a few things, I will make you ruler over many things. Enter into the joy of your lord.'*
>
> *Then he who had received the one talent came and said, 'Lord, I knew you to be a hard man, reaping where you have not sown, and gathering where you have not scattered seed. And I was afraid and went and hid your talent in the ground. Look, there you have what is yours.'*
>
> *But his lord answered and said to him, 'You wicked and lazy servant, you knew that I reap where I have not sown, and gather where I have not scattered seed. So you ought to have deposited my money with the bankers, and at my coming I would have received back my own with interest. Therefore, take the talent from him, and give it to him who has ten talents.' For to everyone who has, more will be given, and he will have abundance; but from him who does not have, even what he has will be taken away. And cast the unprofitable servant into the outer darkness. There will be weeping and gnashing of teeth."*[1]

"Thanks, Terry," Jack said, then to the class, "Did you hear what the servant said, '*I was afraid, and went and hid your talent in the ground?*[2]

"And did you hear the master's response, *You wicked and lazy servant?*[3]

"I'll tell you folks, I don't think this parable simply *happens* to be in the Bible. I don't think the Holy Spirit one day chatted with Matthew about bulking up his book by tossing in some incidentals. I don't think the point is unclear that we are each given talents—not financial units as used here, but gifts and skills, abilities and aptitudes. And I don't think this issue of *our* stewardship of talents entrusted to *us* is extraneous to the conduct of our lives… irrelevant to the core of our purpose… invulnerable to Jesus' judgment.

"On the contrary, I think this is one of the most important and most dismissed messages in God's word. I think this is a remarkable lesson about fear, about service, and about life. And I encourage you to make this Scripture your focus in your quiet time and prayer time each morning this week. As you do, be prepared for God's moving in your life. And… who knows… maybe it is into *you* that God wants to implant… or simply reveal… a talent, a calling, a dream. If you say that—given your circumstances—you doubt it, I would say that if God can impregnate a virgin with a child, he can impregnate you with a dream.

"Before we move away from this matter of dreams, I want to share with you one more brief thought. In your pursuit of God's will, be particularly careful of two threats. I say this in the context of something we read a few weeks ago by Theodore Austin-Sparks who said that we often find ourselves in some great battle and expect God to enter on our side to fight for and deliver us. He said that that is not the case, that God doesn't *deliver* us, that instead he *enlarges* us.

"That, I believe, will be true… but I also believe that *this* can be true: Just as God wants to use you as the principal device through which he intends to bring about his purpose, it can also be you… *you*… who may unwittingly be the biggest obstacle in this process. To illustrate, think of God's means of delivering his will as being a garden hose. As water freely flows through a hose so he intends his blessings to freely flow through you. But he cannot do this if at the end of the hose you restrict the flow by imposing *your* will… specifically, your will in the form of pride or fear… *pride* that keeps you from asking for the help of those who could assist… *fear* that keeps you from risking the opinion of those you respect.

"I don't suggest that this is an easy matter. I don't suggest that you act imprudently. And I don't suggest that you pursue your vision at the expense of others pursuing theirs—*ever!*

"What I do suggest is that you be conscious of these two shadow demons. What I do suggest is that pride and fear can unconsciously affect your life and God's will. And, what I do suggest is that you not unintentionally inhibit how God may expand you."

Pausing, Jack looked them in the eyes and carefully said, "If you feel chosen, selected, directed to do something God-led, then *pray* like it. *Think* like it. *Act* like it."

Pausing again, he said, "Some in this room, perhaps several, might say, 'I did that: I pursued …but I failed.' To you I would ask 'by whose definition did you fail: by yours?... by the world's?... by God's? How can you *know*, how do you *measure*, how do you *count* the lives you touched… the examples you set… the lesson you taught?

"Thinking of this, I am reminded of the children of a good friend of mine who told me that seeing how their father dealt with a major setback had been one of the most inspirational lessons of their lives. I know that in talking to him—I'll call him Matt—*I* was inspired. It came about one summer evening years ago as we sat on his deck watching the sun set. It was days after he had been fired… *fired.* The circumstances of his dismissal are relevant, so I'll summarize them: He was the marketing director of a small company that specialized in manufacturing lawn irrigation products for a limited number of large retail distributors who then sold the hardware under their private brands. Occasionally a retailer would develop a unique feature which gave their product a competitive advantage. These were called proprietary features, with proprietary meaning Matt's company would manufacture these for them on the handshake agreement that—without the consent of the developer—they would not include the feature in products they manufactured for other clients. A feature developed by one client proved particularly popular. Owners of the company saw opportunity for a major increase in sales, market share, and national presence if the retailer would allow other customers to use it. Matt approached the client. The client declined. The owners told Matt to use it anyway. Matt said no.

"As we sat on his deck, the inevitable question from me came up, and I asked, 'Matt, how are you doing?' I expected him to express concern about holding on to the house… anxiety about keeping the kids in college… anger about the wrong thing happening from doing the right thing. To my surprise, he said, 'We're going to come out of this. My biggest concern is that I will have been found faithful, on the other side, when we do.' I knew he wasn't talking about marital but spiritual fidelity, and then he went ahead to tell me about the last verse of Psalm 33. It was the first time I had paid attention to it, and—as you now know—it has become one of my favorites. The verse says, as you have heard me quote before... *our heart shall rejoice in Him, because we have trusted in His holy name*.[4] The emphasis is not in the thanksgiving *after* something has been done, but the joy in trusting *before*."

Still talking conversationally, Jack said, "That night, Matt became an inspiration… a picture… an icon to me of what a faith-filled man should be in the toughest of times.

"I believe only the inspired can inspire. In large part, his inspiration came from the Scripture I just quoted.

"In large part it came from his wife, Susan, whose confidence in him never wavered… or if it did, she never let him know it. By the way, I don't think it ever wavered because I believe she knew his faith and knew the God Matt was depending on to enable him to take care of the family.

"And in large part it came from Matt's knowledge of the Bible—not only of specific verses like the one I just quoted which feeds the mind, but characters who become mental models who feed the soul… role models who give us strength and patience, if not understanding, in that which we are experiencing.

"As evening moved from dusk to dark, we talked about these characters and the models they represented to him. Particularly, we talked about those who seemingly ended up in the *wrong* place for doing the *right* thing. We spent a lot of time talking about *the* classic example of this—Joseph in the Old Testament—and we talked about the clear lesson Joseph teaches: to never… *never*...," Jack paused, looked at the class, searching their eyes for understanding of this essential truth, then continued firmly, "…hear me on this… to never... *never*... judge God's love… by your circumstances."

Glancing at the floor, Jack formed his thoughts, then said, "Before I speak about Joseph, this man of *faith*… this man who conscientiously pursued what he deemed to be God's code of conduct… I want to speak about two people who *violated* God's trust, who acted *contrary* to God's will… and examine how God treated them. I want to do this because there may be some in this room who are thinking 'you don't know what I have done… you don't know how I have sinned… you don't know how far from God and his love this has placed me.' If that is what *you* are thinking, I want you to revisit the Bible's most famous story in Genesis and the world's most grievous sin in Chapter 3.

"The story is Adam and Eve.

"The sin was disobedience in their eating the fruit of the tree of knowledge of good and evil.

"The *eternal* consequence of their act for mankind is recorded in Romans 5:12: *sin came into the world through one man.*[5]

"The *immediate* consequence for *women* is recorded in Genesis 3:16 where God says *I will greatly multiply your pain in childbirth, in pain you will bring forth children.*[6]

"The *immediate* consequence for *men* is recorded in verses 17 through 19 where God says *cursed is the ground for your sake; in toil you shall eat of it all the days of your life.*[7]

"And the *immediate* consequence for *both*—though only man is referred to—is in verses 23 and 24 which says *Therefore God sent him out of the garden of Eden... and He placed cherubim at the east... and a flaming sword... to guard the way to the tree of life."*[8]

Jack stopped speaking. Then into the stillness of the room he said, "Now, I want you to see what God did *after* multiplying women's pain in birth and cursing the ground from which man through toil would bring forth food, but *before* sending them out of the garden. Open your Bibles to Genesis 3:21." After giving them a moment to find the passage, Jack quoted the verse, saying, *And the LORD God made for Adam and for his wife garments of skins and clothed them.*[9]

Jack looked at the class and said, "Weeks ago, when we began this farewell series, I said that there are three questions you need to apply to every verse: *What* is being said? *Why* is it being said? *How* does it apply to my life?

"You don't need me to interpret this inconceivable, inexplicable, incomprehensible act of God's ongoing love, compassion, understanding toward these two who had just damned the world.

"And you don't need me to explain his ongoing love, compassion, and understanding toward you... irrespective of what you've done, irrespective of what you feel you deserve, irrespective of how far you feel you are from his care."

Jack glanced at the floor again, then continued, "I want to return to the point I was making about the example set by Joseph.

"This is a great story about bad things happening to good people after doing the right thing ...about remaining faithful in adversity... about never judging God's love by your circumstances.

"This is a story that demands study, understanding, and application, whether your information source is the book of Genesis in the Bible or *The Ballad of Little Joe* in a Veggie Tale video.

"And this is a story of one of the most dramatic, most sweeping, most decisive epics in world history—the story of the conception, gestation, and birth of the nation, Israel."

Jack paused, looked over the class, then began, "You may recall the early events in Joseph's life. You may remember that he was favored by his father, Israel... that Israel gave him a coat of many colors... that Joseph had a dream of the moon and sheaves bowing down to him... that he told his brothers the dream meant that they would bow down to him... that—because of this interpretation, the coat, and their father's obvious favor—his brothers were insanely jealous... that they sold him to a caravan bound for Egypt... that they told their father he had been killed by a lion... that in a slave market in Egypt, he was bought by Potiphar, an officer of Pharaoh... that Joseph excelled in serving Potiphar and was made manager of his household... that—for reasons we'll explore in a moment—he was sent to prison where his interpretation of dreams eventually led him to Pharaoh... that Joseph accurately interpreted Pharaoh's dreams... that Pharaoh made him his second in command to prepare Egypt for, as the dreams predicted, seven years of famine... that the famine also struck Canaan and drove Joseph's ten brothers to Egypt to request food... that the official they met there was, unknown to them, Joseph... that he eventually revealed himself and engineered the relocation of the entire family —his father Israel, all eleven brothers, their children, everyone—into Egypt... that over the next 400 years in Egypt—in its economic, political, and military womb—Israel's family grew into a people of millions... that there arose a Pharaoh who *knew not Joseph* and, fearful that they might overthrow the government, enslaved the children of Israel... that Moses was found in a reed basket, raised by an Egyptian princess, and called by God to free his people... that Moses led them from Egypt in the Exodus, prepared them for self-rule at Mt. Sinai and, after 40 years of wandering, saw them enter the land promised, fulfilling the original covenant God had made with Abraham.

"This fulfilling of God's covenant, this entry of God's chosen people onto the world stage to eternally influence humanity, was a profoundly long and remarkably delicate process. But few moments in the process were as *pivotal*… as subject to *failure*… as dependent upon *character*… as the blinks-of-an-eye seconds in which Joseph made the decision to do what was *right*.

"Would someone find and read Genesis 39 from about verse one through twenty?" After a moment, Dean Camp read aloud from the NIV:

> *"Now Joseph had been taken down to Egypt. Potiphar, an Egyptian who was one of Pharaoh's officials, the captain of the guard, bought him from the Ishmaelites who had taken him there. The Lord was with Joseph and he prospered, and he lived in the house of his Egyptian master. When his master saw that the Lord was with him and that the Lord gave him success in everything he did, Joseph found favor in his eyes and became his attendant. Potiphar put him in charge of his household, and he entrusted to his care everything he owned. From the time he put him in charge of his household and of all that he owned, the Lord blessed the household of the Egyptian because of Joseph. The blessing of the Lord was on everything Potiphar had, both in the house and in the field. So he left in Joseph's care everything he had; with Joseph in charge, he did not concern himself with anything except the food he ate.*
>
> *Now Joseph was well-built and handsome, and after a while his master's wife took notice of Joseph and said, 'Come to bed with me!' But he refused. 'With me in charge,' he told her, 'my master does not concern himself with anything in the house; everything he owns he has entrusted to my care. No one is greater in this house than I am. My master has withheld nothing from me except you, because you are his wife. How then could I do such a wicked thing and sin against God?'*
>
> *And though she spoke to Joseph day after day, he refused to go to bed with her or even be with her. One day he went into the house to attend to his duties, and none of the household servants were inside. She caught him by his cloak and said, 'Come to bed with me!' But he left his cloak in her hand and ran out of the house. When she saw that he had left his cloak in her hand and had run out of the house, she called her household servants.*
>
> *'Look,' she said to them, 'this Hebrew has been brought to us to make sport of us! He came in here to sleep with me, but I screamed. When he heard me scream for help, he left his cloak beside me and ran out of the house.' She kept his cloak beside her until his master came home. Then she told him this story: 'That Hebrew slave you brought us came to me to make sport of me. But as soon as I screamed for help, he left his cloak beside me and ran out of the house.' When his master heard the story his wife told him, saying, 'This is how your slave treated me,' he burned with anger. Joseph's master took him and put him in prison, the place where the king's prisoners were confined."*[11]

"Thanks, Dean," Jack said, then, looking over the class summarized the story: "One man in one moment held true to what was right, and the consequence—on world history, on my friend Matt, on Matt's children—is incalculable. And that leads me to say this to those of you who have in the past… who may be at this moment… who will be in the future… facing a decision and measuring the consequence, do as Matt did: Look to God, look to the Bible, and look to this man Joseph for courage, inspiration, and hope.

"I add 'hope' to this summary because, as Matt pointed out to me, that is an important part of the last verse of Psalm 33. Together, verses 21 and 22 in the King James versions says this: *For our heart shall rejoice in him, because we have trusted in His holy name. Let thy mercy, O Lord, be upon us, according as we hope in thee.*[12] The NIV puts it this way: *For in Him does our heart rejoice, because we have trusted—relied on and been confident—in His holy name. Let Your mercy and loving -kindness, O Lord, be upon us, in proportion to our waiting and hoping for You.* [13] Simply put, this says 'bless me Lord *according*—meaning to the extent, to the degree, to the level—that I place my *hope*, my *trust*, my *expectation* in you.' I could spend the remainder of the hour exploring the life lesson at the end of these two brief verses, but I want to spend the balance of the time talking about the life lesson at the beginning of the verses... about *rejoicing*... about *joy*."

Standing quietly for a beat, Jack smiled and said, "I find it interesting that... for those of you who joined me for the first time 12 Sundays ago... the teaching point has come full circle... that we are back to that which Jesus emphasized that last night with his lesson of the vine... that we are back to this word, joy... that we are back to Jesus saying these unimaginable words as he walked toward those unspeakable horrors: *I have told you this so that my joy may be in you... and that your joy may be complete."*[14]

Glancing at the clock, he said, "Our time is about up. I want to leave you with two things. First a poem by Helen Steiner Rice, *Someone Cares*, that says the source of *joy* is in *giving*.

A very favorite story of mine
Is about two seas in Palestine
One is a sparkling sapphire jewel,
Its waters are clean and clear and cool,
Along its shores the children play
And travelers seek it on their way,
And nature gives so lavishly
Her choicest gems to the Galilee.
But on to the south the Jordan flows
Into a sea where nothing grows,
No splash of fish, no singing bird,
No children's laughter is ever heard,
The air hangs heavy all around
And nature shuns this barren ground.
Both seas receive the Jordan's flow,
the water is just the same, we know,
but one of the seas, like liquid sun,
can warm the hearts of everyone,
While farther south another sea
is dead and dark and miserly—
it takes each drop the Jordan brings
and to each drop it fiercely clings
it hoards and holds the Jordan's waves
until like shackled, captured slaves
the fresh, clear Jordan turns to salt
and dies within the Dead Sea's vault.
But the Jordan flows on rapturously

As it enters and leaves the Galilee,
For every drop that Jordan gives
Becomes a laughing wave that lives—
For the Galilee gives back each drop,
Its waters flow and never stop
And in this laughing, living sea
That takes and gives so generously
We find the way to life and living...
Is not in keeping, but in giving."[15]

Jack smiled as his mind ran to a tangential thought, then said, "Could I enter a statement from a secular source into this spiritual theme of giving. I was surprised to read this several years ago. The first time I saw it, it was attributed to Picasso. I've since seen possible attributions to Shakespeare and others. Irrespective of who said it first, I like the simplicity, the clarity, the truth in what is said... maybe that's because I believe this should be the universal refrain, from all of us, for all of life."

Turning to the whiteboard, picking up the marker, Jack wrote:

> The meaning of life is to find your gift.
> The purpose of life is to give it away.
> Picasso

Turning back to the class, Jack said, "The second thing I want to leave with you—and the last thing I want to ask of you—is this: Become a Galilee... become a giver... become a Godsend.

"Specifically, I want you to do this... listen to me... I want you to do this: I want you to start your own, private, personal, Little Mission. I want you to look around your world and find a cause that needs your help, a group that needs your encouragement, a mission that needs your talent.

"Now, a 'mission' is different from a 'ministry.' A ministry is *ongoing*. A mission is *intermittent*. A ministry is what you do for your family, friends, colleagues, and others close to you on a routine, daily basis. A mission is what you do for those you don't know and who don't know you... those who are awaiting delivery of your talents or touch to improve their lives. Your Little Mission may take the form of teaching an immigrant to speak English... collecting old laptops for Guatemala preachers ...sponsoring at-risk kids of imprisoned parents to a Christian summer camp... buying and distributing gloves to the homeless in winter... providing a small scholarship for books for struggling ministerial students."

Pausing for a moment, considering whether to speak of what had just come to mind, then deciding he would, he looked up at the class and said, "Surprisingly… remarkably… invariably, it is—to the person doing the giving—'no big deal.' There is no better example of this than our daughter-in-law, Allie, who happened to mention something a couple of weeks ago. Here's the story: Over the July 4th holiday, we were with our kids and grandkids. One afternoon as Allie, Kelli, and I watched our grandsons play in the water, we asked when they would be coming to see us. She said she'd have to check her Saturday schedule, but didn't believe it would be long. Soccer season was over and Saturday obligations were rare, so out of curiosity I asked. She said she spent some Saturday nights with a friend of a friend… a person she had heard about when her friend, Emily, begged off a Saturday-night dinner invitation because of a prior commitment.

"As it turned out, Emily's commitment was to Linda, a single mom in her early 30s with three children, ages six, eight, and ten. She has no living relatives and a court order protecting the children from their absent and abusive father. She is bedridden because of a rare, incurable, degenerative disease called Mitochondrial Myopathy, or MITO. She is unable to care for her children who also have the disease, who are also bedridden, and who are rapidly declining mentally and physically… the most conspicuous example being the ten-year old who now functions as a seven-year old. Nurses are there throughout the days. Friends are there throughout the nights. And Allie is there two Saturday nights a month. Allie leaves her family in the care of their father to bathe, feed, and tuck away for the night… drives by herself through darkening streets of a large city… to Linda, who is paralyzed from the waist down, where—though drained of energy herself from a day of parenting one boy fully into the terrible-twos and another boy fully into testing the boundaries of a five-year old's world—she sits, reads, naps, and watches the clock… awaiting the time to give Linda's six-year old daughter her 1:00 AM and 5:00 AM feedings through an IV tube.

"No big deal to Allie.

"A Godsend to Linda.

"Find *your* Little Mission... your Mini-Mission

"Look for that which is out of the ordinary—giving to United Way doesn't count.

"Make it somewhat sacrificial in time or money or both—keeping in mind that your primary responsibility is your daily ministry.

"Make it something to which you feel drawn—recognizing that this is not simply a punch in the card of life.

" Do it anonymously—not only are we not after punches, we're not after points.

"And do it in love—for, as 1st Corinthians 13:13 says, *And now abide faith, hope, love, these three; but the greatest of these is love."*[16]

Jack stopped. Took a breath. Glanced at the clock. Saw that there was time left, but thought, *that's it... you did it... go... now.* He took another breath, stood there in silence, wanting some way to say 'thanks,'… to say how much they'd meant to him… to say how much he'd miss them. His mind was a blank. He could think of nothing sufficient. Then… into the hanging silence… he simply said, "This is not goodbye."

He turned to ask Beverly to close when from the back of the room a voice boomed, "*Jack!*" Jack looked to the sound and saw a mountain making its way down the aisle between rows of chairs. It was Tug. In one large hand the Education Director held up a book. Jack recognized it as his own and thought *Tug! Autograph? No!*

Tug arrived at the front, stood before Jack and said, "Jack, we have known for some time that this moment was coming. We have also known for a longer time how you felt about autographs. But this is our turn, and it is my privilege on behalf of the church and your class to present to you this…."

Tug held out to Jack his book.

Jack looked at Tug, then at the book.

With emotions running from curious to stunned, Jack took the book, glanced at Tug, looked back at the book, and opened it. Across the first page was a handwritten message in blue ink from the senior pastor… across the second was a note in day-glow yellow from a kindergarten teacher… across the third was a wish in green felt-tip from a janitor… and across the next and the next… for scores of pages… notes and wishes, regards and goodbyes… in gel pens and Crayon, Sharpies and ball points …in small script and large caps, with loopy dots and colored hearts… all signed… all autographed …all tearing at Jack's heart.

The first jolt hit his throat as he choked back the lump.

The next hit his chest as Tug crushed him in a bear hug.

The last hit his eyes as he pulled away from Tug and turned away from his class….

Epilogue

Twenty minutes later Jack took Kelli by the hand, whispered, "It's time," and led her from the classroom through remaining well-wishers into the hallway.

From there, still tightly holding her hand with his right, his book with his left, he guided them out of the building and across the parking lot to his car.

Once they were in, buckled, and fighting for smiles, she said, "Don't go yet."

Surprised, he shifted to neutral, pulled on the brake, and again took her hand to encourage her. To his further surprise, he saw that she didn't need encouragement, that she was actually smiling… broadly.

He then heard her say as she opened the glove box and removed a small package, "I have a going-away gift for you."

"You're kidding," he said as he looked at her and the package, and marveled again at the strength and fortitude of this woman. "What is it?" he asked as he finally took the small wrapped box.

Still smiling, proud of him for who he was, proud of herself for what she had done, she said, "Tapes… recordings… of these last lessons… for your next book… *Jack's Last Class.*"

###

Your Takeaways and Action Items from this Chapter

Takeaway 1

(page__)

Takeaway 2

(page__)

Takeaway 3

(page__)

Your Takeaways and Action Items from this Chapter (cont.)

Action Item 1

(page__)

Action Item 2

(page__)

Action Item 3

(page__)

What Now?

I hope *Jack's Last Class* has blessed you as much in the reading as it did me in the writing.

I want to close with this question: *What now*?

I'd like to suggest this simple answer: *Share it.*

First, post your review and stars☆☆☆☆☆ on Amazon, then—if you feel this is a story that should be shared—here are 15 ideas. For starters, pick three:

1. ☐ Give copies to local faith-based Shelters for battered women and children.
2. ☐ Give copies to local faith-based Sober Homes for recovering drug/alcoholic-addicted.
3. ☐ Give copies to local faith-based Homes for PTSD and civilian-life re-entry vets.
4. ☐ Give copies to faith-based Halfway Houses for released women and men inmates.
5. ☐ Give copies to your church library, Education Director, and small group leaders.
6. ☐ Give a copy to local newspaper religion writer.
7. ☐ Give two copies to local parochial school libraries.
8. ☐ Give two copies to libraries of local senior citizen and assisted-living communities.
9. ☐ Give two copies to barber, stylist, dentist, doctor, attorney for waiting-room reading.
10. ☐ Give a copy to the chair-bound due to dialysis, chemotherapy, disability, or accident.
11. ☐ Give copies to police, military, hospital, workplace, or college-campus chaplains.
12. ☐ Keep six copies at home to give when occasions arise to a handyman, neighbor, etc.
13. ☐ Send a copy to a deployed service member, college student, distanced career starter.
14. ☐ Call family and friends and start a Zoom Bible study, post on Facebook.
15. ☐ Pray for America: That we fulfill the vision of a people *guided* by God, *ruled* by law, *founded* and *fostered* by a culture of mutual respect, open civility, and neighborly care.

Source Notes

Chapter 1:

1. International Standard Version (ISV)
2. New International Version (NIV)
3. New International Version (NIV)
4. Ray Van Der Lann – Faith Lessons: Old Testament (video)
5. *Napa Stories* by Michael Chiarello
6. New International Version (NIV)
7. *Napa Stories* by Michael Chiarello

Chapter 2:

1. International Standard Bible Encyclopedia
2. International Standard Bible Encyclopedia
3. King James Version (KJV)
4. International Standard Bible Encyclopedia
5. International Standard Version (ISV)
6. International Standard Bible Encyclopedia
7. *CONFIDENCE*, by Rosabeth Moss Kanter
8. New International Version (NIV)

Chapter 3:

1. International Standard Version (ISV)
2. *Mere Christianity* by C.S. Lewis
3. New International Version (NIV)
4. New International Version (NIV)
5. New Century Version (NCV)
6. New International Version (NIV)

Chapter 4:

1. *Mere Christianity* by C.S. Lewis
2. *Mere Christianity* by C.S. Lewis
3. King James Version (KJV)
4. New International Version (NIV)
5. Amplified Version, Classic Edition
6. Amplified Version, Classic Edition
7. New International Version (NIV)
8. English Standard Version (ESV)
9. English Standard Version (ESV)
10. Amplified Version, Classic Edition
11. American Standard Version (ASV)
12. English Standard Version (ESV)
13. International Standard Bible Encyclopedia
14. International Standard Version (ISV)
15. New King James Version (NKJV)
16. New International Version (NIV)
17. New International Version (NIV)

Chapter 5:

1. *The Holy Spirit* by Billy Graham
2. *The Holy Spirit* by Billy Graham
3. International Standard Version (ISV)
4. King James Version (KJV)
5. International Standard Version Encyclopedia

6. International Standard Version Encyclopedia
7. King James Version (KJV)
8. International Standard Version (ISV)
9. International Standard Version (ISV)
10. International Standard Version (ISV)
11. International Standard Version (ISV)
12. International Standard Version (ISV)
13. International Standard Version (ISV)

Chapter 6:
1. International Standard Version (ISV)
2. King James Version (KJV)
3. International Standard Version (ISV)
4. International Standard Version (ISV)
5. International Standard Version (ISV)
6. New International Version (NIV)
7. *The Green Letters* by Miles J. Stanford
8. *The Green Letters* by Miles J. Stanford
9. *The Green Letters* by Miles J. Stanford
10. King James Version (KJV)
11. *The Green Letters* by Miles J. Stanford
12. *The Green Letters* by Miles J. Stanford
13. *The Green Letters* by Miles J. Stanford
14. *The Green Letters* by Miles J. Stanford

Chapter 7:
1. *The Case for A Creator* by Lee Strobel
2. *The Case for A Creator* by Lee Strobel
3. *The Case for A Creator* by Lee Strobel
4. *The Case for A Creator* by Lee Strobel
5. *The Case for A Creator* by Lee Strobel
6. *Westminster Shorter Catechism*

Chapter 8:
1. John 14:9 - New International Version (NIV)
2. *Whatever Happened to the Human Race* by Francis Schaeffer
3. New International Version (NIV)
4. New Century Version (NCV)
5. English Standard Version (ESV)
6. King James Version (KJV)

Chapter 9:
1. New International Version (NIV)
2. New International Version (NIV)
3. Young's Literal Translation (YLT)
4. Webster's Bible (WB)
5. americanhumanist.org/what-is-humanism/manifesto3/
6. Text of Address by Alexander Solzhenitsyn at Harvard Class Day Afternoon Exercises, Thursday, June 8, 1978
7. www.americanhumanist.org
8. *The Screwtape Letters* by C. S. Lewis

Chapter 10:
1. Focus on the Family, Robert Veldarde
2. *Mere Christianity* by C. S. Lewis
3. *The Holy Spirit* by Billy Graham

4. New King James Version (NKJV)

Chapter 11:

1. *You Don't Have to Take Your Clothes Off to Cheat* by Carolyn Susman of the Palm Beach Post
2. *Emotional Infidelity* by M. Gary Neuman
3. *Brain Dump* by C. L. Howell
4. New King James Version (NKJV)
5. New King James Version (NKJV)
6. New International Version (NIV)
7. New International Version (NIV)
8. New International Version (NIV)
9. International Standard Version (ISV)
10. International Standard Version (ISV)
11. New International Version (NIV)
12. New International Version (NIV)
13. New International Version (NIV)
14. New Living Translation (NLT)
15. New Living Translation (NLT)
16. New International Version (NIV)
17. International Standard Version (ISV)
18. Improbable Victories by John P. John
19. English Standard Version (ESV)
20. King James Version (KJV)
21. King James Version (KJV)

Chapter 12:

1. New King James Version (NKJV)
2. New King James Version (NKJV)
3. New King James Version (NKJV)
4. Psalm 33:21, American Standard Version (ASV)
5. New American Standard Version (NASV)
6. New American Standard Version (NASV)
7. New American Standard Version (NASV)
8. King James Version (KJV)
9. English Standard Version (ESV)
10. New International Version (NIV)
11. New International Version (NIV)
12. King James Version (KJV)
13. New International Version (NIV)
14. New International Version (NIV)
15. Someone Cares by H. S. Rice
16. New King James Version (NKJV)

Fictional People and Places: The following people and places were created by the author to carry the narrative from an isolated selection of Scriptural passages to a cohesive story:

People: Jack Kirk, Kelli Kirk, Chuck Wilson, Dee Dee Devonshire (and her dissertation), Dr. Mark Taylor, Ted Taylor (Tug), Sandra Blake, Dianne Downing, Beverly, and a host of class members who played cameo roles in asking questions, quoting Scripture, and accommodating guests. Allie Kirk and Linda (MITO) are real people and events with changed names. Poems in Chapters 3 and 8 are by the author.

Places: Chicago's off-campus seminary program, Bernkirche Theological Seminary (a seminary by a different name existed in Switzerland in the 70s-80s which served as a model for BTS), Geneva LeFinfintel Ballet Academic, and Madison-Mason University.

Non-fictional People and Places: Dr. Bruce Wilkinson, Paul Harvey, Dr. Abraham Maslow, Peggy Noonan, Pew Research, Westminster Assembly, University of Bern, Helen Steiner Rice, and all cited/footnoted above.

Note to Group Leaders

My experience has been that the smaller the Group Leader's role in this study the better. This because the format of Takeaway questions from their weekly reading leads members to identify segments that are most important to them and initiate discussion themselves.

So, I encourage postponing any summary of the chapter by Leaders until the end of the session, and begin the session by randomly picking a person and asking, *"What was your Takeaway Number 1?"* Allow all the free flow of comments and discussion from that person and the group that follow, then ask the member to their right the same question.

Repeat until all have shared thoughts on Takeaway Number 1, then begin again with the person who started the first round by asking, *"What was your Takeaway Number 2?"*

Repeat.

Bill Hawkins

Bill with his and "Jack's" roadster

Bill is a graduate of the University of Oklahoma, a life-long Texas resident since, and a first-time author.

In addition to writing, he paints (watercolors) and sells his artwork to cover the costs of giving away copies of *Jack's Last Class*; hosting the *jackslastclass.org* website; and producing *JLC* in paperback, e-reader, and audio formats for sale through Amazon.com.

Copies for chaplains in Afghanistan

His founding faith was encouraged by his parents, inspired by his maternal grandmother, and fostered in his early years by a small church in a wheat and cattle community in northern Oklahoma.

Experiences in Vietnam, business, civic service, travel, and churches have further shaped his worldview, much of which is expressed through his alter ego, Jack Kirk.

Bill and his wife of 50+ years live in Houston, Texas.

bill.hawkins@jackslastclass.org

"I have told you these things, so that in me you may have peace. In this world you will have trouble. But take heart! I have overcome the world."

John 16:33 NIV

Made in the USA
Monee, IL
04 February 2022

90632832R00104